TYRA & BJORN

VIKING GLORY BOOK THREE

CELESTE BARCLAY

Published by Oliver Heber Books

Lord Tennyson may have said, "'tis better to have loved and lost than to have never loved at all," but this book is dedicated to anyone who has fought for their love. And won.

Happy reading,

Celeste

SUBSCRIBE TO CELESTE'S NEWSLETTER

Subscribe to Celeste's bimonthly newsletter to receive exclusive insider perks.

Have you read *Their Highland Beginning, The Clan Sinclair Prequel?* Learn how the saga begins! This FREE novella is available to all new subscribers to Celeste's monthly newsletter. Subscribe on her website.

Subscribe Now

VIKING GLORY

Leif
Freya
Tyra & Bjorn
Strian
Lean & Ivar

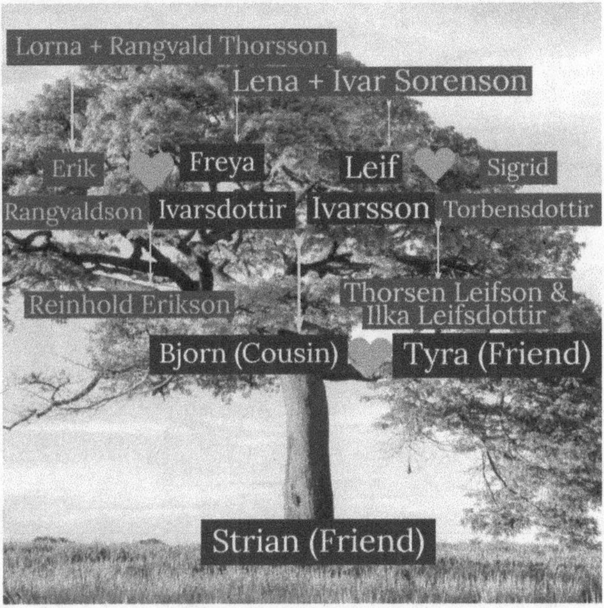

Lorna + Rangvald Thorsson
Lena + Ivar Sorenson
Erik Rangvaldson
Freya Ivarsdottir
Leif Ivarsson
Sigrid Torbensdottir
Reinhold Erikson
Thorsen Leifson & Ilka Leifsdottir
Bjorn (Cousin)
Tyra (Friend)
Strian (Friend)

PROLOGUE

10 Years Ago

Tyra Vigosdóttir extended her arm to Bjorn Jansson and jerked him from the ground where she had just knocked him onto his backside. She slid her foot under the hilt of his sword and kicked it until her hand wrapped around the handle. She handed it back to Bjorn with a smirk.

"Maybe one day you'll be able to keep up. Today isn't that day," Tyra goaded.

They had been sparring once more, and the result was typical. Tyra knocked Bjorn onto his arse time and again, despite being a woman, two years younger, and only coming to the middle of his chest. They had been sparring since they were children, and at seventeen, Bjorn resented Tyra, who was only fifteen, still being able to best him. He was a renowned warrior in his own right, but somehow Tyra knew him better than he knew himself. She was always at least one, but usually three, moves ahead of him.

Before Bjorn could thank her, she spun on her heels and marched away, her honey-blonde braid swinging down her back. Bjorn grimaced as he recalled the loathing he had seen in her eyes as they fought. For the longest time, there had been a teasing glint as she bested him, but for the last three moons, there had been anger and disgust. He accepted that he deserved it, but it still stung.

He moved to the side of the training ring and stepped into the shadows as he took a long draw from his water skin. He watched as Tyra spoke to their friend Strian. Bjorn wanted to grimace at the sight of Strian and Tyra together, but he knew it was not Strian's fault. Bjorn's mind wandered to when his friendship with Tyra ended three moons ago. Bjorn remembered as though the events were happening before his eyes. The early spring weather was unseasonably warm and after training, Bjorn looked for Tyra as he usually did. He did not make a habit of talking to her or standing near her, but having been in love with her since he was seven, he was always drawn to her. When he was unable to find her but spotted his cousins Leif and Freya, he wondered where Tyra had disappeared to. She and Freya were best friends and rarely apart, so he made his way to his cousins as he looked around.

"You seem to be missing your other half," he grinned at Freya.

"Tyra was hot and wanted time to soak, so she went to the fjord."

"Alone?" Bjorn's heart began to race. Tyra was a force to be reckoned with when she was armed, but she would be vulnerable while undressed and alone. "Why didn't you go with her?"

"She said she wanted some time to herself," Freya shrugged. "We aren't one person. We do things alone."

Bjorn grunted as he walked to the tree line, then ran until he spotted the fjord to his left. He slowed his pace, cautious not to make his presence known in case someone did lurk within the trees watching Tyra. He drew his sword as he approached the shore. He scanned the area, but could not hear nor see anyone else. His chest was tight with alternating pangs of fear and anger for Tyra's foolishness. He sheathed his sword and waded into the water. He had seen Tyra's blonde head at the surface as she soaked the rest of her body. She spun around, with a knife pointing at him, when she heard his splashes.

Tyra's eyes opened wide as she took in Bjorn standing knee-deep in the water with a look of fury on his face. She had seen him angry countless times, his wrath usually directed at her for beating him, but this rage was far more intense than she had seen before.

Bjorn's mind screamed that his chest and cock would detonate simultaneously as both throbbed. He had been with more than one woman, and he had seen different body types over the years, but he had seen nothing as beautiful as the water nymph who stood before him. She was exquisite, with long legs and slender hips. She had broad shoulders and muscles from years of training. Her breasts were not as large as those that usually drew him, but they would easily fill his hands. He forced his eyes from the thatch of dark hair that protected the place he most wanted to be at that moment.

"Bjorn?" Her hushed tones barely carried to him.

He did not respond except to continue walking toward her as he pulled his fur cloak from his shoulders. He stopped just inches before her and swung it around her shoulders before pulling her into his embrace.

"What were you thinking?" Tyra did not miss the real distress in his voice. "Why would you come here alone?"

"I wanted time to think."

"About what? What could be so important that you would allow yourself to be vulnerable? You might have a knife, but what if there had been more than one man, and you're already naked?" His voice hitched as he squeezed his eyes shut to banish the image forming in his mind. He was certain he might be ill if he allowed his imagination to envision her being assaulted.

"I needed to think about how I felt about someone."

A crushing weight descend upon Bjorn's shoulders as he scooped Tyra into his arms and walked to the shore.

"Who?" he grunted.

Tyra's blue-hazel eyes gazed into Bjorn's brown ones. They had looked each other in the eyes countless times; after all, they had known each other since Tyra's birth. This time the electricity fired between them.

"You," she mouthed, no sound coming out despite her effort. Bjorn lowered her to the ground as he brushed away the hair sticking to her neck. He lifted the soaking strands from beneath his cloak.

"Me? What were you thinking?" His voice came out barely more than a whisper as his breath brushed across Tyra's nose and cheeks.

"That you would never hold me as you are now." Tyra smiled but was unable to look at Bjorn, instead staring over his shoulder. She shocked herself that she just admitted that aloud. He had just seen her naked, and now she was confessing that she desired him. She had never been so exposed.

"Then we are opposites in yet another way. My mind can't stop thinking of finding ways to stand as we are now." He brushed the back of his fingers across her cheeks. "Tyra, you frightened me coming here alone. I can't bear anything happening to you. Do you not realize how precious you are?"

Tyra had no answer for that question. She had not felt precious since her parents died. She swallowed several times as she tried to keep the lump in her throat from choking her.

"Oh, Tyra," Bjorn murmured before his mouth descended to hers.

His kiss was soft as he did not want to scare her. He was not blind to the fact she kissed other boys before, having seen it more than once. He nearly tore each boy apart as he struggled to contain his jealousy. He also was aware she could feel the hard ridge within his leather pants. She opened her mouth and swiped the tip of her tongue against the corner of his lips.

Bjorn dove in, needing no further invitation. He cradled her head as he tightened his hold around her waist. She mewled as his tongue tangled with hers, and her hands ran over his chest to his shoulders before weaving into the hair at his nape. She pressed her body against his as his cloak slid open. Her breasts caught between them, the tight peaks that were her nipples puckered from the cold water and desire. His hand roamed up her ribs until he swept his fingers along the side, and at her moan, he pressed it between them. He groaned as his hand filled with her supple flesh. His cock continued to strain against his pants, but his conscience strained too.

"Tyra, we have to stop." Bjorn pulled away.

"Why?" It was her turn to question him. "I've coveted this for so long. It's unreal that I'm standing here with you."

She dropped her head as her hair cloaked her face.

"I never imagined you would ever want me," she stated with honesty that tore at Bjorn.

"I've wanted you for as long as I can remember." Her honesty deserved the same from him.

"Then don't stop. Bjorn, be my first."

Bjorn wanted to yell that he would be her only, but he was not ready to make such pledges. He looked into Tyra's eyes, earnestness filling them. It was not just the heat of passion, but a steady gaze. There was nothing he desired more in that moment than to introduce Tyra to making love, initiating her into the pleasures of the skin. He drew his cloak from her shoulders and laid it on the ground. Tyra lowered herself onto the fur as Bjorn undressed, careful to keep his sword unsheathed and within reach. He would not risk her safety. He kneeled between her legs as she reached for him. He rested on his forearm as his hand traveled to the juncture of her thighs. He nearly spilled when he discovered how ready she was to welcome him. His fingers moved as he watched her cheeks flush. As her body crested, he thrust into her. She clenched around him, her inner muscles along with her thighs and arms. He drew out the moment until they both were beyond the point of rational thought.

"Look at me, Tyra."

"I want to, but it's too much. I can't keep my eyes open. Bjorn," she moaned at the end.

Bjorn pulled himself loose at the last moment, bending his head to kiss Tyra once more. It was the most tender kiss he had ever shared. They spent another two hours on the beach as he introduced to her other ways in which they might share their attraction. When they accepted they should not remain away from the homestead any longer, Bjorn led her to the wall and watched as she went to her aunt and uncle's longhouse.

Bjorn had not been this lighthearted since before his parents died when he was five. He was excited to see Tyra the next morning, but he spotted her standing at the door of Strian's home. They were locked in a tight embrace. Bjorn's world fractured around him as he blinked. He watched as they broke apart and spoke. He tried to resign himself to seeing the woman he loved with his best friend, but he could not.

They trained as usual that day, but he avoided Tyra while they were on the field. He saw her confusion, but he struggled to be near her. When two other shieldmaidens, Helga and Gunnhild, approached him, he welcomed their attention. He agreed to meet them that night, and he was aware Tyra witnessed him with the two women. He did not miss the hurt that flashed across her face as she turned her back on him. That night, Bjorn met both women and went through the motions, but his mind and heart would not move past Tyra.

When Tyra arrived at the sparring ring the second morning after what she was convinced had been a life-altering experience, she ran straight into Bjorn's shoulder. He reached out and caught her, but she pushed her hands up as she broke away from him.

"Don't touch me. Don't ever touch me again, you man whore."

Bjorn knew he had upset her, but he had not imagined she would push him away. "Pardon me. You wouldn't want Strian to see you."

"Why would he care?"

"I saw you with him yesterday. I guess now that you're broken in, you are ready to move on."

Bjorn was unprepared for the fist that plowed into his face, nor was he ready for the next one that came under his chin. He reached for his nose, opening his belly for the punch that landed there. As he bent low, Tyra grasped his shoulders and drove her knees into his cods.

"You arse. Yesterday was the one-year anniversary of our parents' death. We were consoling one another."

Bjorn's look of shock was comical, but Tyra was so revolted by him that she found no humor in his realization.

"I hate you, Bjorn Jansson. Perhaps one day I will only mildly dislike you, but right now, I wish you were dead."

Tyra ran away, and Bjorn tried to go after her, but the pain—physical and emotional—doubled him over.

ONE

Present Day

Bjorn watched Tyra as she trained with Freya. He had been watching her like a hawk for the past several months. For years he had a sixth sense when it came to Tyra, always knowing where she was, but an enemy injuring her in a battle against Hakin Hakinsson made him even more vigilant. During that battle, she saved his life by moving between him and an axe-wielding giant who had already broken his arm. Tyra stabbed the man through the belly but took the axe to her chest before Bjorn had the chance to push her aside and sink his blade into the giant's chest.

If Tyra had not protected him, Bjorn would be dead, rather than watching over her like a nursemaid. He would admit that she impressed him with her improvements in such a short time. It had been four moons since her injury, and she was nearly back to full strength. He watched her sweep her leg against Freya's knees and flip his cousin over her shoulder. Freya rolled and came back to her feet as she swung her shield, pushing Tyra back several steps.

Both women locked swords as they bared their teeth at one another. Tyra brought her shield up between them as Freya hacked her sword into the side of Tyra's shield where it lodged. Freya headbutted Tyra's forehead. Both women threw down their swords and shields and launched themselves at one another as they rolled on the ground.

There was no way to keep up with who had the advantage as their positions changed. A smile emerged as he watched the two women go from baring their teeth and hissing at one another to smiling, then giggling, as they tangled together.

"It's nice to hear my wife laugh. There were a few months when I thought she didn't know how," Erik Rangvaldson mused as he watched Freya pin Tyra to the dirt.

Bjorn's upper body lurched forward, but he forced himself not to take a step forward. He waited a heartbeat, then relaxed when Tyra's knee pushed Freya from her.

"We also thought Freya had forgotten how to laugh. She may have fallen in love with you, but she certainly appeared not to like you," Bjorn laughed as he turned to look at his cousin by marriage.

"History has a way of repeating itself, don't you think?"

Bjorn's laugh died as he glared at Erik. Erik and Bjorn had become friends, and Erik had easily joined Bjorn, Leif, and Strian's tight-knit friendship. It was not because Erik married Freya. The bonds of friendship began before that when they fought against their common enemy, Hakin Hakinsson.

"I never would have told you about Tyra if you were going to remind me. I prayed you were too drunk to remember what I said."

"Not nearly drunk enough, but you were definitely drunk enough to make your confessions. But don't worry. They're safe with me. I have said nothing even to Freya, though I'm sure she suspects the truth."

During the week of Erik and Freya's wedding celebration, they had all gotten more inebriated than usual. During a drinking binge, Bjorn confessed his feelings for Tyra to Erik as the men watched Freya and Tyra dancing together. Another man cut in to dance with Tyra, and Bjorn had been beside himself. Erik kept him from making a fool of himself by interrupting Tyra's dance.

Tyra tolerated Bjorn after years passed and her anger cooled. They had antagonized one another since childhood, then there had been a period after their liaison where Tyra refused to look at him unless they were forced to spar. Bjorn bore several scars from Tyra's resentment. These scars came from the nicks her sword and knife cut, along with the wounds her words caused. His guilt had diminished little over the years, and his regret was his constant companion. Now, they still antagonized one another, but the bite was not there in Tyra's words or actions.

The most recent way they got under one another's skin was about Tyra's recovery. The near-death experience convinced Bjorn that he owed her a life debt. Tyra refused to accept it, saying they were even since he carried her to safety and stayed with her while she was unconscious. Bjorn wanted Tyra to take more care with her return to fighting, and Tyra wanted Bjorn to leave her alone.

"I would rather no one discussed how I feel about Tyra. I certainly don't want to talk about it. I said all I have to say." Bjorn hoped Erik would take the hint, and when he looked at his friend, Erik nodded.

"I spoke to Strian this morning. He's gone to the

winter lodge for the next week." Erik gave Bjorn a pointed look. Bjorn nodded before turning to watch Tyra again.

"The anniversary of their parents' death is today." Bjorn would never again forget that day. It was that day that changed everything. It was the day he lost the only woman he ever loved. He wanted to speak to Tyra, but this one day of the year seemed to be the most inappropriate for him to go near her.

Freya jogged over to them and threw her arms around Erik's neck. Erik, in turn, lifted his wife off her feet and lowered his head for a kiss. The kiss was just like every other one the couple shared: far too long and far too intimate for public. Bjorn tried to look away, but he did not miss Tyra's attempt to ignore the couple. Her gaze met Bjorn's, and he watched the wall drop in place just as it did every time they were near one another. Tyra looked at Erik and Freya, then grimaced.

"Since you haven't anything better to do, or no one better to do, let me knock you on your arse a few times." Tyra jutted her chin up as she looked down her nose at Bjorn, an impressive feat since she still came to the middle of his chest.

Bjorn felt like a homeless dog gobbling up any scrap of attention she offered, even if her waspish tongue hurt him. Her biting words never ended, but he was aware he had done little over the years to improve her impression of him. He had lived up to the reputation she accused him of, but it was never for the reason anyone assumed. It was the loneliness that grew from his parents' death that first drew him to his bed partners, then it was an attempt to forget Tyra. It never made him less lonely, and it never wiped Tyra from his mind.

Tyra led the way to the training ring, where they

faced one another as Tyra assessed Bjorn. She took in the arm that the enemy broke the day her connection to Bjorn changed for a second time. She would never forget the giant snapping Bjorn's arm like an oatcake, then drawing his sword back to cleave him in half. Tyra would remember forever the mind-numbing fear she experienced as she watched the only man she had ever loved stand next to death. She pushed her way in front of him and barely blocked the berserker's axe from cutting her in two, but she was not able to stop the blade from sinking into her chest.

The wound was deep and broke several bones. Bjorn gained his footing and plunged his sword into their opponent's chest seconds after Tyra drove hers into the man's belly. Tyra slid into unconsciousness with Bjorn's name on her lips. She woke once in his arms as he carried her back to their camp despite his broken arm. She remembered nothing for several weeks after that except hearing his voice.

Once she awoke, Tyra learned that Bjorn had been driven to the point of violence more than once when people suggested he leave her bedside. He claimed it was the blood oath he made to repay the debt he owed. She tried to discharge that debt because she loathed his controlling nature, but he would not relent.

As Tyra looked him over again, her strategy was already forming. Their swords engaged as they moved on the offensive at once. Bjorn attempted to use his size and strength to make her knees buckle, but she was more agile than Bjorn. Tyra swung at his shield as she danced away. She reset her stance, then lunged for him again. She lifted her sword to bring it down on Bjorn's weaker arm, which held his shield. When he raised his shield high enough, she used her own shield to swipe across his belly, knocking the air from his lungs. He stumbled backwards as Tyra continued her onslaught.

Bjorn regained his footing and his breath. As Tyra prepared to swing again, Bjorn twisted sideways to come around her back. She had expected this move and stopped short before swinging. She twisted the other way and brought her shield down toward Bjorn's head. He ducked, giving Tyra the opportunity to lean all her weight forward to push him forward and off his feet. Her momentum, along with Bjorn grabbing her wrist, caused her to follow him to the ground. Bjorn felt her falling and twisted to land beneath her, which meant she sprawled across him. Tyra looked down at the shock in Bjorn's eyes as he lay there with one arm wrapped around her waist.

"I'm sorry," he whispered.

"For what?" Tyra was unable break her gaze.

"I didn't mean for you to fall."

"That's silly. We were fighting. You should have meant to do more than that."

"That's different. I didn't want you to land facedown, not on your chest." Tyra's trance broke at the mention of her injury. "Don't, Tyra. Don't snark at me because I care."

Bjorn was aware the words were exactly what he should not have said as soon as they left his mouth. Tyra scrambled to her feet and grabbed Bjorn's hand. She tugged with all her strength and brought him to his feet. Then she spat at his feet.

"I don't need or want your protection. I don't need or want anything from you."

As he had so many times before, Bjorn watched her storm away. He could have beaten his own head in with his shield. Unlike so many times before, he did not let Tyra race off, leaving him behind. He followed her as she wound her way through the homestead and out the back wall. He was certain he knew where she was going, and he had a moment of doubt as he followed her to the fjord. He watched her break into a run as she moved further away from their homes. She still carried her sword in her hand, and it relieved him to watch her scanning from side to side.

He, too, carried his sword as he followed her, checking over his shoulder several times. He wanted to yell at her for once more leaving herself vulnerable. All these years later, and she was still wandering off on her own, but now they had an enemy bent on destroying both their tribe and Erik's. She ran to the water's edge, but not where Bjorn expected. The place where she stopped was not somewhere she might wade in. Instead, she stopped by a rune of stones, a stone arch with bones laid out beneath it. There was the hilt of a knife Bjorn recognized as her father's, and a comb beside the bones.

Bjorn considered for a moment leaving her to the solitude of her parents' memorial, but when she dropped to her knees and sobbed, he refused to abandon her. He watched her shoulders shake as tears streamed down her cheeks. He wanted to wait until her tears abated before he made his presence known. He did not want to embarrass Tyra in addition to violating her privacy, and he did not want to add to her list of his transgressions. But as the minutes began to add up, he inched from behind the trees.

Tyra was aware Bjorn had followed her, but she needed to escape everyone else's eyes before she collapsed into a puddle of tears. She wished he would leave her alone, so when she heard him approaching, she whipped around with her knife drawn. She came to her feet as she pointed the blade at him.

"Can't you just leave me alone? Just for an hour? Gods. Why can't you just stop?" She choked out.

"You know that ever since Hakin Hakinsson

started attacking us for Rangvald and Ivar's homesteads, it's not safe for anyone to leave alone. He's no neighbor to us, and he would love nothing more than to capture one of us. We could assume he bled to death, but Freya severing his arm is no guarantee." Bjorn did not, could not, hide the frustration from his voice.

"Just because he's been the bane of our lives no matter how often we fight him doesn't mean you can't give me some privacy!" Tyra screamed as tears continued to stream down her cheeks.

Bjorn sheathed his sword and edged toward her. His heart broke as he watched the woman he not only loved, but admired for her physical and mental strength, fall apart before his eyes. She had not cried despite the excruciating pain from her chest wound, but now she stood there looking lost and hurt. When he was within arm's length, he pushed her wrist done, and she did not resist. He pulled the knife from her hand and dropped it to the ground, pulling her into his arms, and she dissolved. She drew her arms in as she grasped the shirt he wore. He tucked her head against his chest as he rubbed her back and ran his hand over her hair. He said nothing. He had no words, and he was sure nothing would make it better. It had been eleven years since she lost her parents, but Bjorn recognized that the pain was as fresh as if it had just happened.

They stood together for what seemed like forever to Tyra, but she could not bring herself to pull away. She spent every day in torment, in conflict between her love for Bjorn and her dislike of him. As they stood together, she allowed her love to win out, and she absorbed the comfort he offered. She clung to him as though he was the only thing anchoring her to the earth and keeping her from floating away. She breathed in his pine and musk scent, his muscles flexing as he stroked her back and hair. She listened to his steady heartbeat, which calmed her. She turned so she could press her forehead against his chest. She noticed his semi-aroused rod. A sliver of her mind relished knowing he was still attracted to her. A louder part screamed he was attracted to anything he could slip his cock into, but mostly she was relieved that he just held her.

When Tyra lifted her head from his chest at last, Bjorn pressed the same feather-soft kiss to her forehead that he had been scattering on the crown of her head. He said nothing, and she appreciated it. She struggled with what to say, but she knew she should say *something*.

"This day doesn't get any easier no matter how many years pass. I'll never forget returning home from that first raid to find my mother and Strian's mother dead. Our people go raiding in Scotland to come home and find our neighbors killed our mothers and Lena lost her last babe. Our people go to avenge the ones we lost, and Strian and I both lose our fathers. It's so damn unfair."

"I know. Strian goes to the lodge." Bjorn looked out at the water. "When my day comes, I take out a fishing boat and don't return for two days. I take enough ale to keep me warm, but not enough to end up drowned."

Tyra's hands released his shirt and pressed flat against his chest.

"I forget that you understand what this is like. You never speak of them, so I admit I forget. I realize not talking about them doesn't make it hurt any less."

"It doesn't. I don't have a shrine to them, but I sail out to where my father used to take me when he taught me to fish and sail. It's the same spot where Uncle Ivar and I towed their pyres before sending them to Valhalla. That is my memorial."

"I never found out that's what you did. I've seen you come back drunk, but I always assumed you were doing something else."

Bjorn froze as he looked down at her. "You assumed I went to screw on the anniversary of my parents' death? You assumed I dishonored my parents' memory by thinking only of my own pleasure?"

"No! That's not what I meant. I figured you did something more like Strian."

"I doubt that. I think you can only believe the worst in me. Sorry to disappoint you once again."

"Don't say that. Don't put words in my mouth. You are who you are, and I know that. I really did think you were in the woods or at the cliffs to be alone."

Bjorn did not miss the distress in her voice as she tried to convince him she was telling the truth. He did not intend to make the day worse and upset her more.

"I'm sorry. I'm more sensitive about my parents' death than anyone realizes. It's been so long I have a hard time remembering them, but twenty years falls away very fast whenever that day rolls around." Bjorn took a deep breath, and Tyra felt his chest expand. Her fingers clenched his shirt again as she held on. "I've lived a good life and been well taken care of. Uncle Ivar and Aunt Lena have treated me as though I'm their own child, but it doesn't change the fact that I'm not. It doesn't change how much I miss having what Leif and Freya have."

"I know," Tyra whispered.

She looked up at Bjorn, and her heart lurched when she saw the tenderness in his gaze. Her eyes shifted down to his lips as she remembered the kisses they shared all those years ago only feet from where they stood now. When she looked up, she was certain that he was thinking the same thing, because his eyes darted to the beach.

"Tyra," he murmured as his lips grazed her temple. She tilted her head back further and parted her lips. Bjorn took the invitation and poured his love into his kiss. It was languid and gentle as they reacquainted themselves. Bjorn pressed his tongue forward and groaned as she sucked lightly. Their kiss continued until Bjorn tasted the salt of her tears mixed with the sweetness of her breath. He pulled back and saw the tears that soaked his lips. His thumb brushed them away, but she grasped his wrist, stepping back.

"Why couldn't you be the man I need?"

Tyra took several more steps back before running back toward the homestead. This time Bjorn let her go. He watched her as she became a speck in the distance. His heart had a vice cinching and shrinking it; he was fairly certain it had shriveled up and left nothing behind. He had wanted nothing more than to be the man Tyra needed. The last two years had seen him grow more and more hermit-like as he could no longer stand taking a woman to bed who was not Tyra. His dry spell caused rumors and was even a source of taunting from Tyra, but he would not admit to anyone—other than Erik when he was drunk—why he no longer bedded women like he once did.

After his afternoon with Tyra and the disaster that followed, he spent years trying to replace her or at least distract himself. But three years ago, Tyra became the companion of Knud, one of their fellow warriors. While she never moved into the man's home, she slept there most nights. Their arrangement lasted almost two years, and it was during that time Bjorn gave up. He found he did not want to replace her or forget her. He did not want anyone else.

It was on rare occasions, mostly feasts, when he would allow himself to drink to the point where he could use the dark to imagine any woman was Tyra. He had too many demons he wanted to keep hidden to continue living as he had.

TWO

T yra wiped the tears from her face and took several deep breaths before she opened the door to the jarl's longhouse. She heard the women's voices coming from the living quarters, so she turned to the door where she recognized Freya, her mother Lena, and Erik's mother Lorna all laughing. She knocked and entered when a familiar voice summoned her. Freya stood, her brow creased, and came to Tyra. She pulled her best friend into a tight embrace.

"You're sadder than when you left, and I saw you were upset after sparring with Bjorn," Freya whispered.

"I am."

Freya cupped her friend's face and looked at her, but she was unsure of what had upset Tyra. It was more than just grief. When Tyra's face began to crumple, Freya pulled her into another tight embrace. Tyra welcomed the solace Freya offered after the emotionally charged training with Bjorn, the overwhelming need to escape, and the conflicted exchange with Bjorn near the fjord. When she was prepared to face the others, she looked up and nodded at Freya.

They walked back to the women and only then did she notice that Sigrid, Freya's sister-in-law and Lorna's niece, was also with them. She sat with her hands on her rounded belly, watching Tyra. Sigrid offered her a smile and a slight nod, and Tyra was aware Sigrid had had a vision of her. Sigrid's gift of sight had saved their lives more than once, but those visions that involved their private lives were disconcerting.

"Tyra, come sit with me," Lorna spoke softly.

Tyra had grown to admire and respect Lorna not only as the *frú*—the jarl's wife—of her tribe and as Erik's mother, but also as a warrior in her own right. Lorna had lived in the Trondelag for thirty years, but her coloring and accent gave away her Highland homeland. Now, Lorna made space for Tyra. She slid her arm around the younger woman, who in turn leaned into the embrace in a way she only ever did with Lena. There were other motherly women in their village, but none made her feel like Lena, and now Lorna, did.

"Lass, I think it's time you and Freya listened to the story of how I came to wed Rangvald. Sigrid knows it since she is my niece, and Lena was there for much of that piece of history. It's a long tale, the start of our saga, so bear with me."

Freya and Tyra both perked up at the mention of a story they had heard hints of for months, but the telling of the tale had never happened. Even Freya, Lorna's daughter-in-law, had not heard it.

"You both know that Rangvald Thorsson, the mighty warrior," she grinned, "and I met when his tribe, led by his older brother, raided my clan, the Mackays. To understand how things came to pass, you should know who I was before I met Rangvald. I was only six-and-ten at the time, and the daughter of the laird. I only had brothers and I was the youngest of the laird's five children, so I followed them everywhere. When I was a child, my brothers laughed when I wanted a wooden sword to be like them, but my father allowed my second oldest brother to give me his when he moved on to a real sword. I carried my wooden sword everywhere with me and watched each training session my brothers had. I would copy their moves and then practice in my chamber. My parents humored me for years, but my mother insisted I learn how to be a proper chatelaine for our keep and our clan. When I was not in the keep, I was either watching my brothers in the lists or on my horse with my bow and arrow.

"By the time I was ten summers, I was a far better archer than any of my brothers. The winter of my eleventh year was when my first brother was killed. He was on a raiding party, and he never returned home. His loss devastated my parents, and I was filled with guilt being a girl rather than a boy. I felt like a waste after my parents lost their oldest son, so I pushed myself harder and trained more. My parents never made me feel that way. It was all in my mind. At three-and-ten summers, my second brother, who was the youngest of the four, died when he fell from his horse. That left my middle two brothers and me.

"I begged Aiden and Andrew to train me. It took a week of hounding them until I threatened to have some of the other older boys teach me, but I warned them it would have to be away from the keep. They both knew better than to let their three-and-ten-year-old sister go anywhere away from the keep with a group of boys. They agreed, and I joined them in the lists the next morning. They teased the three of us when I showed up in a pair of trews and a leine I'd made for myself earlier that year. The laughing ended when I launched a dirk at the boot of one of the oldest boys. It landed at the tip of the leather and trapped it to the ground. I was fortunate the boots were slightly big, or it would have landed in a toe. I challenged my brothers in front of their friends and the older warriors.

"I embarrassed both brothers, but they decided they would humor me. Neither expected I would be able to hold a sword, let alone wield one. No one was aware the blacksmith's son was sweet on me and made me a sword for my saint's day the year prior. I had given up the wooden sword and trained with a double-handed broadsword designed for my size. As I began to move through the sparring, my brothers discovered I was far stronger than I looked.

"Since I had grown up watching them train, taking note of each of their strengths and weaknesses, they realized they would have to fight in earnest if I wasn't going to show them up. I fought one, then the other, both ending in a draw. Then I challenged them to fight me at the same time. I was far too confident for my own good back then, but I was confident that I had skill. I held my own against them, and some of the other boys decided it would be fun to humiliate me. They claimed my brothers were being easy on me.

"By the end of the first day, I'd broken one arm and two noses. It wasn't my intention, but I was backed into a corner more than once. After that, some of the older warriors spoke to me and asked how I learned so much. I was honest and told them of the years I spent watching and training. They allowed me to come back day after day, and they made sure the younger warriors treated me with respect, just as any other warrior would be. My third brother, Andrew, died one sennight before the raid that brought Rangvald and his men. A fever sickened him and took him in his sleep.

"Rangvald's raiding party arrived just before the sun rose. They swept in like a Highland storm. There was no time to even sound the warning bells. I dressed and grabbed my sword before running to my parents' chamber. My father was already coming toward me, and I remember saying 'I love ye, Da,' and he answered, 'I love ye more, lass.' Those were the last words we said to one another. I moved on to find my mother to take her to the chapel.

"There was no doubt Norsemen would not respect the sanctity of the kirk, but there was a place to hide beneath the floor under the altar. The floor was made of stone, and the moveable one fit so snuggly, it was impossible tell it moved unless they already knew. We used the secret passages to enter the bailey, and I covered my mother with my targe as we ran to the chapel. We were to the door, when a giant of a man stepped in front of me.

"I had never seen such a large man, and all my brothers and my father stood close to six and a half feet. He roared at me then laughed. He tried to push me over as he reached for my mother. I brought my sword down on his arm to sever his hand. He was faster than I expected, even with the injury. He drove his fist into my stomach and grabbed my mother. He slit her throat before I had the chance do anything. I sliced through the arm I had already injured and took his hand from him. I tried to run my sword through him, but a searing pain across my shoulder nearly brought me to my knees. Someone shot me with an arrow. The pain seemed to galvanize me, just as it had the beast in front of me. I swung my sword and aimed the hilt at the man's head. I landed it against his temple, and he tumbled to the ground. I swung around and prepared to launch my knife at whoever held the bow.

"I will never forget that moment. The most

handsome man I ever laid eyes on stood before me. He was just as large as the man I'd just fought, but he was so different. He seemed calmer and less angry than the other warriors. He looked as though he didn't belong with them because he wasn't just plowing through victim after victim. He was methodically picking off my clansmen, but there was a grace to him I'd never seen in another man.

"I snapped the arrow from my shoulder as he turned back toward me and raised his bow. I had already drawn my dirk when he prepared to fire again. He lowered his bow when he saw me, but I threw my knife. He shifted to his left and caught the dirk by the handle. I had never seen any man do that other than my father who taught me how to do the same thing. He stalked toward me, and I was sure he would snap my neck, but he pushed me behind him as he looked past where I was standing. I turned back and found the giant was on his feet again. It boggled my mind how the man I'd severed a hand from and hit in the head was back on his feet, once more ready to kill me. I remember every word of every conversation as though it were happening all over again.

"'Mine,' was all the man who now shielded me said. The warrior I'd fought laughed and tried to reach for me with his remaining hand. 'I don't think so, little brother. I lead this raid, and I shall claim whatever thrall I want.' I understood enough of the Norsemen's language to follow along as they discussed making me a slave. I began to back up when movement caught my eye.

"I looked toward the battlements in time to witness my brother fall from it with an arrow through his chest. I no longer noticed the two men squaring off over me. I ran through the battle to get to my brother just as my father arrived at his side. My father was more aware of what was going on around us than I was. He thrust his targe over me and received a back full of arrows for it.

"Before I figured out what to do next, a large arm wrapped around my waist and hauled me back into the chapel. I looked up to find it was the man who had shot me but also defended me. He pointed to himself and said, 'Rangvald. You?' in broken Gaelic. I looked at him as if he sprouted a second head but remembered the Norse our priest taught my brothers and me. 'I'm Lorna. You shot me, and you saved me.' It surprised him that I spoke Norse, but he put me down and told me to hide.

"None of the other Norsemen had raided the chapel yet. I ran to the altar and slid the stone aside, dropping into the hole below. I slid the stone over it, then someone stood on it. Moments later, the hoard of men entered, knocking over and breaking everything. Voices floated to me, but I didn't understand everything. I was positive it was Rangvald who stood above me, and he never moved even when other feet came near him. He issued orders to collect everything of value, but he never left my hiding spot unprotected.

"It felt like I was down there for a lifetime as I remembered seeing my parents and brother killed. I wanted to hate them all, but I marveled at how one of them chose to protect me. It petrified me that he had claimed me. I was determined to end my life before leaving my keep and clan as a slave. When the noise ended, he moved the stone and lifted me out.

"I looked around, but they had stripped the chapel of everything, even the altar linens. Rangvald watched me as I stepped toward another stone that had a cross etched into it. He didn't stop me as I prayed, asking God to forgive me for taking my own life. I realize now that Rangvald didn't guess what I was doing, but he understood when I drew my dirk and pointed it to my chest. To this day, I don't think I've ever seen him move so fast, except for perhaps when the wolves attacked Erik.

"He threw himself at me, knocking me down, and sending the blade skidding across the floor. 'No, Lorna. No. You can't kill yourself, not after I've saved you three times.' When he said that, and I realized he had saved me thrice, I only nodded. He rolled off me and helped me to my feet and even handed my dirk back to me. I looked at it then him. 'I will not leave here a slave. If you make me, I will be dead before we reach your boats.'

"Rangvald made me an offer that changed my life in a way not even the raid did. Had my family lived, my father would have arranged a marriage for me. He would have set a price for my hand and then let lairds bid on me either for themselves or their sons. He loved me, but he was responsible for the clan. Alliances protected us from one another, even if they weren't able to protect us from the Norsemen.

"Rang promised me I would be a free woman. I would be no one's thrall, and he would allow me to come and go as I pleased. I impressed him with my Norse because I followed what he was saying. I was honest and told him it frightened me to go, but he was kind when he reminded me I had no one left. All my family was now gone, and the Norsemen had wiped out most of my clan. He was as gentle with me as possible as I considered everything he said. He was right; I had no real reason to stay. It would be more dangerous to stay than to go. 'What do you expect of me?' I was afraid of his answer. I expected him to say I would become his concubine or servant, but instead he said, 'I expect you to live.'"

"He watched over me the entire voyage back to Stjordal, making sure none of the men tried to molest me. He somehow convinced his brother Harold not to kill me for amputating his hand, and he threatened to geld him in his sleep if he claimed me as a thrall. I should have known then that Rang was not cruel like his brother, but he was also not a man to underestimate. When we arrived at their homestead, Rang was true to his word. He ensured I was a free woman. But that was all that he did.

"He turned me over to his mother, who detested me from the beginning, and carried on with his life. He was polite when he noticed me and kind when others taunted me. He stood up for me more than once, but otherwise, he left me alone. I watched him with more women than I can stomach remembering. I hadn't any false hopes that he would find me as beautiful as I found him handsome, but it hurt to be abandoned.

"I knew no one there, and I had left at his suggestion. I had no one at home in Scotland, and no one in my new home. As a free woman, I was permitted to come and go as I wanted and allowed to carry weapons. After I had been there for three months, I was lost, unwanted, and useless. I'd seen the other women train, and I envied them their freedom, their purpose, and the respect they received. I decided I had had enough of being ignored by Rang and everyone else. I was in the training yard the next morning before anyone else. I was warming up when men and women began to show up.

"They laughed at me as I swung my sword in wide arches. I hadn't done much with it for almost three months. It was the longest I had gone without training since I was a young child. Rang and Harold arrived, wondering who was being taunted. Harold laughed when he realized it was me, but Rangvald was ready to intervene when I launched my knife at his foot. I pinned the tip of his boot to the ground, just like I had done to the boy when I was a child. He looked up at me in shock then narrowed his eyes, fury beginning to turn his face red. 'Ungrateful,' he snarled in Gaelic. 'Scared?' I taunted back. He pulled the dirk from the ground and sent it hurtling toward my heart.

"Unlike he had in the bailey of my home, I did not step aside. I reached out, grabbed the hilt before it reached me, spun it around and charged at him. My targe was on my back, so he was unprepared for me to roll it forward and use it to ram his chest; he had expected either my sword or my knife. He staggered backwards but caught himself, but I was already moving through thrusts and slices that I had been doing since I was ten. One of his men tried to step forward, but he received the hilt of my sword to his nose.

"Rangvald ordered them all back. We circled one another as I spewed all my pent-up grief and anger at him. 'You brought me here. Convinced me it would be a better life. What do you do the moment our feet touch the ground? Abandon me to a woman who despises me. Abandon me just like every other person in my life.' I didn't even realize what I was saying as the words came out a mixture of Gaelic and Norse. I stunned the crowd, with both my aggressive but skilled fighting and my knowledge of their language. I only used Norse words for the ones I was sure he wouldn't understand in Gaelic.

"Rang understood me better than I realized. He allowed me to vent my spleen. I said horrid things to him, things to this day I wish I could take back. I called him weak, a man whore, a coward, anything that came to mind that even touched on the truth. He was neither weak nor a coward, though I did think him a man whore. I said them because he was not fighting me like he should have.

"Our sparring ended when we disarmed one another and held each other in headlock. He had the chance to snap my neck, but I grabbed his groin. After that day, they welcomed me in the training yard. Rang sparred with me and only gave me partners he trusted. He watched for weeks before he was comfortable sparring with someone else while I partnered elsewhere. I appreciated his acceptance and the way he made others accept me, but I would leave the training field alone, just as I had arrived, when everyone else came and went with friends or lovers.

"He found me one day near the fjord. I was sitting looking out at the cliffs and water. I had been crying, but my tears had dried. He took a look at me and understood. He sat down beside me, picked me up, and plopped me into his lap. He didn't say anything. He looked out at the water just as I had. I stared at him, then turned back to the water. He wrapped his arm around me, and I leaned back.

"We sat like that for a few hours. Neither of us spoke. Finally, the sun began to set, and the temperature fell. When I shivered, he wrapped his cloak around me. He was the first one to say anything. 'I know it's been six moons to the day since you arrived here. You're unhappy, and that isn't what I wanted for you. Do you want me to take you back?' I looked at him, and it was like my chest was caving in. I had fallen in love with him, but he never looked at me the way I watched him look at other women. I was convinced he never would. I was an outsider. But then, I would be too if I returned home.

"A cousin of mine would be laird now, having come from our outlying land. 'There's nothing to go back to. I have no more a home there than I do here. I don't belong in either place.' Rang was silent for a long moment before he began to speak. 'Before I met you, I fought and whored, just as you've accused me. I had little reason to do more. I am not my father's eldest son. I don't get along with Harold very well, so I avoid him.

"'When I met you, something changed. I caught you attacking Harold when he blocked your escape with your mother. I witnessed the damage you did, and I was obligated to defend him as his brother, so I shot the arrow at you. But he taunted you as he killed your mother. He taunted you to torment you, and something inside of me screamed that this was wrong. You had been valiant and brave, but we outnumbered you. If it hadn't been Harold, it would have been someone else.

"'When you ran to your brother's side without care for your own safety, I realized that you would sacrifice yourself repeatedly for your people, for the ones you care about. Then I watched your father do the same, and I understood where you got it from. Thinking you might die where so many other bodies laid was unbearable, along with imagining any man raping your or making you his bed slave. That's why I hid you.

"'When we arrived here, I wanted you to see I'd told you the truth about being a free woman. I gave you space because I didn't want you to ever wonder if I meant to trick you or force you to pay for your freedom. I also didn't want anyone to ever accuse you of being my whore. You needed to grieve, but I know now you haven't done that, have you?'

"I shook my head as I listened to him, unsure of why he was saying all of this. 'Lorna, you've seen what I wanted everyone else to see. You've seen the Rangvald that people expect, but I'm not what you assume. When we arrived, I tried to go back to my old life. I tried to pick up where I left off, drinking and wenching. I know you saw that, but it lost all appeal each time I caught sight of you and how lonely you looked. Lorna, I haven't been with another woman since within a moon of your arrival. I've paid more than one woman to keep quiet about me sending them away.'

"I remember shaking my head, so confused. 'I don't want any of them. I don't want any woman who isn't you. But I never wanted anyone to speak ill of you, saying you are my bed slave or concubine. I didn't want them to claim you bewitched me if I tried to woo you soon after we arrived. I wanted to give you time to adjust. I did all the things I was sure people expected me to do when all I ever wanted were moments like this.' And he kissed me."

Lorna paused for the first time in her story to wipe tears from her eyes and to swallow several times.

"Rang admitted he was in love with me, just as I was in love with him. We coupled there for the first time, looking out to where the fjord met the sea. I had never felt more special and cared for than in those moments. He walked me back to the homestead afterwards, and I returned to the small hut I lived in to prepare for the evening meal. When I arrived at his parents' longhouse, I found him seated with a woman in his lap. He was laughing with her and had his hand on her hip. His mother stepped next to me and informed me that the woman was Rangvald's companion now.

"They had been bedding each other for months, and she told me I should never have come. I was one more mouth to feed and should live like the thrall they intended me to be. I didn't look anywhere but straight ahead, and I said nothing until she walked away. When I looked over, I realized Rangvald was watching me. I had never in my life or since then held such hatred as I did for him in that moment. I felt abandoned all over again, and I despised myself for being a fool, for trusting him.

"I left the longhouse and ran to my hut. I gathered the few meager belongings I had brought with me and the few things I'd gained since I arrived. I knew my way to Lena and Ivar's homestead from conversations I'd overheard many times as the marriage between Rang's sister Inga and Ivar was being planned. I slipped out of my hut without being seen since it was dark. I'd seen the hidden gate in the wall, and it was easy to leave the homestead unnoticed. There were risks to stealing a horse, but I did it anyway. My life was forfeit already.

"It took me four days to ride to Ivar and Lena's. I'd never met either of them before, so everyone was a stranger there. I was more willing to risk becoming a thrall than stay there to watch Rang paw at some other woman when I'd confessed I loved him."

Lena reached out a hand and grasped Lorna's. Lena continued the story as tears began to fall down Lorna's cheeks.

"We weren't sure what to make of the Scots woman who rode into our homestead asking for a place to live and work. Ivar and I realized immediately who she was. There weren't any other Highlanders living near us, and certainly not any women who would arrive with a sword and shield. We brought her inside and listened to her tell her story of the raid, of being brought back to Rangvald's tribe, of living there, and then telling us she was no longer able to stay. She was evasive about the reason, but Ivar and I both were certain it had to do with Rangvald.

"Ivar even asked as much, but Lorna evaded the question without lying. It was a fortnight before Rangvald rode into the homestead. Ivar's tribe did not get along well with Rangvald's then, especially since the arrangement for Ivar's wedding to Rangvald's sister was not progressing. Ivar refused to marry anyone other than me. I'd already been his companion for four years. The state Rangvald was in shocked me. He was supposed to be representing his father and brother as he continued to negotiate the marriage agreement, but he was so drunk he nearly fell from his horse. He looked like he hadn't slept in weeks, and his men said he often talked to himself in Gaelic.

"Once we heard that, we needed no further explanation. Ivar dragged Rangvald to the bathhouse to clean and sober him up. I searched for Lorna, but the moment she realized why, she bolted. She had spotted Rangvald at the jarl's table when she walked in. I will never forget how Rangvald must have sensed her, because it was impossible for him to have seen or heard her. His head whipped around, their eyes met, and Lorna pushed through the crowd to get free of the longhouse. Rangvald was on his feet and over the table before anyone recognized who he was chasing."

Lena stopped there and squeezed her friend's hand. Lorna smiled as she wiped her cheeks again.

"He caught me as I ran to the stables. I was ready to leave, even though this time I had no idea where I would go. I didn't waste time saddling the horse but was mounting bareback when two hands gripped me around the waist and pulled me down. I hissed and spat like a trapped wildcat. I'm not sure what I said, but I'm sure I told him I hated him several times. I told him he was a liar, an oath breaker, and a coward. I told him he had no honor.

"He was well within his rights to kill me on the spot for those things, you know that, but instead he pinned me against his chest and let me sob until my legs no longer held me up. He carried me to an empty stall and seated us in the hay. He waited until I stopped crying then spoke softly, but I heard the pain in his voice. 'I'm sorry you walked in when you did, and I found out what my mother told you. But she didn't tell you the truth. I would never allow anyone to make you a thrall, and no one has any right to tell you, you deserve to be one.' I tried to scramble away from him.

"I didn't care what his mother had said. That was the least of what caused my pain. He pulled me back into his lap. 'Wait,' he ordered, and his voice had an edge I didn't recognize, at least not directed to me. 'I told you I knew what my mother said and that it wasn't true. That woman isn't and never was my companion. She's my younger cousin from the neighboring homestead. You may not have seen how young she is, but she's barely four-and-ten. My brother gave her too much ale, and she sat on my lap to keep from falling over or having any of the men grab her.'

"I listened to what he said, and part of me wanted to accept him, but he had admitted to me already that he had been with other women since he met me. I had no claim on him before, and I didn't have any claim to him then, but it didn't mean I wanted to picture of him bedding someone else. I refused to speak. Rang asked me if I believed him, and I wouldn't say anything. He asked if I would come home with him, I didn't answer. He finally gave up and led me back to the longhouse. He handed me over to Lena and refused to stay in the longhouse if it made me uncomfortable.

"I wanted to tell him to stay, but I was still hurt and angry. I wanted him to suffer, so I said nothing. He slept in the stables with little to keep him warm. I watched him the next morning, a twinge of guilt plucking at my conscience, but it evaporated when I noticed two women walk by. He smiled in a way that

I was convinced no man who was in love would smile at another woman.

"Once again, he spotted me, but it was too late. I locked myself into the chamber Lena gave me and refused to speak to him. Rang spent the entire day outside my door, knocking and calling my name. I discovered he spent the night in the hall because I grew hungry and tripped over him when I opened the door. Rang followed me back into my chamber and nearly got my sword through his gut. He admitted he had bedded each of those women on previous trips and felt obligated to be polite, since he was still supposed to be arranging his sister's marriage.

"He remained a week to conclude business, but he spent more time trying to prove himself to me. He made sure I trained, he made sure I had food when I refused to leave my chamber, and he made sure I had clothing since I'd brought so little and refused Lena's offers. As he made me more comfortable and made it easier for me to stay there, there was no way to avoid witnessing how he was changing.

"I was told about the state he was in when he rode in, but I noticed other things. He was losing weight, he rarely smiled at anyone other than me, and he didn't speak much. I realized these changes were because of me. He worried about what I would think if he smiled or spoke to the wrong woman. I was overwhelmed with guilt for causing his pain, and he shared the same guilt."

Lorna let go of Lena's hand and raised Tyra's chin. She gave Tyra such a kindly and understanding smile that Tyra found herself crying yet again. She had listened to Lorna's story and understood why she was being told this tale.

"I think you understand. I think you see the similarities in our fears and our pain, but I hope you see the similarities in our flawed men. I am certain, without a doubt, that Rangvald has always been faithful to me. After we married, we only spent nights apart when he raided, and I was pregnant with Erik. I wasn't able to raid with him then, but I fought alongside him when I wasn't pregnant.

"The times when I wasn't there, Rang refused to sleep anywhere without his younger brother Sven nearby. He insisted that no one leave him alone at night, so there was no way for anyone to ever claim he had been unfaithful to me and so no woman 'molested' him, as he called it. Harold died not long after I returned from Ivar and Lena's, and we're all familiar with the disaster that was Ivar's trial marriage to Inga.

"Rangvald became jarl soon after that and pledged that if he ever broke his oath to me, then he would no longer be a man who should lead. Tyra, this was a long story, but it is one that causes me both great sadness and great happiness to tell. There was so much pain between Rang and me, but I am so much better for the love we share. Thank you for listening to me."

Lorna hugged Tyra, and Tyra breathed in the other woman's lily-of-the-valley scent. It reminded her of her mother, and her tension slid away from her. Freya moved closer to Tyra and laid her hand on Tyra's arm.

"Tyra, there isn't anyone here who doesn't recognize how you and Bjorn are destined for one another. You have to decide. Are you going to keep punishing him and yourself, or are you going to have more faith in the two of you? One path leads you to the life you've been dreaming of since you were a girl, while the other will leave you both growing old alone. He's not going to choose anyone else. You tried, and it nearly broke you. Tyra," Freya looked at the other women in the room and bit her lip. She wanted to divulge a secret she was not supposed to know. Neither Erik nor Bjorn were aware that she had overhead Bjorn's drunk confession.

When Tyra began dancing with one of the young men, Freya wove her way through the crowd and was going to sneak up on her new husband to surprise him with an offer to escape the crowd. Instead, she heard a truth she had suspected for years. She tilted her head toward the back of the chamber, and Tyra followed her. Freya dropped her voice to a whisper.

"I'm not supposed to know this, but I overhead Erik and Bjorn talking during the week of our wedding feast. Tyra, Bjorn hasn't been with any other women in two years. He's had a few drunken interludes during feasts when he's seen you with other men, but he doesn't want anyone else."

Tyra was in utter disbelief. None of what Freya said made sense to her. She had seen Bjorn around other women and seen him flirt, but she had also heard rumors that he was not as popular as he once was. She never considered it was by his choice. She had assumed he had worked his way through the women, and they denounced him as a cad and did not want him back.

"Tyra?"

"Hmm?"

"What are you going to do?"

Tyra looked at Freya then the other women who chatted together. "I don't know. Does that change anything? He assumed the worst of me, and then became the worst he could be."

"Tyra, you know you aren't being fair. You were Knud's companion for two years. Bjorn may have been with many women, but you practically lived with a man. We all assumed you would marry Knud. Bjorn's never made that kind of commitment to another woman. I know you didn't love Knud, but you were with him for *two years*. Bjorn endured that, endured the rumors that you would wed another man, endured seeing the two of you together over and over, endured it and pretty much swore off all other women. When will you stop punishing him?"

"When I can trust him."

Freya's head jerked back. "Are you worried he would leave you for someone else?"

"Surprisingly, no. I think he knows I would geld him for that." Tyra looked at Freya, then over at the other three women. "You don't know what is to be without family. We've always been like sisters, but we aren't. You always came home to parents and a brother who adore you. Now you have a husband who dotes on you, and you get along with his family. I don't have that. I live with an aunt and uncle who secretly complain that I am a burden. They never wanted to take me in, but Ivar wouldn't let them do otherwise. Even though I rarely eat there and am away more often than I am home, I am still unwanted. Freya, Knud and I barely touched each other for those two years. He overheard my aunt and uncle one night when he walked me home. It upset him so much, he wanted to challenge my uncle. I begged that he not to do so because they are the only family I have left. He offered on the spot to have me live with him, whether or not I wanted to bed him. We were more roommates than lovers. That's why I couldn't marry him. He fell in love with Una, and I had to explain to her the situation. I returned to my aunt and uncle to allow Knud space to court and marry Una."

"Then things have not been as they appear for either of you."

Tyra pressed her lips into a flat link and squeezed her eyes shut as she nodded.

THREE

Bjorn sat beside Leif during the evening meal for the first time in ages. Sigrid sat near Lena and Lorna to discuss baby-related matters Bjorn had not understood when the women began speaking. Now, Bjorn listened as Leif spoke about the upcoming journey to Scotland, but his mind was drifting. He watched Tyra sit with her aunt and uncle along with Strian. He kicked himself for the thousandth time for making the mistake that Tyra had been interested in Strian all those years ago. They were more like brother and sister than friends. Bjorn witnessed how things were strained between Tyra and her relatives, and now that Strian had no family left, he often acted as a buffer for Tyra. He leaned forward as he watched Tyra's aunt launch into some diatribe or an-other directed at Tyra.

"Would you listen just for five minutes then I will let you stare all you want?" Leif's elbow dug into his side.

Bjorn barely spared him a glance as he continued to watch Tyra shift on the bench. He watched her shoulders inch toward her ears as the waves of ten-sion rose from her and reached him.

"I heard you already. You can't and won't go on

this voyage because Sigrid is already halfway through her pregnancy. I don't blame you for staying home with your wife. I would do the same. You want me to lead our warriors along with Freya and Erik. Tyra will command the fleets while we sail, and I am to listen to Strian's sound advice. Leif, you haven't said anything you haven't told me every night for the last sennight."

Leif leaned closer to Bjorn, "I'm so glad you're so sure that's what I said. At least you were listening at some point. I told you, just now, that I learned something today that might interest you. Tyra was not Knud's companion in truth. It turns out, things were so bad with her aunt and uncle that Knud offered her a place to stay, so she had the opportunity to avoid going to her family. They were barely ever lovers. She left when Knud fell in love with Una. She wanted him to have a chance for happiness after all that he did for her."

Bjorn shifted his gaze to Leif, "And how did you come by that information? Did your wife see it?"

Leif growled at Bjorn, still sensitive about some of the suspicious and judgmental things Bjorn said about Sigrid during the early days of her relationship with Leif. "No, Knud told me. When I spotted Tyra running toward the fjord, I asked Knud why he didn't help her. I said they looked like they were still friends and had once been both in love and lovers. He swore it must never get back to Tyra's family, but since he and Una are now married, he didn't see the harm in others knowing."

Bjorn's eyes darted between Leif and Tyra. His gaze remained on Tyra as she wrapped her arms around her middle, guarding herself against her aunt's ongoing barrage. Bjorn watched Strian try to intervene, but Tyra's uncle began to raise his voice. When his anger turned to Tyra, Bjorn was done watching. He was away from the table and crossing the room with little care who he bumped into.

"Tyra, you're needed at the docks. Something is wrong with the hull of two boats, and your boat builders need you to instruct them on how to proceed."

Bjorn was confident it was a plausible lie. There was no one within a hundred leagues who did not recognize Tyra was the greatest sailor alive. People spoke of her as though she were part goddess, a daughter of sea goddess *Rán* and *Ægir*, her husband. Over the years, she had formed the best team of carpenters and woodworkers to be her shipbuilders. They consulted her on most boat projects, and other ship captains wanted her workers to do their repairs.

Tyra looked over her shoulder at Bjorn, her brow furrowing. She looked him in the eye and understood what he was doing. She nodded and climbed from the bench, excusing herself. Strian stood but moved to take Bjorn's seat at the jarl's table. Bjorn led Tyra from the longhouse into the brisk evening air. He rested his hand at her elbow and waited for her to pull away or brush him off, but she did neither. They walked to the docks even though they both knew there was no need. They stood together as the aurora borealis lights flickered across the sky.

"Leif and I feared them as children," Bjorn whispered. Tyra turned her head to look at him, and he nodded. "We worried it was the gods looking to steal children at night. He would climb into bed with Freya. He did it until we were nine summers."

"What did you do?" Tyra turned to stand before him.

Bjorn shrugged and looked back up at the sky. "What was there for me to do? I didn't have a sister or brother to go to, and my cousin had already run to his sister. I remained in my chamber and pulled the covers over my eyes until I was sure I would either suffocate or fell asleep."

"I never would have guessed. To me, they were the souls of our loved ones waving to us. I found comfort in that after my parents were gone. I know that's not the case, but it helped me to feel less alone."

"I wish I had thought of it that way." Bjorn looked down and caught Tyra looking at him. "What was your aunt saying to you? Why did your uncle yell at Strian and then turn to you?"

It was Tyra's turn to shrug, but it did not satisfy Bjorn.

"Don't shut me out. Not again. Not today."

"You're asking a lot of me for one day, Bjorn."

"I worry about you," he whispered. "And it upsets me that anyone, especially your family, mistreats you."

Tyra rolled her shoulders back and closed her eyes. "My aunt called me a failure for not convincing Knud to marry me. She told me I would be too old for any man to want me and that I had a choice once I return from this mission: find my own husband, accept the one they pick for me, or leave their home and not return. Then my uncle yelled at Strian for not asking for me even though he knows Strian is more my brother than anything else. My uncle said Strian shouldn't be sitting at our family table if he had no intention of actually becoming family. He didn't say it outright, but he reminded Strian that he has even less family than I do. He made it sound as though, because of his uncle Einear, Strian would be lucky if our family or any other family welcomed him. Everyone knows it wasn't his fault Einear betrayed Ivar and killed his own brother. All over a worthless woman like Rangvald's sister Inga. Anyway, you came just as he was ready to launch his attack at me."

"I know. When he stood and looked at you, I couldn't ignore it."

"Thank you. Strian would defend me, but I also don't want my uncle to ban him from sitting with us. He's always kept his thoughts to himself, but something has been different lately, and he is even more reserved than usual. I worry about him, Bjorn. His leg healed, but something has changed within him. He goes through all the motions, and he's stronger than he ever was, but he seems so hollow. It's as though he's given up."

"I know. I've seen the same, and I've been thankful until tonight that he sits with you and your family. I wasn't aware things were so bad between all of you."

Tyra's laugh held a hard edge. "When haven't they been bad? Unlike Jarl Ivar and Frú Lena did with you, my aunt and uncle didn't want to adopt me. Ivar forced them. My uncle never cared about his sister, so he doesn't care about his sister's daughter. My aunt is just a spiteful woman, and my cousins are becoming spoiled and nasty. That's why…" Tyra trailed off, and Bjorn would not complete her thoughts. He guessed she would not appreciate knowing he was aware of her arrangement with Knud.

"Where will you go tonight? Back to their home?"

Again, her laugh held no mirth. "Definitely not. You've brought me to where I planned to sleep."

Bjorn looked at the boats, then Tyra, and shook his head. "You can't mean you would sleep on your boat."

"Why not? I do it all the time."

"What?"

"Yes. I spend more nights on my boat than I do anywhere else. My aunt and uncle assume I'm with a man and don't care except that no proposals have come my way, and I get the peace I want. Besides, I like my boat."

"I know you do. You may as well be the tenth daughter of *Rán* and *Ægir*, but that doesn't mean you should be pressured into retreating to your cabin to find a place you belong."

Embarrassment and discomfort at the reminder that her family did not want her flooded her. She realized Bjorn meant well, but her nerves were raw from all that transpired that day, including her relatives telling her they never cared that today was the anniversary of her parents' death. It was just like any other day except it reminded them of the burden they carried. She had told no one that this was how her morning began.

"We aren't all so fortunate to have a jarl and *frú* for an uncle and aunt. Not all of us have a jarl's longhouse to return to. Not all of us had the spoiled upbringing of being the jarl's favorite, his second son."

Bjorn reeled back as though she slapped him. "I'm not Ivar's second son. I am reminded of that every day since I sleep in the chamber that should have been his second son's, but alas, none of Lena and Ivar's other children lived long enough to claim it. I know exactly where I live. I know exactly who I am. I am there by the mercy of the gods and their generosity. I was only five when my parents died. I was a child who would have starved if they hadn't taken me in. I wasn't old enough for my family to marry me off when my parents died. I didn't have any options but them."

As soon as the words left Bjorn's mouth, he wished he swallowed them. Tyra staggered backwards and waved him away when he tried to support her.

"I had thought I'd marry soon after I moved in with them. I thought I'd found someone who would want to marry me. No greater fool than me to have thought that."

Tyra ran to her ship and jumped onto the deck. For the second time that day, Bjorn watched her disappear as she left him behind, regretting the past and the present.

<hr>

Tyra ran along the deck until she reached her cabin, but rather than slam the door shut, she left it open just enough to observe Bjorn standing alone on the dock. She expected him to storm away, so she was unprepared when his shoulders slumped, and his head hung to his chest. He stood like that for so long that Tyra started to worry. When she decided to go back, she paused because he sat and tilted his head back to look at the night sky.

Tyra remembered he said the aurora lights scared him as a child. She remembered Bjorn was a happy child, fearless to the point of being reckless. She had a hard time reconciling what she had learned with what she was certain she knew. It made her wonder how much was a façade, how much of his recklessness was to make up for how scared he must have been when he had no parents. Perhaps his brazen acts were an attempt to join his parents in Valhalla. He was right. He lived at the mercy and generosity of Ivar and Lena, and he was lucky they were loving to him. She had been wrong to point out he was not their child.

The deaths of their infant children, the stillborn births and miscarriages, were a sensitive topic for everyone, so to point out Bjorn was a substitute had been unkind. Guilt began to eat at Tyra when she recalled the various unkind words she had tossed at Bjorn over the years. She began to worry he might not have deserved all of her caustic remarks.

Bjorn watched the lights flash across the sky. The old fear seemed foolish now, but it had terrorized him as a child. He had never admitted to anyone but Tyra that they scared him. He knew they scared Leif because he had snuck into Leif's room more than once to discover it empty and to learn later that he was in Freya's room. He never admitted he was lonely and frightened, because he did not feel right denying Leif of his sister's help. Instead, he did as he told Tyra. He buried his head beneath the covers. Now, he watched the greens and yellows dance behind the clouds, and he tried to view them the way Tyra did. He liked the idea that the lights were his parents waving to him. His thoughts reverted to them when he was alone, but he struggled remember what they looked like.

The guilt of forgetting them had plagued him for years, and the love he carried for Ivar and Lena made him feel like he failed his parents' memory. He moved to the edge of the dock and looked down at the water. More than once he considered sailing out and not returning, instead joining his parents where their pyres burned. The only thing that stopped him each time was knowing he would die but never join them in Valhalla. His death would not be in battle or in the glory of serving his people. He would not feast with the gods or his mother and father.

The goddess Freyja would not select him to join her in *Fólkvangr*. He feared his death would have no honor because his death would not happen while avenging someone. He would not be honored for dying to avoid bringing shame to his family. Just the opposite, he would shame himself. Bjorn had fought for his people time and again, and he was proud of his service. But they would view taking his own life as weak when he knew in every other sense he was anything but. He had survived the loss of his family and too many battles to count. Bjorn would not shame his surviving family, but it did not change the fact that he struggled with the decision for years.

Bjorn looked over his shoulder at Tyra's boat and another wave of failure crashed over him. He had failed her as a friend and a lover. He had caused her pain ten years earlier just as he did now. Her words from earlier that day rang in his ears, "Why couldn't you be the man I need?" He had asked himself the same thing many times since his one tryst with her. It was a crushing realization each and every time that he was not that man and probably never would be.

Bjorn's head hurt, and the weight of the world seemed to crush him. He needed to escape for a while. He looked at the water again. He was happiest when he sailed, and he would rather swim than walk. He stood and removed his cloak, his sword belt, his knives, his boots, his leather pants, and his shirt. He walked to the end of the dock and dove in, swimming as far as his lungs allowed, until his chest burned and forced him to the surface. He looked back at the shore and noticed Tyra running along the dock, stripping off her clothes as she sprinted.

FOUR

Tyra watched the anguish play across Bjorn's face as he stared at the night sky. It was impossible to ignore the dejection he managed to hide from the rest of the world. She felt like an intruder, spying on him during his most vulnerable moments, but she feared what he might do. She kicked herself for never considering that she and Bjorn might suffer the same grief. She had been so consumed in her own feelings, and Bjorn's loss had been so long ago, that she did not stop to consider he might still be suffering.

Now her unkind words and taunts were petty and childish. She had an inkling of why he felt duty bound to keep her alive. He did not seem to fear his own death, but the possibility of losing those he cared about bothered him. While Tyra did not deny she loved Bjorn, she had always feared his feelings toward her were more out of obligation. She doubted that now. As she watched him, her heart expanded with love for a man she had had a hard time tolerating. She loved him for the man she knew him to be, even though she could not rid herself of her grudge or her animosity when she came into contact with him.

Her mouth went dry when he stood and disrobed. His body had been a marvel when she saw it all those years ago. She had seen him shirtless frequently over the years, and it never failed to stir her, but he was bared in his full glory right before her eyes. She had never seen anything so incredible. His chest seemed broader now that she glimpsed how it tapered to his narrow hips. The muscles in his buttocks flexed with each step, and the muscles in his legs jumped with each movement. His abdomen had more ridges than she realized when she noticed how they created a vee to his hip bones and the tuft of dark hair between his legs. He was still the most endowed man she had ever seen. As he walked past her ship, she ducked behind her door until she was sure he passed her. She stepped onto the deck in time to watch his back muscles bunch and ripple as he dove in. She stood staring as she waited for him to surface.

As the seconds ticked by, unease creeped up her spine. He seemed to have been underwater far too long. He was the best swimmer of them all, but even for him, too much time passed. Fear spiked through her as she waited. The bay was deep enough for their ships, but their hulls were shallow. She worried he hit the bottom, that the seaweed trapped him. She worried something attacked him. She just worried.

Tyra pulled off her boots then ran along the dock, pulling off the rest of her clothes. She was diving from the dock when she caught his head emerging. She swam out underwater, but she came up before she reached him. She looked at him while treading water. They were several feet apart, but his surprise still registered. He swam toward her, and she spotted the caution in his gaze. Tyra began to kick and met him halfway.

"You were underwater so long," she murmured.

"You were watching me?" Tyra turned her head away and nodded. "Why?"

She shrugged, but she was not sure he could see the movement. When he asked again, she was sure he either had not or it did not satisfy him. "Because I didn't like how we left things. My words were thoughtless, but I held yours against you when you spoke the truth. I've been thoughtless more times than I'll ever be able to remember." Tyra looked at the water then toward the cliffs. "I regret now all the jibes I've made over the years. I never once considered your feelings other than to hurt them. I've been angry about how life treated me, and once that anger included you, you became an easy target. I'm sorry."

Tyra looked him in the eye as she offered the apology. Bjorn took a deep breath as he listened to Tyra's admission. He looked into her hazel eyes and saw her remorse. He reached for her hand, which hovered at the surface. When she did not reject him, he pulled her toward him. She came without a fight, their knees bumping into one another.

"That morning, the morning you were hugging Strian, my mind screamed you rejected me. I was sure you used and abandoned me. I never thought about the date. I only wanted to hide the pain and save face. It was like one more person I cared about left me behind," Bjorn's voice broke as he continued to look at Tyra.

"Oh, Bjorn."

Bjorn brushed a tear from her cheek before it had the chance to travel far. He wrapped his hands around her waist and pulled her flush to his body. She wrapped her legs around him as she cupped his face.

"I was so hurt and angry. I never considered how it must have appeared to you. But why didn't you talk to me?" Tyra murmured.

"Because Strian was hurting just as you were. I wasn't going to take something else from him."

Tyra's heart broke as her mind flashed to the innumerable things Bjorn had done over the years, putting others ahead of himself. She had chided herself for loving a selfish man. At that moment, she was realizing her heart had known all along what her mind refused to admit. Bjorn was a good man. That was why she had loved him since they were children. Bjorn rolled onto his back and began to swim them back to the dock.

"What're you doing?" Tyra asked.

"I'm taking us back to shore. I'm not making the same mistake twice. I—"

Tyra gasped and released him. She pushed him underwater and swam fast and hard to the dock, and Bjorn emerged spluttering. He turned and swam after Tyra. He reached the dock just as she pulled herself from the water.

"Mistake? Fine. This was a mistake. I should have known."

"Tyra, wait. Will you never give me a chance to explain?"

"No."

She swept up her clothes and ran to her boat. This time she slammed the door when she reached her cabin, leaning against it as the tears flowed. She wondered if her rejection was premature. Had she rejected him to avoid him rejecting her first, or did she have a legitimate reason to be insulted? Tyra did not know, and she did not want to think about it. She toweled herself off and climbed into her bunk. She closed her eyes, but sleep evaded her until she let her mind drift to the few times she and Bjorn had been alone. Her heart ached, but she fell asleep.

Bjorn dressed himself and made his way back to the longhouse. Before he reached the door, Gunnhild approached him. Her smile was a clear invitation, and Bjorn considered it. He wanted to convince himself that Tyra rejected him for the last time and that he was ready to set aside his love so that he might move on. He smiled back at the woman who had pleasured him several times over the years. It had been during feasts when he was drunk and lonely. This time he was sober and lonely. She took his hand and led him to her home.

Bjorn followed her in and groaned when she pressed her body against him. He had been semi-aroused when he held Tyra, forcing his body to remain in check so as not to scare her. Now it responded with need. It had been so long since he had been with a woman, and he had not forgotten Gunnhild was talented. Her hand traveled to his cock and rubbed its length.

Bjorn tangled his hands into her hair as he returned her kiss. She pulled at his laces until he sprang loose and stroked him as his kiss grew more desperate. Bjorn was aware what he was doing was wrong. It was wrong to be with Gunnhild when he was in love with Tyra. He was sure Tyra would not forgive him if she learned he bedded Gunnhild right after holding her naked body against his own. And he knew it was wrong because it was not Gunnhild he pictured thrusting into, not Gunnhild he envisioned as he surged toward release. It was only Tyra. It was only ever Tyra, whether he was alone or with a woman.

Bjorn's body crept closer to release. He was only moments away, but when Gunnhild sank to her knees and licked him, his eyes flashed open. It was not Tyra he was looking at. He tried to pull loose. "No, Gunnhild. I can't."

But it was too late. His climax overcame him as his seed surged forward, splattering against Gunnhild's lips and chin. He tilted his head against the door and banged it several time, regret coursing through him where pleasure had been only moments ago.

"Still picturing that bitch. She won't have you between her thighs or in her mouth." Gunnhild purred as she stood. She was unprepared for Bjorn to grab her hair and swing her around to bang her back against the door.

"Don't speak about her like that. You know better." He barked as he yanked her hair.

Gunnhild pushed her arms up between them and shoved him back before picking up a jar beside them. She brought it down, but Bjorn stepped away and grabbed her wrist. "She'll whore for other men, but she doesn't want you. You have the chance to enjoy me but instead, she has you by the balls and isn't making you come. When are you going to be a man and get over her?"

"You question my manhood after I showered you with my seed?"

"And who made you find your release? Tyra? Ha!" Her laugh was harsh and cruel. "I don't think so. Does your cock even work if you're not thinking of her?"

"I suppose neither of us will ever know because I wasn't thinking about your cunny."

Bjorn yanked her away and stepped out her door. He made a beeline for his chamber and threw his sword belt down, then threw his boots across the room. He was disgusted with himself for using Gunnhild, for giving into temptation so easily, and for still being in love with a woman who did nothing but reject him.

Bjorn wondered how he could love a woman who

could not stand him. It was beyond unrequited love; it was pure masochism. But he loved her for the person she was, not what she thought of him. That was how his love endured so many years. If he had based it upon her opinion of him, it would have fizzled long before their meeting by the fjord all those years ago. He slipped into bed, loathing himself and feeling worse than he had an hour ago when he considered sailing away.

The next fortnight fled by as preparations continued for their upcoming voyage. Tyra and Bjorn ignored each other by silent agreement, but Tyra noticed that Gunnhild and Bjorn avoided each other with thinly veiled bitterness. She wondered what occurred between them to create such animosity. She had her suspicions, since it began after she joined him in the bay. Her stomach churned each time she pictured Bjorn with another woman, but she was reasonable enough not blame the man. She had rejected him. Again.

Tyra had forced herself to admit it was never Bjorn who rejected her but always the other way around. A thought, an explanation, niggled at the back of her mind, but she did not understand why she kept doing it. It was too painful to reflect upon for long. It brought a sense of loss and regret over time wasted. To Tyra, regrets were useless, but regrets plagued her now.

"Freya, which ship are you taking? Will you sail the shallower hull again or will you go with the larger one?" Tyra asked.

"The shallow one. It worked well the last time, especially when we needed speed."

Erik walked up behind his wife and wrapped his arms around her. "Do you plan to leave me in your wake, since mine will sit heavier in the water? You assigned me most of the supplies."

Freya laughed as Erik nuzzled her neck. Tyra watched Freya wrap her arms back around Erik, but she also witnessed one hand slide between them. Tyra looked down at her maps, but she did not restrain her smile. She was happy Freya relented and admitted how she felt for Erik. She had been a bristly bear when she was unwilling to confess she loved Erik as much as he loved her. The poor man had followed her around like a homeless puppy, trying to get her attention. Their scouting trip to Scotland was the cure, and they came back observing Erik's Scottish heritage of handfasting. They were ostensibly married when they sailed into the docks. A pang of jealousy struck Tyra as it often did when she looked at Leif and Sigrid or Freya and Erik, but she was happy for them.

"If you two aren't going back to your chamber, perhaps you'd look at these maps. I need your help completing the waterway you took from where you left Grímr behind to Erik's family's keep. We may need to use your shallow boat and some of the others if we sail inland."

"Erik would be best at helping you, or have Lorna look them over." Freya looked around and called to her mother-in-law. When Lorna arrived, she looked at the maps and tsked before shaking her head. "Lass, this is off by leagues. Who helped you with this? My son?"

Tyra caught the teasing in the woman's voice. She nodded and laughed aloud when Lorna tapped

Erik's cheek. "He can't steer his way out of a herring barrel. It's a good thing Freya looks after him."

Erik harrumphed but unfolded his arms when Freya gave him a smacking kiss and whispered none too quietly, "He knows how to find the most important port."

Erik lifted his wife around the waist, before tossing over his shoulder. "We'll be back. My wife needs a lesson in my navigation skills." They were running to the jarl's longhouse before anyone replied.

"Newlyweds," Lorna mused as she moved around pebbles that represented various landmarks, then took the burned stick Tyra used to mark the skins that made her maps. As Lorna worked, she spoke to Tyra.

"It seems you didn't get much from my long-winded story. Now you're ignoring each other. What will you do when you are back to relying upon each other for your lives?"

"We don't have to. I will partner with Strian—" Tyra halted when she realized Bjorn would not be partnering with Leif, since his cousin was not going. That meant Bjorn and Strian would partner. Freya now fought alongside Erik, and Lorna would partner with her husband Rangvald. Ivar was remaining to oversee both his and Rangvald's settlements. This made her the odd one out.

"Exactly. You will have to trust him when you partner with both him and Strian. Neither of those men will trust anyone else to fight alongside you. That means they need to be able to trust you, too. I'm sure that won't be an issue with Strian, but can you say the same with Bjorn?"

"Yes," Tyra was emphatic. "It doesn't matter what is happening between us once we're in battle. I will always protect my friends and family. They come first."

"And if he saves your life again or the other way around? Will we suffer a repeat of the last six moons? Both of you snapping at one another, denying what lies between you?"

Tyra stood up and looked at the older woman. Lorna was still the most stunningly beautiful woman she had ever seen. She appreciated how humble the woman was about her appearance, but she used it to gain an advantage in battle. Men were either too distracted by her or underestimated her. Tyra admired her skills, and now that she had learned Lorna's history, she respected her even more. She had seen the similarities in her relationship with Bjorn as Lorna recounted about her story with Rangvald. Tyra just did not know how to fix her own actions.

"Lass, will you take a word of advice from someone older and perhaps a wee wiser?" Tyra nodded. "You have one life to live. You've known the man your entire life. I was told he was with his mother the day you were born, and his mother attended yours at your birth. Everyone knows you have been in love with each other for years, but no one speaks of it. Perhaps they should, then maybe neither of you would be so miserable. In this life, you can love, or you can lose. Right now, you are losing time and opportunities for happiness. No one guarantees you happiness, but when the chance is there, you're an eejit not to take it. Give the man a chance. Do that, really truly do that, and I'm sure he won't disappoint you like you assume."

Lorna gave her a hug and a kiss to the temple that had Tyra leaning into it. Lorna felt it and gave her an extra squeeze. "I'll always be by your side, lass. Just look for me." Lorna stepped back onto the dock and spoke with Ivar and Rangvald. Tyra looked out and spotted Bjorn watching her, but he turned away before she waved.

That evening, Sigrid cast the runes, reading her collection of bones and stones. The others waited with bated breath as she seemed to slip into her trance. She had not spirit walked since her first journey with Leif and the others. Her husband would not allow it, it had frightened him so badly. Now she eased out from her meditative state and looked around.

"Hakin is dead. Freya succeeded during the last attack. He bled to death. But Grímr lives and is healed. He has been training, but I did see where. Now that his wretched wife Inga is no longer running a slave trade, he has little money. It seems he will be hiding. There were both mountains and open fields, which describes most of the Highlands. The men wore black plaids, but they were not such a motley group as before. These men fought together and are very well trained, as if they were an army rather than random mercenaries."

"Lass, did you sense any names? You wouldn't recognize them, but I might," Lorna inquired.

"No, Aunt Lorna. The only name was Grímr's. It screamed at me. The Mackays, MacLeods, and Sutherlands joined us again. It did not seem like you had to travel that far once you arrived at the Mackays."

"That's all right, lass. I have an idea now of where we will have to go," Lorna grimaced. "I can wager a guess who we will meet. There only three choices. The Sinclairs, the Gunns, or the Rosses. It wouldn't surprise me if it's the Rosses, since they live closest to where the three territories join. The Rosses and Mackays have no love lost between them. I hope the flames of hell reach as far as Ross lands. They will fit in well with the Devil."

Everyone stared at Lorna, who only shrugged. She rarely referenced her Christian upbringing, so it was a startling reminder when she spoke of it.

"Bloodthirsty and lusty. Just how I love you." Rangvald slapped her backside before they excused themselves for the night.

FIVE

They set sail the next morning, with Tyra's ship leading the fleet. She relished the feel of the sun on her skin as the wind swept her hair from her neck. She wore it loose while they sailed because she enjoyed the feel of the wind lifting it from her back. It almost made it seem like she might take flight. Tyra was in her element when she was at the helm of her ship. She had been leading the fleet since just before her parents died. She had been four-and-ten when her father insisted that Ivar allow her to captain his ship and show the jarl her innate skills. It took one fishing voyage and a storm that broke apart four other boats to prove to the others she had a gift for sailing. The boat she captained suffered the least damage and the nets, trawling when the storm rose from nowhere, filled to bursting while the storm shredded all the other ones.

When asked how she steered the boat through the storm when she had never been at the helm before, she shrugged and told the others the waves told her what would happen. She just had to look and listen. After that, no one doubted her ability. Her first two expeditions were spent waiting with the ships rather than going ashore to raid. Once her parents died, no one had the authority, other than Ivar, to stop her from fighting. She remembered Bjorn staying silent while everyone argued with her. He was the last to speak up, telling the others she would either survive or die, but better they partner her before they landed than go into the fight alone. That was when Strian, Bjorn, and Leif began fighting as a trio, allowing Freya and her to go ashore to fight together. She resented Bjorn's flippant comment about her life, but now she realized he had done exactly what he needed to defend and protect her.

The first five days of their voyage were uneventful, so Tyra spent most of her time at the helm. She continued to enjoy the sensation of the sun beating down on her, and she guessed her skin was darkening. She suspected that if she looked in still water, she would find a smattering of freckles across her nose and cheeks. She breathed in the tangy salt air as she looked around at the other ships. Tyra observed Freya and Erik standing at the rails of their ships, speaking to one another. Tyra was aware Erik spent the night in Freya's cabin with her, since they were still newlyweds, and it was a luxury to have the privacy.

When Freya was ready to captain her own ship, Ivar insisted his only daughter have a space with a door to keep the men from seeing her. By extension, Ivar insisted that they provide the same to Tyra, who was much like a sister to Freya. Her eyes skipped to the door of her cabin, and a jolt of jealousy stabbed through her chest knowing she would not be retiring with a lover that night. As if that was not bad enough, as she looked to Bjorn's ship her gaze alighted on Gunnhild, who was assigned to her crew.

The woman worked hard and said very little, so Tyra attempted to forget she was there. Tyra noticed Bjorn talking to his crew, a mixture of men and women, as they rotated who sat to row. She looked over her shoulder to catch a glimpse of Lorna sitting in the crow's nest of Rangvald's ship. She did not bother to resist smiling at the sight of the woman who, at times appearing matronly, sat watch high above the water. Tyra grinned at Rangvald's bellows carried, ordering his wife down or his wife's equally vocal refusal to leave. Apparently she was comfortable. She scanned the rest of the fleet comprising ships from Ivar and Rangvald's fleets. She noticed a man she had never met, standing at the helm of a boat off to the port side of her stern. He was handsome even from a distance. She watched his tawny hair blow in the wind, much like hers did. He held the tiller, wearing only leather pants and a fur pelt across his shoulders.

The sun was warm only because Tyra had several layers on. She marveled at how the brisk air or the freezing spray of the surf did not affect him. No man had drawn Tyra's attention in a long time, but she discovered she was very curious to discover who this man was. She turned away to find Bjorn watching her. He was too far for her to read his expression, but she sensed he was not pleased to witness her staring at the other man. She wanted to smirk, since the knowledge that he and Gunnhild had done something after her swim with Bjorn stung. Tyra's nose twitched. She sniffed and called her first mate over to take the helm. She was scaling the mast before her first mate asked what was wrong.

"What do you see, Tyra?" Bjorn called over.

Tyra shaded her eyes as she looked to the horizon. She sniffed again and was sure she smelled the storm before she spotted the waterspout far in the distance. Tyra watched the clouds vibrate and counted before the next one. She could not hear the accompanying thunder, but she deduced from how close the bolts were, the storm was strong. Her father taught her that the sounds of the waves had the ability to swallow the warning thunder before it would reach them. This storm was still a great distance away, but Tyra understood how the weather shifted at sea.

"There's a storm brewing," she called to Bjorn. "We have some time, but it will get very rough. Pass the word that everyone needs to leash themselves or the storm will sweep them overboard."

Tyra shimmied down the mast and began giving orders to her crew as she checked the items stored in the hull. Once the rowers pulled all the shields over the sides and secured them under the benches, there was little to do but take the helm again. Tyra watched Bjorn speak to Erik and Freya even though no voices carried to her. She had already told her first mate to pass the word to the ships nearest theirs. She looked back to her stern and spied the handsome warrior again. He looked at her and nodded once before returning his gaze to the water, but she caught his grin. She twisted back around, annoyed that he was laughing at her for looking at him. Staring might have been a better description, but she was not willing to admit it.

She ordered her sails to remain raised as the wind began to pick up. She called out orders as she turned her boat parallel to the rising waves. They were not large enough yet for her to worry about them broaching. Instead, she wanted to make as much progress as possible before the wind inevitably blew them off-course. By sailing parallel to the waves, the current would knock her back to the route she wanted rather than pushing her away. Or at least that is what she hoped. The raindrops began as fat beads of water bouncing off her hair and nose. She looked up to the sky as the wind picked up. She ordered the sails lowered and the crew lashed to the deck. She handed the tiller over to her first mate as she climbed the mast again.

"Tyra! Tyra, get down!" Bjorn's voice carried on the wind. Tyra sensed he was irate without looking down at him, but she ignored him as she scanned the seas. She observed the storm crashing just a few leagues ahead of them. Tyra watched as the swells shifted and grew with each surge.

"Breaking waves! Bows forward, sails down, oars in," she called to the captains close enough to catch her orders. The others would follow those in front of them. She slid down the mast and made her way to the rail, looking over the edge at how the sea churned below her hull. She peered into the depth as water rushed below her hull. She did not notice any hint of a cross current, and she thanked the gods for that.

"Tyra!"

Tyra stood up and found Bjorn standing at the rail of his ship yelling at her. He wanted her tied to the tiller, but her stomach dropped as she looked past Bjorn's shoulder.

"Bjorn, no! Hurry! You must tie down!" She pointed wildly as Bjorn furrowed his brow at her. She waved and pointed.

"Wave!" She screamed as the first one crashed over Bjorn's bow. He grabbed the rail and hung on before the water swept him over the side. He kept his head tucked until the water settled. He stood and glared at her.

"See!" He called back to her. Tyra was certain her ears deceived her. The insane man would use his near drowning as a lesson to her. She shook her head as she tied the rope around her waist. She watched him do the same.

For the next twelve hours, the raging sea battered and bashed their fleet about like a child's toy spinning around a drain. Tyra ordered the crew to huddle between the benches. She gripped the tiller with both hands as she tried to keep her bow pointing into the waves, but it was getting increasingly difficult as the wind shifted and rather than heading into the swells, they now chased the fleet. This was far more dangerous as they surged up and under the hulls. The screams carried on the wind as the seas tossed boats that floundered.

Tyra tried not to look back but focus on the waves around her. She accepted that her voice reached none of the other captains, so she relied on hand signals to tell those near her when to point their bows into the wave and when to angle into them. This avoided crashing into a wave head on when the water surged behind them. She prayed to Thor and *Rán* to be kind and merciful, even though the gods were rarely known for mercy. She watched the lightning and counted the time between the strike and the clap of thunder. When there was no time between them, she realized they were nearing the eye of the storm.

Just as fast as the wind and storm blew in, it subsided. While Tyra listened to cheers, intuition told her the storm was not done with them. They had survived one side of the storm. They were in the eye and would soon pass back into the punishing gale.

"Stay tied down! No one move!" Tyra bellowed. She noticed Freya and Erik watching her. She strained to find Strian and Bjorn, but she breathed again when she was certain they were looking at her. She signaled for their bows to point forward and to follow her. She gave the signal for everyone to remain lashed to the hulls.

Tyra listened to the voices on the wind as her friends carried out her orders. She wished she knew if Rangvald and Lorna caught glimpses of her gestures, and if they did, that they understood what they meant. Her mind jumped for a moment to the handsome man, but it whipped back to the storm as the next round of waves breached her bow.

Tyra fought the tiller as it tried to lift her from her seat. She pulled hard to keep them on course, hands wrapping around her as he first mate anchored her to the bench. She counted her blessings for at least the hundredth time over the years that her first mate was a foot taller than her and nearly a hundred pounds heavier. She would go nowhere while he held her down. She nodded her head as she continued to steer them through the second round of the storm.

The storm ended with the waves calming and the sun trying to rise behind them. They had sailed through the night and made it to morning. When Tyra was confident no imminent danger remained for her to climb the rigging, she scurried up the mast. She looked in all directions, but the sky was clear as if the storm evaporated into the heavens. She surveyed the damage to the ships around hers. Some looked like the waves grazed them, but others listed. Much of the fleet limped along like an old man with aching joints. Tyra leaned as far forward as she dared to assess the damage, but a voice hollering her name made her roll her eyes and scoot back down to the deck.

"Woman, you shall be the death of me!" Bjorn's ship sailed closer to hers now as they had all shifted position even though Tyra's ship led. "I do not intend to die in these waters when I have to fish you out. We made it through the storm, but you would break your neck falling from your own mast."

"Bjorn."

"I know my name."

"You're overreacting. Besides, you are absolved of your duty to protect me."

She watched as Bjorn's gaze shuttered, and he backed away without a word or even a nod. She held her breath as he began ordering his crew to examine their ship for damage. Tyra returned to the tiller and tried to estimate their location.

———

By midmorning, Tyra was certain they were not as far off-course as she feared. The storm pushed them south which was the direction they wanted to travel. It also pushed them west toward the Orkney Islands. Before the sun set, she glimpsed the first hints of land off her bow. She suspected they were the chain's uninhabited islands, but they would have beaches and timber. Those were her priorities for her own ship and the rest of the fleet. She guided the fleet toward them, and the sun sank below the horizon as they came ashore. The ships in the fleet's rear tethered together so they would not float away, and the crews wove their away over benches and planks until they waded in.

Tyra had to tap on Strian's arm as he swallowed her in his embrace. He whispered into her ear.

"He was right. You took unnecessary risks. You might not like him ordering you about, but he cares. We all do. His voice just happens to be the most strident."

Tyra nodded as she gave him one more squeeze. Freya was behind her when she turned, and the two women embraced as they shared their fear and relief with no need for words. Once her friends were sure everyone was hale, they worked with the others to set up camp near the beach. It was too late to assess the damage. Once people built fires, watches were assigned, and a sparse meal eaten, everyone gave in to exhaustion.

As the sun rose once more in a bright, clear sky, Tyra walked around the hulls, making note of which needed the most urgent care. Bjorn and Erik were checking with captains for injuries that needed tending, while Freya and Strian determined the boats and crews they lost. Rangvald and Lorna hiked a ridge near to the beach. They set off to scout for any of the lost boats and to get a lay of the land.

"You have the natural talent everyone says you do," a deep voice came from over Tyra's shoulder. She sensed who it would be before she turned, but she still was not prepared for how dazzlingly handsome the man was. She took in his broad shoulders and the smattering of hair on his chest. He was nearly the most handsome man she had ever seen. There was only one man she found more attractive, but she forced her mind from Bjorn.

"Thank you. I'm glad to have it when I can keep my people safe."

"Perhaps the tales are true then. You are the tenth daughter of *Rán* and *Ægir*."

"Hardly," Tyra's voice hardened. She despised the comparison because it ignored her real parents. It was already becoming hard to remember what they looked and sounded like. The man held his hands up as he smiled at her, his white teeth shining in even rows.

"I meant no offense. I intended to appreciate the fortune the gods offered us."

Tyra nodded as she moved on to the next ship. The man followed her as she ran her hand along the wood planks.

"You're aware of who I am." She added nothing beyond that. She would not state her curiosity but let him decide whether he would take the bait.

"I am Fritjof."

Tyra looked over him, and something in the back of her head made her wonder if his name was true. *One who steals peace.* He smiled once again, and she pushed the meaning aside.

"It's nice to meet you. You sail for Jarl Rangvald?"

"Yes. I'm a distant cousin to the jarl and Erik."

Tyra nodded as she continued to survey the ships. She would ask Erik later about the man. Before their conversation progressed, Strian came back to her side.

"Tyra, there isn't as much damage as we expected, but there are a few holes and deep gouges that need repairing. Your carpenters will be busy for the next few days. I'll send my crew and Bjorn's to fell trees and bring them back. In the meantime, we are meeting."

Tyra watched Strian's gaze flick past her as he

assessed the man standing behind her. His face re-
vealed nothing, but Tyra knew him well enough to
sense Fritjof did not impress him. She would ask
Strian later about the man, too. She looked back at
Fritjof and smiled.

"It was nice to meet you."

"And you, too."

SIX

Tyra twisted her back and leaned her head from one side to the other as she tried to release the knots forming from standing over a log, running a rasp over it to remove the bark. She pushed her shoulders back and ignored the cracks along her spine, but she flushed when Fritjof stepped forward just as her chest thrust forward.

"You work very hard and at a great many things. You are a mapmaker, a shipbuilder, a sailor, and a carpenter. Is there anything you can't do?"

"Yes. Plenty," she grinned.

"Such as?"

"Cook. I can't cook, and I don't sew very well. I mean I can do these things, just not very well."

"If those are your only failings, then you are still nearly perfect."

A growl filled her ears as she instinctively reached for his pelt and pulled him forwards lest Bjorn walk into him with a log under his arm. She glared at him and at Strian, who carried the other end. Strian chuckled and shrugged. Bjorn scowled when he realized all he had done was bring the two closer together.

"Thank you," Fritjof murmured against her hair

as he cupped her shoulders. She found her hands resting on his chest. His skin prickled as if it would singe her fingertips. She looked into eyes that were dark brown. They reminded her of someone else's eyes, but they lacked the warmth she was used to in Bjorn's gaze. Fritjof's seemed to assess her as if he was sizing her up. Whatever he found must have pleased him because he pulled her closer.

"Would you dine with me tonight?" he asked.

"As long as I am not needed elsewhere."

<hr>

The rest of the day passed as Tyra's shipbuilders sawed and hammered, preparing to repair the worst of the damage the next day. When it was too dark to continue work, and everyone was hungry and tired, Tyra called it quits for the day. She found the others, but they were chatting rather than planning or strategizing. She looked around and spotted Fritjof who watched her. She smiled, and he walked toward her. He brought a bowl of pottage someone cooked earlier that evening.

"I think you earned your supper tonight."

"Thank you. I am starved." She took the bowl, and they found a place to sit against one of the felled logs. Tyra blew on the steaming food as she looked across the rim at him. Fritjof cocked his head as he watched her eat.

"How are you not married yet?" The question, nearing on accusation, shocked Tyra, and she choked on the food that burned the back of her throat.

"I beg your pardon?"

"No man claimed a seat next to you, and you agreed to dine with me. That tells me you're unwed or at least your man is not on this voyage."

Tyra lifted her chin and peered into smoky

brown eyes. "I'm not married because I don't want to be."

Fritjof nodded as he looked around. Tyra was sure he noticed the others watching them, but Tyra ignored them. "Then why are aren't you someone's companion?"

"Who says I'm not?"

"The same reasons I know you're not married."

"Perhaps I like my freedom."

"Freedom to choose?" Tyra nodded as she guessed where the conversation was going. "Then who do you choose?"

Tyra smiled behind the bowl and continued to sip as Fritjof waited. When he looked around and grew uncomfortable with the silence, Tyra placed her bowl beside her. "I haven't given it much consideration."

"I believe I can give you much to consider."

Fritjof ran his hand over her knee as she watched his gaze linger on her lips. Tyra tried to focus on Fritjof, tried to enjoy his attention and touch. It was not unpleasant; it just was not exciting either. She looked at the handsome man in front of her and remembered Lorna's words about having only one life. She accepted she and Bjorn were not meant to be, and she was tired of lonely nights.

Tyra wanted to lose herself with someone who wanted her. She figured if Bjorn had moved on with Gunnhild, even for a night, she would do the same. She was not looking for any form of attachment. She was looking for pleasure and release. She imagined Fritjof might provide that.

Bjorn watched from across the fire as Tyra conversed with a man he did not recognize. He admitted the other man was good looking, having listened to several other women comment on him throughout the day. He looked at Erik and cocked his head in Tyra's direction, raising an eyebrow. Erik looked beyond him and shrugged.

"He's not a bad man, but he also is interested in himself. As long as she doesn't set her hopes on a future with him, she'll come out no worse for wear."

Bjorn hissed at Erik's choice of words, and his friend looked guilty.

"I just meant he will not harm her or take advantage of her." Erik leaned forward, letting go of Freya long enough to murmur to Bjorn. "You know, if she is ready to move on, then you should, too. Do you want to grow old alone? Do you want to die without making the most of life? There's always the chance you die in the next battle, and what? You've been living a celibate life like a Christian monk for no reason than to punish yourself."

Bjorn nodded, aware there was truth in Erik's words. It appeared Tyra was moving on and would enjoy the man's company for the night. He looked away as nausea gurgled in his belly and tried to push its way up his throat. His sights landed on Gunnhild and another woman, Solvi, who he had bedded several years ago. He smiled at the women as they chatted together. He stood and nodded his head toward the woods. The woman exchanged a glance before walking toward him.

"Come to your senses?" Gunnhild purred. "You're lucky you have such a big cock and a talented tongue, or I might not be so forgiving."

"It has been a long time," Solvi chimed in. "You shall have to refresh my memory."

Both women stepped forwards and ran their hands over his chest. He tried to pay attention to the women as their hands drifted over his middle to his cock. It was only slightly awake, but it perked up as the women's ministrations grew more forceful. He tried to concentrate and enjoy the attention, but there was only one thing to envision if he wanted his body to comply.

Tyra watched Bjorn walk away with the two women clinging to his arms. It strung to watch him entertain anyone else. She was no virgin, and it was no secret. She had not been one for ten years, and she had had more than just Knud as a partner in her past. Being a shieldmaiden was perilous work. With no guarantee of life but a surety of death, one learned to take pleasure when it was available, as there was a surplus of misery in battle. However, it had been a long time since she shared a bedroll with any man. She forced air through her nose as she built her courage.

She surveyed the camp, and her eyes returned to Fritjof. He was handsome, and he watched her as she decided he would do as well as any other. Loneliness had crept into her heart unlike ever before. The brush with death during the storm, followed by watching Bjorn choose not one but two women, made her decision seem more reasonable. If he found comfort, so would she. She smiled at Fritjof, and he stood, reaching for her hand. She met him halfway and with a smile, they turned to find their own spot among the trees. She had not made it far when she sensed eyes upon her. She looked around and found Bjorn glaring at her. Her eyes darted to his companions before she lifted a brow to him in defiance.

He had no claim to her, no right to stop her. Why now? She knew, just as he did, that she could find solace when she wanted. He had proven it true for himself. However, it did not stop Bjorn from disentangling himself from his surprised, then angered, partners. He stomped over to her and placed his hands on his hips, glaring at her wordlessly.

Once again, she raised her eyebrow to him. He looked at Fritjof and growled. The other man had the audacity to chuckle. Fritjof raised his hand, saying, "Shall we?"

She nodded once and made to step around Bjorn. He grasped her upper arm and pulled her toward him. He bared his teeth and hissed for the man to leave. Fritjof shrugged and chuckled again.

"Bah. Too much work for one night," Fritjof said. "Find me when your keeper is already busy plowing someone else."

Tyra bit her tongue as she opened her mouth to ask Fritjof to stay but watched him hold out his arms to Gunnhild and Solvi. The women giggled and led him into the trees.

"He was quick to replace you," Bjorn grumbled.

"No faster than those two bitches in heat replaced you."

Bjorn shrugged, "Doesn't bother me, if we might try being honest."

"Honest? You want honest? How about, I can't stand you and wish you would stay out of my life." Tyra shrank back from the harshness of her own words.

"Someone has to protect you from yourself."

"And that someone has to be you? I don't need your protection. In fact, the only person I need protection from is you."

"Very well. Run and catch him. Join in. See how you feel about yourself in the morning."

"I can think of how I would feel. Pleasured and satiated."

Bjorn's laugh was hollow just as he felt. "Of course. I'm sure that's it."

"And you know otherwise? From Gunnhild?"

Tyra regretted the words when agony and torment haunted Bjorn's gaze. Bjorn looked at Tyra for a long moment before he looked at the camp. There were a handful of women he had bedded over the years sitting around the fire, some even with their husbands or companions. He was tired of playing this game, dancing this dance, with Tyra. He was too heartsore to keep up a façade any longer. He would make sure she understood, and then she could decide, but he was done trying.

"Ingeborg," he called out to a woman about to sit down.

Tyra gasped as she watched the buxom blonde walked toward them. She was familiar with the woman Bjorn had slept with many times over the years. She had even feared the woman might become Bjorn's companion, if not his wife.

"Hello, Bjorn. Tyra." Ingeborg smiled at them both, but Tyra caught the lust flare in the other woman's eyes as she looked at Bjorn. Tyra had an urge to slap her.

"Tell Tyra."

Tyra looked at Bjorn and then at Ingeborg. She looked just as confused as Tyra felt.

"Bjorn, are you sure? You made me swear never to tell anyone, and I assumed that included Tyra."

"What?" Tyra looked back and forth. "What am I not supposed to know?"

She waited as Bjorn watched her, and Ingeborg wrung her hands.

"Bjorn?" Tyra whispered.

"Tell her, Ingeborg," Bjorn growled.

"All right," Ingeborg sighed. When she spoke, she made sure her voice did not carry. "Tyra, you know Bjorn and I were intimate for quite a long time. We've even come together again in recent years, but not often, mind you." Ingeborg bit her lip but plowed on when she caught the nervousness on Tyra's face.

"Bjorn swore me to secrecy and paid me well to keep his secret. Tyra," Ingeborg paused yet again. "It was your name he called out. He called me by your name and would never look at me."

Tyra stood there stunned. She had not imagined this would be the secret Ingeborg divulged.

"Thank you," Bjorn murmured, and Ingeborg nodded before returning to the fire. Before Tyra said anything, Bjorn called out to another woman, Eira. The woman approached them, but her smile dropped when their faces turned toward her.

"Tell her."

Eira looked at Bjorn and nodded once before looking at Tyra. "It was your name. He never said mine, refused to look at me. He made me promise not to tell anyone, and he paid me well for it."

"Thank you," Bjorn gazed into the fire rather than at either woman.

"Wait," Tyra reached out to stop Eira. "I don't understand. You two were together many times. It didn't bother you?"

Eira looked at Bjorn before looking at Tyra, and Tyra deduced the answer. Eira still loved Bjorn. Tyra squeezed the woman's shoulder and forced a smiled. Bjorn opened his mouth to call out another name, but Tyra could not bear it.

"Stop." Her hushed tones carried across the few inches that separated them. Bjorn looked at her and waited. Neither of them seemed able to say anything. After several drawn out moments, Tyra dislodged the lump that sat at the base of her throat. "Why? Why did you do that? Why tell me?"

"Because it's time you knew."

Tyra tried to back away, shaking her head. She held her hands up as if to create a barrier between them. Tears gathered at the corner of her eyes. "It doesn't change anything, Bjorn."

"Doesn't it? Doesn't it change everything?"

"No. It can't."

Bjorn stepped forward and grasped her arms. He pulled her, and she stepped into his embrace. She let him wrap his arms around her. She rested her head against his chest as she breathed in his fresh scent. He had bathed earlier that evening, and she smelled the pine from his soap. He stroked her back as she fisted his shirt as she clenched her fingers closed. Tyra relaxed into his arms until the sounds coming from the trees nearby drifted to them.

"Gunnhild, yes. Right there." Tyra and Bjorn froze as several grunts and a long moan followed. "Solvi, that tongue of yours."

"Finally, a man who uses my name. A man with a cock that works on its own."

Tyra pulled away from Bjorn as she looked aghast at the trees.

"So much for a secret," Bjorn muttered. He looked at Tyra and recognized humiliation rather than embarrassment. He reached for her again, but she shook her head before dashing away.

Bjorn wanted to bash his head against a tree trunk. He could not win for trying. No matter what he did, no matter how honest he tried to be, Tyra rejected him. Bjorn watched her settle near the fire, and something in him fractured. He found a jug of mead and walked down to the beach. He would drown his sorrows rather than watch all the happy couples curl up together.

Tyra noticed Fritjof, Gunnhild, and Solvi return from the woods. She watched as they engaged in a sloppy kiss with all three swiping their tongues, a sight that was obvious even from the other side of the fire. Tyra watched Fritjof walk to his tribe's side of the camp before she watched Gunnhild make her way toward their camp. Solvi settled next to another man.

"Gunnhild," Tyra called out, careful not to draw attention. She waited until the woman stood before her. "Sit. Please."

"Why, princess? Angry that both men you want prefer bedding me?"

"Angry that only one of those men remembers your name?" Tyra looked up at Gunnhild as the other woman glared down at her. It tempted her to rise to her feet, but she knew Gunnhild would view it as a challenge.

"Enough. I just want to understand something, then I won't ask any more of you. If you want to sail on another ship, I will arrange it."

"Very well. What?"

"Has it always been that way? I mean, we heard what you said. Has it always been like that?"

Gunnhild sucked in a breath that whistled through her teeth. "Yes. At least once he'd bedded you, or at least I assume that's what happened because he never talked about you before that day he spied you hugging Strian."

"You know about that?"

"I watched the whole thing. It was impossible to miss the hurt and rejection, so I used it to my advantage. Helga and I both did, but it was your name he kept whispering."

"Didn't that bother you?"

"You must not remember what he can do with that cock and tongue, or perhaps you never had time to find out. I can keep a secret for what he can do."

Tyra rose to her feet, feeling much more sober than she knew she was. "If it didn't bother you, then why taunt me? Why bother trying to goad me and hurt me?"

"That has nothing to do with Bjorn. I just don't like you. You're privileged and entitled all because Frú Lena was friends with your mother, and you got to play with Freya as a child. You think it makes yourself equal to Freya. You're not. You have no relations with the jarl's family, and you're nothing but a penniless orphan. You should remember your place."

Tyra forced herself to keep her face neutral despite the vitriol spewing from Gunnhild.

"It would seem my place is under, or perhaps on top of, Bjorn since that's where he wants to be." Tyra sniped.

"Bitch."

"Bitch with a man who wants her enough to pretend every other woman is her."

Gunnhild lashed out, but Tyra's instincts overcame her heartache. Tyra grasped Gunnhild's wrist and twisted it before pressing it back.

"You won't be able to row with a broken wrist, and if you can't row, then you are worthless. Would you like us to leave you behind? Would you like everyone to watch me beat you? Or would you like to answer my last question?" she pressed harder against Gunnhild's arm.

"Fine. What do you want?"

"What was the price for your silence, or was it just enough to let him fuck you?"

"He paid good coin along with bringing me pleasure," she sucked in another whistling breath, "And he threatened me. More than once I said something against you, and those are the only times in my life I feared death. I worried he would kill me, so I kept my mouth shut around others."

"Thank you. That's all I wanted."

Gunnhild shook out her wrist and smirked. "I'd

get off your high horse and ride him before you miss your chance altogether. He's waited ten years for you, but he's virile and will need sons. He can't wait for you forever."

Tyra watched as Gunnhild found a spot near the fire and cradled her wrist. Then she looked toward the beach. The sliver of rational thought left cautioned her not to follow Bjorn to the beach, but the rest of her thoughts lurched in his direction, and her body followed.

Bjorn sat with his jug of mead between his bent legs. He took drags from it until the last drop washed down his throat. Now, he watched the waves lap along the beach and bang against the hulls of the anchored fleet. He laid back and covered his eyes with his forearm. Despite not being able to see her, Bjorn knew when Tyra arrived on the beach. He was tucked away beside a log, and now that he was lying down, he knew she did not spot him. He waited until her footsteps came near him. He did not have it in him to go another round with her. His head and his heart hurt too much for any more rejection. He deepened his breathing and stilled his body. He knew when she found him, but she did not rouse him.

"Why can't I ever tell you what I need to say? Why do I ruin everything every time?" Bjorn inched his arm from his eyes, but she was already running back to the camp. He closed his eyes and let the alcohol carry him into a land of dreamless sleep.

The fleet and its sailors remained on the small island for three more days while Tyra led the repairs. She avoided everyone but Freya, and even then, it relieved her that her friend spent more time with Erik than her. She spent each night after her confrontation with Gunnhild in her cabin. Bjorn watched her retire to her ship and slipped to the beach to stand watch. He did not trust so many men knowing she slept isolated from the others. The nights were uneventful, but neither of them slept well.

SEVEN

Tyra led the fleet into the bay below the Mackay keep, the alarms ringing as Erik and Freya waded ashore. Lorna and Rangvald's bickering carried on the breeze as they followed Freya and Erik to the shore.

"Alex," Erik's voiced boomed. "Come greet your favorite cousin. And me." A dark head that resembled Erik's appeared over the battlements.

"Freya? And Lorna? Erik, ye should have mentioned both of ma favorite cousins are here. Plus ye. And Rangvald." It was only moments later before Alex Mackay and an entourage of guards made their way to the tops of the cliff. "And ye brought friends. Ready for another round of hide-and-go-seek with yer friend, Grímr?"

"I am. Are you?"

"We've been impatient for yer return. We've been getting along with our neighbors too well, and I fear ma men will grow soft. Bring yer people up. They can set up camp just outside the bailey wall."

Freya waved to her along with Strian and Bjorn. They each waded ashore and followed the two couples to the crest of the cliff. Tyra had to admit the looming structure that greeted them impressed her. It was even more impressive on level ground than from the sea. She watched Alex greet his family, and once more she was left out. She stood between Strian and Bjorn, and she sensed all three orphans felt the same longing.

"Shall we?" Strian muttered.

Rangvald and Lorna led their group as Lorna looked at how the land had changed since her last visit several years ago. Freya and Erik hung back to walk with their friends, while Alex cast Tyra appreciative glances and a wicked smile. She looked at him and admitted to herself that he was just as attractive as Fritjof, if not more, but his resemblance to Erik made it seem wrong to look at him. Bjorn's tension was palpable as Alex turned toward her.

"Erik has nay manners. He failed to introduce me to ye," Alex directed his words at all three of them, but it was clear he spoke to Tyra.

"I'm Strian, and this is Tyra and Bjorn."

Alex grinned as he locked forearms with the two men, a clear struggle to determine whose grasp was stronger. His touch was much gentler when he grasped forearms with Tyra. "A pleasure to meet ye. And where is the great Leif I heard aboot? And his wife Sigrid?"

Freya piped in, "My brother and Sigrid remained at home because she is carrying my first nephew."

"Nephew? How can you be so sure? Perhaps it's a wee niece for me to spoil," Erik teased.

"You shall spoil that child no matter whether it's a girl or a boy."

"True, wife, and I'm sure I will learn from your example."

"Likely."

Tyra watched Freya and Erik banter before she looked to Alex. He was not watching his cousin. Tyra ducked her head but smiled. She glanced at Bjorn to see he was not paying attention. She looked up and followed his gaze, but she could not tell what he saw. He seemed to stare into space.

"Bjorn?" she whispered. He did not answer and walked faster. Tyra looked at Strian, but he shrugged as they watched Bjorn walk toward the loch rather than follow the others to the keep.

"Do we wait?" Strian whispered.

"I don't know. I don't know what's going on."

"Neither do I. He only looks this way when he sails out for his two days each year."

Tyra looked back to Bjorn as he skipped stones across the loch. Lorna came to stand with Strian and Tyra.

"You wouldn't remember this, but Ivar sent men with Rangvald and me during one of our voyages here. Bjorn's father was one of them. We traded with my family, and Rangvald and I introduced Ivar's people to the Mackays, forming an alliance of sorts. We brought back many things, and one was sickness. Bjorn's father was home three days before he and Bjorn's mother died of the illness. Bjorn had been staying at the jarl's home, so he played with his cousins. He never saw his parents before they died. His father understood he was growing ill and insisted Bjorn stay away. His wife refused to go. She wanted to tend him, and she died beside him."

The news knocked the air from her, and from the stricken look on Strian's face, he felt the same way.

"You go to him," she nudged Strian. "I only cause him pain."

Strian nodded before moving toward the loch and Bjorn. Remorse flooded Tyra once again as she remembered the unkind things she had said and what she allowed her mind to conjure about Bjorn. She remembered his parents died of a sickness, but she had never learned the details. She did not know he had not seen his parents before their death. She had learned more about Bjorn in the past moon than she had known during their entire lives.

———

It was three days before Freya and Erik led the Norsemen from Castle Varrich with Alex and his men beside them. They agreed to give the visitors a few days to recover from the arduous voyage and for the Norsemen to train alongside the Highlanders with the hope they would learn from one another. Despite a few squabbles, it was a success. The two armies shared tactics and strategies, the Norsemen learning how to anticipate their enemies while the Highlanders learned several moves that they would have considered savage if they were not so effective.

During those three days, Bjorn was unusually withdrawn and quiet. He said little but trained harder than most. He drove himself to the brink of exhaustion, so he fell into bed every night too tired to think about where he was or the pain that came with that realization. He knew they would go to Mackay land, but he never expected it would hurt so much to be where his father became ill. He failed to drive away the ache that settled into his heart, no matter how many drams of whisky he downed during the evening meal. He itched to ride out and not look back.

There was nothing to make him lighthearted and jovial like he was at home. He did not miss Tyra's covert looks of concern, and once they would have excited him and filled him with hope. Now he was numb. His entire life changed because his father vis-ited this keep. It was almost as if his father's ghost lingered with him, and rather than miss his father, he was livid. Anger swirled through him even though he knew this anger was unreasonable. He remembered his father loved him and his mother above all else, so his father would never have intentionally brought illness to kill him or his wife. That did not change how Bjorn felt. He had been cheated out of a family for as long as he could remember.

When they rode out from the Mackay keep, Bjorn did not look back. He resolved to return to his ship rather than step foot into the bailey. He was certain he would not return without losing a part of his soul. He looked ahead of him to where Freya and Tyra rode side by side, and Erik rode with Alex. Bjorn began to relax as life shifted back into the predictable. He appreciated riding beside Strian.

Before his marriage, Leif would have engaged him in conversation for the entire ride, usually about women that they either had bedded or wanted. Strian offered companionable silence, and it was what Bjorn needed. It soothed his nerves as the tension drained from his shoulders and neck. He leaned from side to side as it cracked, and he breathed a sigh.

"You sound like an old man," Strian chuckled, speaking for the first time since they rode out four hours earlier.

"I feel like one some days. We have lived a long life at over a score."

"True. We have done better than many of our friends, but they feast with the gods while we eat these oatcakes the Highlanders call bannocks. I call them dusty turds."

It was Bjorn's turn to laugh. He had to agree with Strian, but he preferred the Highlanders' dried beef over the Norse pickled herring. He had never liked them, but he had eaten so many over the years, he was sure he was part fish. "We should be able to hunt tonight and enjoy fresh meat. I could eat three rabbits on my own with room left over in my belly."

"You can stick with your measly rabbits. I would prefer a side of beef."

"You've always been drawn to heifers."

Strian gave him an obscene gesture before grinning. "I like something to hold onto when I plow my fields."

"I didn't know you were a farmer."

"I am a man of many talents."

The men laughed together, and Bjorn had to admit it was nice to banter with his friend. Strian was the most discreet of the three men who grew up together. He did not speak of his conquests. Bjorn was not even sure if he had any, but he was never short of options and offers. Strian never boasted of any specific woman, but Leif and Bjorn were aware he had been with some of the most beautiful women in their tribe when they were younger.

Bjorn looked around as they passed through an open field. Everyone was on the lookout as they moved into an unprotected meadow where an attack might come from any direction. His gaze landed on Gunnhild and Solvi. They sneered at him as they both turned to smile at Fritjof, who rode at the front of Rangvald's contingent.

Bjorn did not flinch, since he found he did not care about anyone's opinion of him. He glanced at Tyra, and nothing registered with him. He had once cared about her opinion above all others, but there was not even a twinge now. He wondered if he was still numb from his reaction to being at Castle Varrich or if he was moving on from Tyra. He looked around again and cast his gaze over the women from his tribe and Rangvald's. None of them stirred him. He wondered why he was disinterested in all women.

The combined army of Norsemen and Mackays rode for three days before they came to the place where Mackay land met Sutherland and MacLeod territories. Warriors from each clan awaited them. Bjorn watched as representatives rode forward to speak with Alex, Freya, and Erik. Freya laughed and Erik growled at least once as the two men greeted Freya with greater fervor than she did with either of the men.

Bjorn watched as both men looked at the Norsemen, and he would have laughed at how soon their gazes reverted back to Tyra, but his jealousy decided it was a good time to roar back to life. Bjorn supposed he had exhausted his libido just he had the rest of him as he watched Tyra smile when Freya introduced them. He caught the genuine expression she offered and how it lit up her already-beautiful face. His body reacted as it always did, his mind flooding with misplaced possessiveness.

As they moved on, Tyra fell back to ride between Bjorn and Strian when Alex, along with the Sutherland and MacLeod leaders, rode beside Freya. Bjorn did not bother smothering his laugh as Erik maneuvered his horse closer to Freya's. The poor man was stuck. He would never let his wife ride with an unprotected side, so it meant at least one man had to ride alongside her now that Tyra rode with her friends. Erik decided his own cousin was the least of the three evils and got Freya between him and Alex. The other men laughed as Erik bared his teeth.

However, it was Erik's turn to grin when Freya grasped the front of his shirt and pulled him in for a kiss that left no one in doubt of how she felt about her husband. Bjorn glanced at Tyra from the corner of his eye, and he caught the look of jealousy flash across her face. She did not envy Freya for having Erik's love, but she longed for what the couple had. For the thousandth time in his life, Bjorn wished Tyra would relent so they both might have what Freya and Erik shared.

EIGHT

Bjorn had to admit that Andrew Sutherland and Kenneth MacLeod, heirs to their clans, impressed him. They were mountains of men, much like the rest of their warriors. It was obvious the men from each clan respected their leaders. The men followed with confidence and did their leaders' bidding because they wanted to, not because they feared Andrew or Kenneth. It reassured Bjorn, since they would enter battle with these men.

"We shall water the horses up ahead," Andrew called out. The warriors numbered well over one hundred, so it was not a quick event to allow each horse to drink its fill. While they stood around waiting, Tyra, Bjorn, and Strian joined Rangvald and Lorna as they spoke to Alex, Andrew, and Kenneth.

"We ken they've moved their camp. After their mad dash after us, they rejoined the handful they left behind and traveled further south. Our scouts reported they found a welcome when they arrived on Ross land. Nae surprising that the bastards would be bosom buddies with invading savages," Kenneth snarled before he realized how the visitors might react.

He looked around to find hands on sword hilts,

glares shooting daggers at him, and a few snarls. He opened his mouth to apologize, when Lorna dissolved into giggles. It was not long before the others were laughing too.

"I'm sorry, Rang. I tried nae to laugh and let ye have yer fun, but the poor lad looked like he was about to pish himself." Lorna continued to giggle. "Oh lad, dinna take it personally. Yer da was a pain in ma arse when we were weans. Let him ken I had ma fun at yer expense, and that if he wasna such an auld man and could still sit a horse, I would have had ma laugh at his expense."

Every head swung around, shocked Lorna's accent come back in full force. Her burr was always present and lent a softness to her words, but they had never heard her sound like the Highlanders.

"What?" Lorna looked at her husband and son.

"Your Highlander is showing, my love."

"Och, aye. I suppose it is. I lived half ma life here. Auld habits die hard, ye ken."

"I ken." Rangvald's laugh rumbled from deep in his chest as he leaned forward to kiss his wife's forehead. "You can practice your brogue with me later."

Everyone but Erik laughed when the older man winked at his wife. Erik rolled his eyes, used to his parents and their open displays of affection.

Kenneth shifted in his saddle as he tried to regain some semblance of authority. "I meant nay insult."

"You didn't insult us. You are right. Grímr and his men are savages. That's why we came to end him and his recruitment of mercenaries," Bjorn spoke up, taking pity on the man who looked to be close to his own seven-and-twenty.

"Aye well, we werenae so impressed with what we learned the last time ye arrived," Kenneth mused. "When we learned of Hakin's plan to attack Rangvald's settlement before Ivar's, then him kidnapping

Erik's cousin Sigrid, we kenned we were in for a fight. I canna say how I understand why he thinks a seer would bring him victory."

"After Leif and Freya, Strian, Tyra, and I sailed to Hakin's home, we found few people there. Thank the gods Leif isn't here to remember finding Sigrid bound to an altar, about to be sacrificed," Bjorn explained. "Leif's order to burn the settlement only riled Hakin more. You can't be surprised that, after having no home and losing so many warriors to skirmishes with us, Hakin turned to Scotland to recruit mercenaries."

"We tracked them to the border of Ross land but didna cross over. We suspect they came ashore on Mackenzie land, staying close to the border with our territory," Andrew MacLeod spoke up. "They must want to stay close to the coast. Sutherland land is far too wide for them to cross and still have an easy escape route."

"That means they sailed all the way around the tip of Scotland. They must have anchored their boats in the Minch," Lorna looked to the west as though the coast were visible despite the distance. "MacLeod, did yer da ken this?"

"Nay. We havenae been home, Lady Lorna, since we discovered they'd crossed into Ross land. We sent a messenger with our suspicions but nae since we confirmed it," Kenneth answered.

Lorna looked at her younger cousin, Alex. She seemed to assess him, and when he did not disappoint, she shared her thoughts.

"Alex, ye ken we canna all continue to ride on. If Grímr put in at Mackenzie land, then ye ken they are a good distance from Andrew's home. It's too far for Andrew to ride and tell his da and still help ye. Ye're on better terms with the Mackenzies than the MacLeods are. Ye and Andrew must ride to the coast to let the Mackenzies ken what's happening on their land, and if ye find them anchored there, ye must fire Grímr's ships. They canna be able to leave Scotland with more fighters."

Alex and Kenneth exchanged a look and nodded. Everyone recognized that Lorna spoke the truth. If they burned Grímr's ships, it would not matter how many men he recruited. He would be unable to leave Scotland until he had new ones built. That assumed he ever made it back to the coast to discover what happened to them.

"Grímr excels at this game of cat-and-mouse. Lorna is right. We must burn their ships in case they can hide then run back to the coast. We need these Mackenzies on our side," Rangvald interjected.

"Without his wife Inga's money coming in, he must be getting desperate. We need to cut off his means of escape." Erik added.

"Aye, ma cousins have the right of it," Alex nodded his head. "Then this is where we split up."

Alex shook hands with everyone until he came to Lorna, who pulled him in for a motherly embrace.

"Lad, I kenned yer father, and I am glad he led our clan after ma father died. Ye remind me of ma da, which tells me ye are doing a fine job. Yer da would be proud of ye. I witnessed how well yer people live and how they both respect and like ye. Ye will help the Mackays prosper and thrive once again." She gave him a peck on the cheek before she gathered her horse's reins. She called out, "We ride."

The Sutherlands led the Norsemen further south, and there was only a slight sense of trepidation as the Norsemen were forced to put their trust in a clan that had been adversaries to their only allies. Andrew

Sutherland ended any doubts the first night when he approached Rangvald.

He extended his arm to Rangvald saying, "We both stand to lose if the Rosses and these savages," he winked, "form an alliance. The Rosses are kenned to be dirty fighters. They have the ear of our king, so they dinna need to fight fair. They will attack, then run back to the king to tattle, saying they were the innocents. When we fight them, we fight to leave naught to tell the tale. I amnae in any mood to tell ma father we failed. He isnae a forgiving mon. I will lead our warriors to Ross land if I have yer vow ye will fight both Ross and Norsemen."

Rangvald clasped Andrew's forearm and shook it vigorously. "You have my word, which means you have the oath of every Norseman and woman here. They have sworn upon their sacred rings fealty to their jarls. That binds them to any oath I make. Besides that, my people and Ivar's have lost many at the hands of Grímr and his brother Hakin. There are many who came to avenge their loved ones. Me included."

"Yer family tree is a wee complicated. Do ye mind explaining how ye all seem to be related to one another? I thought our clans were bad."

Rangvald's smiled died, but he nodded.

"Ivar was supposed to marry my sister Inga, but he refused. He was in love with the woman he's now married to, Lena, who's Freya and Leif's mother. Even though I succeeded in bringing her home from Ivar's, she was still sent to an arranged marriage with Grímr. Her need for revenge ate at her and ultimately cost Inga her life. She had an affair with a man from Ivar's tribe."

Strian shifted uncomfortably as Rangvald spoke of his uncle.

"The man happened to be Ivar's second-in-command," Rangvald continued. "He sold secrets to Hakin in exchange for a promise that he would have Ivar's land. Long story short, Inga led Hakin and Grímr by the nose. She was the mastermind behind the plots, and she was the one to figure out how to pay for the mercenaries."

"But she's dead now, aye?"

"Yes."

"How'd she die? I dinna suppose she came along with her men to the battles."

"I killed her." Rangvald looked Andrew directly in the eye. "And I am not done getting my revenge."

There was no one present who did not understand the significance to Norsemen of making an oath and vengeance. The pact was sealed.

It took another two days to ride far enough into Ross land to meet a sentry. There had been much speculation as to why the Rosses did not post scouts closer to the border. They understood when they crested a hill to find a warband of a hundred men waiting. The Norsemen and Sutherlands outnumbered the Rosses and had the advantage of fighting from the top of the hill. As Andrew called his archers forward, Bjorn looked around, his intuition screaming for attention. The hair on the back of his neck prickled, and he sensed there was more danger lurking. Bjorn pulled his shield from where it hung on his saddle. He backed his horse out of the ranks as he scanned where they came. His eyes strained, but he was sure there was a glint of steel.

"To the rear! They surround us!" Bjorn called out as another warband raced forward. "Shield wall!"

The Norsemen on horseback dismounted and

slapped their animals on their rumps before joining the others as they interlocked their shields and held them over their heads. Bjorn pulled Tyra next to him as the first arrows rained down on them. He had no time to catch whether she glared at him like he expected. He scanned for Erik and Freya, ready to defer to them, but he did not spot either of them.

"They rode too close to Andrew. They are fighting with the Highlanders. Freya was picking them off with her bow," Strian called several people down.

"Open and guard," Bjorn said to Tyra and the man beside him. They tilted and lifted their shields as he stood tall enough to survey the oncoming force. It relieved him to find the enemy was on foot with none on horseback. The Norsemen stood a better chance.

"Archers, prepare!" Bjorn called as he crouched down. "They advance on foot. We keep the shield wall no matter what."

Bjorn thumped the hilt of his sword against his shield, and the others followed, creating an intimidating rhythm.

"Archers, release!" Bjorn ordered. As a one, shields parted as archers stood to launch their arrows. Those without bows held their shields to protect the archers until they crouched again. They repeated this pattern four more times before Bjorn issued his next order. "Forward!"

Keeping their shields still locked together, the warriors stood and marched in unison until arrows pelted their shields. Screams of pain came from within the force, but they closed ranks as gaps formed and warriors fell away. They continued to progress until Bjorn called a halt. He ordered the archers to send another volley of arrows. Only moments later, more arrows sunk into shields and flesh.

"Open and guard," Bjorn said once more. He stood just enough to peer through the shield wall and assess their enemy. They were much closer together than he expected. Once he crouched again, he issued his next set of orders to the Norse army. "We must stand and fight as one. Keep the shield wall, we fight back-to-back for as long as we can. We don't stop until we defeat them. On my word."

Bjorn stood and pointed this sword to the enemy then pounded his hilt twice.

"To Valhalla!"

The Norsemen surged forward with their battle calls as they beat their swords on their shields. Many guffawed at the look of shock, then terror, on the Highlanders' faces. These were not coastal Highlanders. They were not used to facing the Norse.

Bjorn's shield slammed into the first man he saw as he pushed the other man's shield out of the way and thrust his sword forward. He withdrew it and moved on to the next man as his fellow warriors maintained the shield wall for as long as possible. He was aware Tyra was still by his side, but he did not dare look over to her lest he lose his head in the process. Strian's voice came from further down the line, issuing orders to keep the fighters together.

As the next wave of Highlanders slammed into the Norsemen, the shield wall broke apart, and it became a melee. Tyra thrust and swung with ease, glad she was as well healed as she thought. The scar across her chest tugged, but she was as strong as she had been before her near-death injury. She swung her shield down on a man's shoulder as she thrust her sword into his belly. She twisted when she sensed someone behind her.

Tyra sliced diagonally and cleaved the man in half, relishing the blood as it splatted across her belly. She ran forward with the others as she collided with one Highlander after another. She glanced around and found she was no longer near Bjorn. She ducked as a sword cut through the air near her head. Tyra lunged forward, using her shield to break the man's nose. When he stumbled back, she followed through, bashing his head with her shield until blood gurgled from the man's mouth. She looked again, but neither Bjorn nor Strian were within her sight. Tyra had separated from the others, but she noticed Gunnhild struggled with a man twice her size. She fought valiantly, but the woman's arm was already bleeding profusely.

Tyra whipped a knife from her wrist bracer and flung it at the man's throat. It embedded deep within, and a geyser of blood shot forward, spaying Gunnhild. She looked back in the direction from where the knife flew and found Tyra watching her. Gunnhild nodded before both women ran to each other, moving to fight back-to-back. There was no time for grudges if they wanted to survive.

"We must move back near the others before they cut us off. We are winning, but you and I will be dead if we can't get back to the others," Tyra panted.

"Agreed." Gunnhild pointed her sword to an opening in the fighting. "There. On three. One. Two. Three."

Both women charged forward, swinging their swords as men approached from each side. They stopped when they reached the main Norse force. Their chest heaved as they grinned at one another.

"Don't think this means I like you, princess," Gunnhild laughed.

"Don't think this means I can't beat your arse," Tyra grunted.

"He's not worth my efforts. He'll never want anyone but you. Don't miss your chance. Stop being a fool." Gunnhild tossed at Tyra before running to meet an opponent head-on.

Tyra stood stunned for only a moment before necessity required that she focus or lose her head. She fought alone as she plowed through one enemy after another. The bloodlust coursed through her veins even as her lungs burned and her arms ached. Her legs shook as she braced herself against a man who looked like he would swallow her whole. She used her smaller size to her advantage, pushing her shield to protect her as she sliced her sword across the back of the man's knees. He lurched forward as he collapsed. His weight was too much for Tyra to hold against. She fell backwards as the man landed on her. She struck out with her fists, as the man tried to wrap his hands around her throat. She jerked her knee up, trying to jam it against his cods. She made the man grunt, but it didn't slow him.

"Don't damage those. I'm about to use them when I stick my cock in you. I like having women on the battlefield. Much more enjoyable." The giant wrapped one massive paw around her throat as his other hand grasped her breast.

"And I shall geld you before I plunge my knife into your heart." She flicked a knife from her other wrist bracer. She brought it down with all the might her arms mustered. The man howled as it sunk into his shoulder.

"You shall pay for that, bitch."

"I doubt it." She pulled the knife free just before the man lurched backwards to gain leverage to plow his fist into her face.

She thrust the knife into his throat all the way to the hilt. The man's eyes widened before his upper body landed upon Tyra. The man was dead, and his weight trapped Tyra until suddenly it was gone, and she was being pulled to her feet.

Bjorn stood before her, a fierceness on his face she rarely experienced. Bjorn grasped the back of her head and pulled her in for a rough kiss that was over far sooner than Tyra wanted. "Don't die. We're not nearly done with each other yet."

Tyra grabbed a handful of his shirt and pulled him back in. "Don't kiss me unless I can kiss you back."

She pressed a kiss to him before they broke apart prepared to strike the men running toward them. Bjorn slashed the man who charged him and looked back to where Tyra did the same the man approaching her. He reached back and hooked his hand into her belt. He tugged her with him as they covered each other's back. Bjorn ran to where Strian fought beside one of Rangvald's men. It forced Tyra to stumble over bodies even though Bjorn called out warnings. The last body she hopped backwards over was one she recognized. She looked down to find Fritjof's sightless eyes staring toward the sun. She bent over and closed them before she, Strian, and Bjorn formed a triangle to protect one another. They fought together until there were no Highlanders left.

The three friends looked around at the Norsemen still standing and counted. They had lost a quarter of their force. Bjorn tasked a handful of warriors to check for wounded and to organize the dead into piles for burial. The rest trudged along the hill until they determined how the Sutherlands fared. Rangvald and Lorna joined them having fought at the other end of the line. The older couple looked as though they had gone for a walk. Tyra worried she might collapse on the spot while it appeared like Lorna had not broken a sweat. Tyra shook her head as Lorna wrapped her arm around the younger woman.

They came to the top of the hill and realized the

fighting had ended with the Sutherlands victorious. Most of the Highlanders who were their allies remained on their horses or stood cleaning their weapons. They breathed a collective sigh until a scream rent the air. Freya leaped over three bodies before sliding next to a man lying prone. She rolled him over, and the collective sigh became a collective gasp. Lorna took off, and the others struggled to catch up with the mother running to her son.

"Don't you dare die, Erik, or I'll cut off your cods," Freya sobbed as she cradled her husband's head and leaned over to feel his breath.

As the others reached the couple, Erik's eyes fluttered open. "If you do that, how will I ever plant a babe in your fine belly?"

Freya swatted his chest, making his cough. "Not funny. I thought—"

"I know, my love. But not today. I wouldn't leave the others to suffer your temper if I rudely died. Come here, princess." He lifted his hand to brush Freya's hair from her face. "Don't cry. Your nose will turn red, and then I shall have a hard time taking you seriously."

Freya hiccupped a laugh as she sucked in a deep breath.

"Help me up, princess."

Freya pulled Erik to his feet as he wrapped his arm around his ribs. Lorna stepped forward to look at her son, but she respected Freya's right as his wife to tend to him.

"Lorna, I believe we shall need you to tend to your son."

"Let's get him somewhere I can get a better look."

"You know I'm alive and awake. I can hear you and speak for myself."

"Hush," the women barked in unison.

/ NINE

Tyra stepped away, relieved Erik only had the wind knocked out of him when he cracked his rib. She needed a moment alone to collect herself. She walked toward trees that grew just beyond the battlefield. Tyra whistled several times until horses trotted toward her. She recognized her own mount along with the ones of her friends. She wrapped her arms around her horse's neck and leaned against it. She ran her hand along the smooth hair as the horse nickered and nodded its head. Tyra had raised the horse from when it was a colt, and they had the bond needed between fighter and steed. The horse rested its head over her shoulder as it nipped at her hair.

"Stop that, you silly man."

"He's a lucky one." Bjorn's voice came from over her shoulder. She looked back to find him stroking the flank of his own horse. Before she said anything else, Bjorn nodded and walked back toward the others.

Tyra stared at him with her mouth agape. She was sure Bjorn would have said something about the kisses they shared on a battlefield of all places, but he acted as though they barely knew one another. Once she stopped feeling flustered, she followed him back, leading the other horses to their owners. They spent the rest of the day and well into the night burying the Sutherlands who died and building a funeral pyre for the Norsemen.

Each group faced their dead as they carried out their rituals. It was a somber crowd once they settled in to make camp. It was too dark for them to move on, and it assured them that no one lurked nearby. There was no guarantee if they continued to travel. Bjorn and Tyra both helped hunt while Freya tended Erik, whose injuries were not as grave as his wife made out. Lorna organized the evening meal while Andrew Sutherland and Rangvald helped build the many cook fires that glowed against the darkening sky. Tyra stood near Strian and Bjorn as they skinned the animals.

"I found my three rabbits, but no cows for you," Bjorn laughed at Strian.

"I'm sure I can feed my hunger nonetheless." Tyra caught Strian tilting his head toward one of the shieldmaidens from Rangvald's army. She understood that they were not talking just about rabbits.

"You two are disgusting," she hissed.

"Then don't listen, little sister," Strian teased before taking a rabbit and a couple of squirrels to the fire he built.

This left Bjorn and Tyra alone together again. Bjorn reached over and plucked one of Tyra's rabbits, but before she had the opportunity to complain, he began to skin the animal for her. Tyra offered her thanks, and they continued in silence. Tyra came close to cutting her finger off when she found she was looking at Bjorn more than she was the animal she was preparing to cook. His hair had come loose and grime still streaked his face, but he had never looked more handsome. His brown eyes snapped between her and the animal he chopped.

His muscles rippled as he worked, and Tyra found her mouth going dry. She had stood near Bjorn almost every day of her life, but he seemed bigger, stronger, even more masculine than her ever had before.

"Why do you keep staring at me? Is there something on me? Are you disgusted at my filth?"

"Wha—what?" Tyra stammered. "You are no dirtier than I am. I was trying to figure out how to thank you for rescuing me once more."

Tyra slammed her mouth shut when she realized what she said. She waited for Bjorn to pounce on her words, but he shrugged as he returned to gutting the rabbit before him.

"I saw you fighting him, then I looked over and saw him land on you. There was no way you were going to push his dead weight off you."

"Thank you."

"You're welcome. If your rabbit is ready, I'll take it to the fire."

Tyra was once more stunned that he said little more to her than the necessary pleasantries of working near one another. She handed him her meat and watched as he walked away. The camp was subdued as the group ate, but once the meal was through, the mead horns and whisky jugs began to pass around the fires. The bloodlust was wearing off, and now the warriors welcomed the warmth and escape the alcohol provided as they tried not to recall about what they endured.

Erik grunted as he sat down, but he passed a jug of whisky to Bjorn who took a healthy swig. It moved to Strian before Tyra sniffed it. The smell alone made her cough. She let the liquid pass over her lips and tongue, tasting it. When she realized it had a smoky and peaty taste that she liked, she took a long swig too. She feared she would go up in flames as it burned down her throat and landed in her belly. She wiped her arm across her lips to muffle her cough.

Strian clapped her on the back, her cough unpreventable. She pushed him away before taking the jug back from him. Prepared this time, she took several long swallows as the heat slithered along her arms and legs. She was ready for more when she remembered she had to share with the others. The others laughed as she passed it to Freya who shook her head.

"Oh, no. The last time I was here, I was sure I was drinking mead, but they added whisky to it. I'm aware of what it can do to me."

Erik pulled her closer and did not even flinch when Freya bumped into his injured side. "I remember, too." He kissed his wife in a way that had Freya standing again and dragging her husband away by the hand. Tyra handed the jug to Strian, but he was looking at the woman he had been watching earlier.

"Go on. Don't wait until the night is over." Tyra nudged her shoulder against his. Strian grinned, and Tyra wondered why she could not find herself attracted to Strian. He was just as handsome as the other men, and it would have solved so many of her problems. But when he tousled her hair, she remembered why she thought of him more as a brother.

Rangvald and Lorna sat with their own people and the Sutherlands, so that left Tyra and Bjorn alone with the jug of whisky. They looked at one another before scooting closer together. Tyra pretended to hand the jug to Bjorn before bringing it back to her lips. She took another healthy swig before Bjorn took it from her with a laugh. He took several draws before he wiped the back of his hand over his mouth. He offered Tyra the jug, but she shook her head. Her head already weighed a hundred pounds but was moments away from floating away.

Bjorn put the jug down between them and looked at the stars twinkling above them. There were no lights flashing across the sky, but the stars looked like someone had thrown sand into the night, and it hung suspended over their heads. Tyra watched the fire as the flames hypnotized her. Her head lowered to Bjorn's shoulder, and it felt so right that she did not fight it. He shifted to wrap his arm around her waist, resting his hand on her hip. Tyra put her hand on his thigh as she shifted to curl into him. She realized what she had done when Bjorn sucked in a breath. She looked down at her hand then up at Bjorn as he clenched his jaw. She twisted further then reached back to move Bjorn's hand from her hip to her backside.

"What are you doing, Tyra?" He whispered.

"Something I dream about everyday but never let myself do sober." She ran her fingers up the inside of his thigh until she got dangerously close to the cock she watched swell.

"Don't do this, Tyra. You will regret it, and you'll break my heart." Bjorn's voice was little more than a hoarse murmur.

"Break your heart? Like I usually do? Is that what you really want to say?" Bjorn did not respond as his hand stroked her backside. She tilted her head up to look at him once more, and she watched the muscles in his jaw tick. "What if I already regret everything else?"

He looked into her hazel eyes, her pupils dilated and her eyes glassy. He wanted to kiss her with every fiber of his being, but he would do nothing that she might hold against him later.

"You're worried I will blame you for anything that happens. You fear I'll say you took advantage of me," Tyra's hand grazed his cock as she rested it on his belly. Each muscle jerked and tightened as her fingertips glided over the ridges. "Bjorn, I have no one to blame but myself. I've held a grudge against you for something I was sure was the truth. You've already made me realize I was wrong that day. We both were. Rather than talk to one another, we both assumed the worst. Bjorn, you've always been there. No matter what I've said to you or about you, you have never given up on me. It's aggravated me and made me lash out, but it's the same steadfastness that I have always admired about you. You are brave, but so are the other men of our tribe. I understand now, though, that you are far braver than I ever realized. You have endured trials that few remember or give you credit for overcoming. Bjorn, you haven't smiled since we left home. I miss it. I miss the way you make me laugh despite how you annoy me. I miss you."

"What do you want from me, Tyra? How many times am I supposed to come running only to have you kick me? Why can't you see, or rather accept, what every other person who sees us knows immediately?"

"And when you're done?"

"Done?"

"Done with me and leave."

"Woman, I have been in love with you since I was seven. Do you think I will ever be done with you?" Bjorn growled as he lifted her chin.

He lowered his mouth to hers as she opened to him. He brushed his tongue along her lips then the back of her teeth. He opened wider as he tried to devour her. His kiss poured his love and frustration into her. He did not touch any other part of her than where their lips met. His hands dropped away from her backside and her chin. He pulled away as abruptly as he began the kiss. Bjorn looked into Tyra's hooded eyes, but whatever was there was not what he searched for. Or perhaps it was. He stood up and swept the jug off the ground before walking into the tree line.

Tyra watched Bjorn walk away with the jug of mead, and she envied him. She looked around and found one for herself. She had grown up with three large boys as her closest friends. It meant both she and Freya learned to drink with them, and they both developed a high tolerance. Bjorn's kiss had sobered her, or at least her mind was convinced it had. Tyra pulled the cork from the jug and tilted it back. She had half the jug before stopped herself. She looked to where Bjorn sat against a tree, facing away from the camp, away from her.

She was in no condition to pick a fight and win, thanks to the effects of the alcohol. But she did not want to fight anymore. She could not. She would not. She pushed herself onto her feet and waited for the world to lurch or spin. When it stayed as it was supposed to. She pushed her shoulders back and walked toward the trees. When she walked up to the tree where Bjorn sat with his legs stretched out, she was not sure if he was asleep since his eyes were closed.

"What do you want now?"

It surprised Tyra how sober he sounded too, but she knew he had to feel much the way she did. She was not entirely drunk, but she was not totally sober, either. She stepped a foot over him and lowered herself to straddle him.

"Doing what I need to. What I can't stop thinking about. What we both need. Bjorn, I've loved you since I was five. I've always loved you, and that's why you're the only one who has the power to hurt me and scare me."

She pulled at the laces of her leather pants, kneeling high enough to push them down from her hips. She then pulled Bjorn's laces as he watched her.

When he sprang free, Tyra moaned as she wrapped her hand around him. It had been so long since she felt him against her. She stroked him until he groaned and pulled her in for another kiss. Once more, it was as if he tried to devour her. She wanted to do the same. Tyra wanted to be so close she might crawl within his skin. She ran her other hand under his linen shirt as she raked her nails over his belly.

"I've never wanted to hurt you or scare you, Tyra. I have only ever wanted you to be happy and safe."

"I know. But when my mind screamed I couldn't have you, my heart ached with despair. Life has been off kilter for so long. The few times I imagined we had a chance, after, well, after that time, I pushed you away before you were gone."

Bjorn wrapped his hand around Tyra's and stopped her. He was certain he would expire on the spot, but he forced them both to focus on the conversation.

"But I never wanted to go anywhere. Why do you think I would leave?"

"Because those I loved the most left me." Tyra's eyes filled with fat tears, and Bjorn swept his thumbs below her lashes to wipe them away. He encircled her in his arms and pulled her against his chest. He kissed the top of her head.

"I understand. Better than you can imagine. Every time you've turned me down was like losing them all over again, but I am a glutton for punishment. I keep coming back on the hopes that one of these days, you will accept me."

Tyra shifted and grasped his cock again. He guided her hips, and together they lowered Tyra onto his rod. Neither moved, both reveling in how right it felt for their bodies to finally join again.

"Bjorn."

"I know."

As their lips fused together, this kiss was slow and languid. It was an exploration as they held one another, only their mouths moving. The kiss seemed to last forever until they both had to pull back for air. Bjorn ran his fingers along her chin and cheek where his stubble abraded her soft skin.

"I'm sorry if it hurts. I've made it red."

"You've marked me as yours."

"Do you mind that?"

"No. I want more. I want to be yours, Bjorn. I've kept us apart too long. No more." Tyra rocked her hips as Bjorn groaned.

"Tyra, this changes everything. If you have any doubts, leave now. If we continue, I will claim you as my own. I will kill any man who touches you. I will never forgive you if you betray me."

"Bjorn, there's never, ever been anyone else. You're the only one I've loved."

Bjorn dug his fingers into her bottom as he thrust into her.

"Mine," she moaned as she sank deeper onto Bjorn's cock.

"Yours. It's all I've ever wanted."

Bjorn rolled them and pushed Tyra's pants down to her ankles. He thrust into her over and over as she struggled to pull her shirt over her head then do the same to his.

"More. More. I want it all."

"And you shall have it, Ty. You have my heart. Now you shall have my body and my soul."

Bjorn kissed a scorching trail along her neck as he worked his way down to her breasts. He laved his tongue over her puckered nipple. His tongue was rough as he circled it then suckled hard enough to make her yelp. He hesitated a moment, worried he hurt her, but when she dug her fingers into his back, she made it obvious she wanted more of the same. He alternated breasts as he kneaded one and suckled the other.

Tyra writhed under him as the pressure and ache grew low in her belly. She moaned as she thrust her hips to meet Bjorn each time he surged into her. Her fingers tangled in his hair as she pulled his mouth back to her. She nipped at his lips, catching his bottom one between her teeth. He growled as she tugged. Her need and aggression pushed him over the edge. He fought to maintain control.

"Tyra, don't fight it any longer. Find your release, my love. I can't hold on much longer."

"Then don't."

Tyra buried her face against his neck as her climax ripped through her, milking Bjorn's cock. Her muscles clenched around him, drawing him in. He tried to pull out, but Tyra yanked on his hair and trapped his hips with her knees.

"Stay," she begged. "Together."

Bjorn held her against him as his seed shoot from him as his cock surely brushed her womb. His body seemed boneless when his cock stopped twitching within Tyra. She stroked his back with feather soft caresses. Her hold on his hair softened until she only rested her hand against his scalp. Once more, he tried to pull out, but her whisper was the same as before.

"Stay."

"As one," Bjorn breathed against her neck.

"Yes. As one." Tyra smattered kisses along his shoulder and collarbone.

They lay like that until Bjorn's body failed to meet his mind's demands. He slipped from her and rolled so he would not crush Tyra. She slid from him and unlaced her boots before pulling her pants from her ankles. Bjorn sat up to do the same. Once they were both undressed, Bjorn pulled his fur cloak over them. He mindlessly ran his fingers over her petal soft skin. His body and soul rejoiced at finally making love to Tyra, but his mind would not overlook one detail.

"Ty, I didn't pull out. I spilled inside you."

"I know. I wanted you to." She leaned up on her elbow. "I mean, I'm not trying to trap you now that I've stopped running. I just wanted us to be joined through it all. I wanted—" Tyra was unsure how to describe it without sounding sentimental.

"You wanted what I did. You wanted us to be as one with nothing between us anymore."

"Yes."

"I don't think you're trying to trap me. I fear you will think I have done that to you. What about a babe? I didn't think you wanted to be a mother."

"Someday. But you're right, I don't want that now. I will ask Freya for some of her pennyroyal. I know that is how she keeps from getting with child."

"Someday." Bjorn whispered. Tyra leaned back over him and pulled his face to look at her.

"With you." She kissed him with a gentleness that surprised them both. It was beyond tender. "I love you, Bjorn Jansson."

"And I love you, Tyra Vigosdóttir."

They dozed in one another's arms until the sun began to peek through the deep blues of early morning. Bjorn stirred first, but Tyra's eyes popped open. Bjorn held his breath, waiting for the hammer to fall. He waited for Tyra to scramble away, swearing to never look at him again.

"Why are you holding your breath, Bjorn? It's making your ribs stick in me, and it's not very comfortable."

Bjorn was unprepared for Tyra to tickle him. The air whooshed from his chest as he rolled to look at her, but she pushed his shoulder as her body followed him as he lay on his back once more. She ground her mons against his already stirring sword. She sheathed him and began to rock as her head fell back. Her hair had come loose from its braids some time during their previous lovemaking.

The blonde strands whispered across Bjorn's thighs as her breasts pressed toward the heavens. Bjorn sat up, wrapping Tyra's legs around his waist. She rode him as she would her horse, her hips rolling as he gripped them. He pushed her down onto his length as his mouth latched onto her breast. Her moans spurred him on as he guided her into a harder and faster rhythm.

"So deep, Bjorn."

"I know, my love. Gods, you are so tight. You shall make me finish just when we've gotten started."

"So good... Nothing like it... So good..." Tyra only managed to exhale phrases as her body seized control, and her brain raced to catch up.

Bjorn cradled Tyra in his arm as he twisted them and pressed her back against the ground. Bjorn's pace was slower this time as he thrust into her, circling his hips before pulling back and starting the pattern again. Tyra mewled each time he seemed to have sunk to the hilt but found just a tiny bit more to press into her. The pressure against her hidden button was bringing her closer to release as her body raced toward the finish.

She rasped her teeth against his shoulder as her need coalesced into a powerful climax that shook her from her core to her extremities. Her heart surely skipped a beat as she clenched around Bjorn.

"That is the first of many before I am done with you," Bjorn groaned as he thrust and circled again. Tyra whimpered as her hips continued to rise and meet Bjorn's. He pushed her over the edge again and again until her body could take no more. "Look at me, Ty. I would see you as you find your release with me."

"I can't. It's too much. I can't keep them open." Her mouth formed a perfect oval as she moaned out her last release. It was more than enough for Bjorn as his body followed hers, once again spilling inside her. His release was even stronger than earlier in the night. He was stunned by how it wracked his body, and his arms shook as he tried to hold himself above her. He lowered himself to his forearms, but even then, his muscles shook as tremors ran through them. He kissed Tyra's nose, her forehead, and each cheek before pressing his tongue between her lips. She pulled down on his shoulders, but Bjorn did not want to crush her.

"Let me hold you, please." Her soft entreaty was more than Bjorn could withstand. He allowed his chest and belly to press down on hers as he swept the hair from her damp temples. "I won't break."

"I know, but you are precious to me. In moments like this, I want to show you that."

Tyra looked into Bjorn's eyes and found honesty there. She strained to kiss him before resting her head on the ground with her eyes closed. Her fingers continued to play in the hair that covered his nape and upper back.

"As much as I don't want to, we need to dress and go back. The others will have already figured what we've done, but I don't want them to worry. And I definitely don't want any of the men to come looking for us only to find you uncovered." Bjorn handed Tyra her pants, which she pulled on as she grumbled. "Hurry, my little woodland nymph."

Bjorn's laugh died as they both caught the soft sound of leaves rustling. The sound did not come from their camp. They both drew their swords and came to their feet. Despite still being naked, Bjorn tucked Tyra behind him as she had not put her shirt back on. He scooped it up and handed it back to her.

"Ye should have listened to yer mon, but I dinna mind a look at those sweet tits now he isnae panting over ye." The leader of the band of ten men stepped forward. He glanced at Bjorn, who stood ready to pounce. "Nae bad, ma friend. I ken why she was moaning like she was in heat."

The man rubbed his crotch as Bjorn growled, but he refused to take the bait. He would not leave Tyra unprotected. Once he was certain Tyra was dressed, he let out a whistle that pierced the silence of the woods.

"Ye shouldnae done that." The men rushed forward and grabbed both Tyra and Bjorn. One man swept up Bjorn's clothes before they were both tossed onto horses. The man who took Tyra tried to squeeze her breast, but he was unprepared for her to jerk her head back and butt him in the face.

Tyra swung an elbow into his gut before wrapping her hands around his neck and throwing all her weight forward, unseating the man from the saddle and bringing him over her shoulder. She grabbed the reins and made the horse rear before its hooves came down on the man who dared touch her. She spun around to look for Bjorn, but a fist smashed into her face and everything faded to black. Tyra heard Bjorn roar her name, but then there was nothing.

TEN

Bjorn watched Tyra fight the man who dared touch her, and he was proud of how she defended herself, but he fought against the three men who restrained him when he witnessed the leader ride up beside her and drive his fist into her face. She fell from the horse, and Bjorn was sure she broke her neck from how she landed. The man who knocked her from the horse dismounted, threw her across his saddle, and mounted behind her.

The men bound Bjorn's hands before Tyra was back on the horse. The entire attack was over in a matter of a few minutes. They were being carried away before any of the Norsemen arrived at the trees. Bjorn whistled once more, and he heard a response, but a fist slammed into his face too. He shook it off, refusing to give in and not be able to watch over Tyra. Bjorn would not take his eyes off her until they reached safety. He took a punch to the kidneys that doubled him over.

It was impossible to determine which man rode behind him, but he had to be enormous to control Bjorn when it had taken three to restrain him only moments ago. His only consolation was the man's horse would not last riding double, and even though

Tyra weighed only a fraction of what he did, the leader's horse would tire sooner, too.

The group of ten men and their captives rode in silence for a couple of hours before, as Bjorn suspected, the horses that carried two riders began to flag. They turned off the path and followed a deer trail to a stream. Bjorn tried to keep track of their route, but the men doubled back and crossed their own tracks to the point where Bjorn did not know if they were coming or going. When they reached the water, the man behind Bjorn dismounted, then pulled Bjorn from the horse, letting him land hard in the dirt. Before he rolled away, his pants landed on his head.

"Cover up, mon. I dinna need yer naked arse against me anymore."

"Worried it'll keep making you hard?" Bjorn taunted.

"Just how I'll need it when I hump yer woman."

The Highlander was not prepared for how fast Bjorn moved, even with his hands bound. Bjorn roared as he grabbed one the man's ankles and pulled hard enough for the Highlander to fall. Bjorn was on top of him in an instant, bringing his bound hands down as one mighty fist. He pounded away as blood squirted from the man's nose and lips. He leaned back far enough to plow his fists into the man's throat several times before the others pulled him away. It took four men this time to restrain him as he kicked out when the first two grappled with his arms. Bjorn stilled, and the men released his legs. He spat on the man who had not moved from where he landed when Bjorn attacked him. One of the men who had restrained his legs checked on the colossus on the ground. He ran his fingers along the man's neck then shook his head.

"He's dead," the man was incredulous.

"As he deserves," Bjorn said. He swung his head back and crashed it into one of the men holding him. It was enough of a surprise for the man to relax his grip. Bjorn pulled away and swung at the other man who held him. Hands still fisted together, he brought them down on the man's temples. When he was free, Bjorn drove his fists into the base of the man's nose, shoving it into his brain. The Highlander was dead before he hit the ground. Bjorn was ready to tear through the remaining men until the leader pulled Tyra from the horse. He held a knife to her throat. He cocked an eyebrow in challenge to Bjorn. Bjorn stilled but hissed when anyone came near him. He snatched his pants and struggled into them as best he could without the freedom of having one hand at each of his sides.

Tyra's head pounded as she became aware of movement around her and the roar of an injured animal. She blinked her eyes to find Bjorn naked and pounding his fists into a man's throat. Tyra realized it was no injured animal but an enraged Bjorn. She kept her head lowered and listened as someone announced the man was dead. Tyra feigned unconsciousness as she sensed someone moving behind her. She feared she would bite the tip of her tongue off as she kept from yelping when a man pulled her from the horse and a knife pressed against her throat. She dared not swallow despite the temptation.

She made her body remain limp as she hung like a rag doll. She waited for the man to lower the knife from her throat. When his arm passed over her breast and drew to her side, she seized her opportunity. The man had not bound her hands, and that was his greatest mistake. She grabbed his arm with enough space between her hands to bring his forearm down over her raised knee. She delighted in hearing a crack before she dug her nails into his wrists as she spun and pulled him around her. Tyra swiped her foot out, forcing him to the ground. The leader of the attackers grabbed ahold of her hair and yanked her back. She lost her balance, but not before she wrestled the knife from his injured arm. She pointed it at his throat and let the momentum of being pulled to the other side do the work for her. She slit the man's throat, then drove the knife into the hollow at the base of his throat.

Tyra scrambled to her feet and rushed to Bjorn, who held his hands out. The knife made short work of the rope. She handed him the knife as she pulled one from her boot. She had not even realized she had pulled them on in time, but she remembered stepping into them as Bjorn thrust her shirt into her hands. Bjorn's back bumped hers as they both held up their knives, daring any of the remaining men to approach. Tyra bared her teeth and snarled.

"I'd fear her more than me," Bjorn taunted. "She doesn't like it when people rough me up. Very protective."

Bjorn and Tyra scanned the men who surrounded them, confident that even though it was seven to two, the odds were in their favor. However, it startled them when applause floated from the trees nearby. They remained ready to strike until Grímr stepped forward.

"Anyone who underestimates a shieldmaiden deserves the death he gets." Grímr's grin looked more like a sneer. Tyra tried to stifle her gasp as Bjorn went rigid behind her. They both stood, and Bjorn's hand brushed against hers. "Bjorn Jansson, and would that be Tyra Vigosdóttir? Such luck. Not as good as getting Leif or Erik, but just as beautiful as Freya. And just as lusty from what I hear."

Tyra and Bjorn kept their faces impassive, but Tyra was sure they were both wondering if Grímr was antagonizing them or if he knew anything about her and Freya.

"I have spies everywhere. I know Freya is no better than a cheap whore, always ready. And you, my dear. Apparently, you have a body to make men sin. Lucky me. I'm already a sinner."

"So, you're a Christian now?" Bjorn tried to change the subject. "Sold yourself to the Christian devil?"

Grímr flicked his glance at Bjorn. "Whatever I am, I shall have a good time riding her," he leered at Tyra.

"And if I rip your cock off first?" Tyra purred. If someone did not listen to her words, they might think her voice was seductive. "And what if I shove your bollocks down your throat? I doubt you'd be very hard after that. What should I do with your cock if I have it and don't want it? Shove it up your own arse?"

"Vulgar. But I find that rather hot."

"What do you want?" Bjorn interjected.

"Didn't I just tell you?" Grímr licked his lips, and Tyra wanted to wretch. "You mean beside fucking your woman in front of you? Ah, well, I should like to finish what my worthless brother and my whoring wife started. Now that I don't have to share my spoils with them, I'm enjoying myself even more."

"Because you don't dirty your hands. You got one little cut on your leg, and you were too scared to fight after that. Does your new God like cowards because you know ours don't?" Bjorn shifted so Tyra was no longer in Grímr's line of sight.

"Those are big words for an outnumbered man who has a woman he'd rather not see raped. I would suggest you try sugar over vinegar if you want her to only end up raped and not dead."

"I'd prefer death," Tyra muttered.

"That can be arranged. After my men and I get what we want from you." Grímr gestured to the line of men who stepped forward. There were easily fifty visible to Tyra and Bjorn. Seven they could defeat, but fifty would see them dead before the fight even began. "Not so much to say now? Just as well because I was tired of hearing your pitiful whining."

"It's your voice you've been listening to." Bjorn grinned. "It does sound like a petulant child."

"You really do want to discover what I will do to Tyra, don't you?" Grímr flicked his wrist, and one of his men ran forward.

Tyra did not even flinch when she plunged her knife into his groin and pressed down on the hilt. Blood blossomed across the man's leather pants.

"She cut off my cock," the man wailed.

"Shall I take off your balls too?" Tyra did not wait for an answer before plunging her knife into the man's belly. She pulled the knife free and ran her tongue against the flat side of the blade. She forced herself not to throw up, but she would make her point.

"She's crazy."

"Bloodthirsty wench."

"Nae worth having ma cock lopped off."

"I dinna need that cunny."

The whispers and comments rippled through the men just as Tyra intended. She wiped her knife across the dead man's shirt before tossing and spinning the knife, catching it at the last minute. She did it several times as she passed her glance over the men who assembled around Grímr. She licked her lips and tilted her head to the side. Tyra raised her brows before smiling seductively.

"She is *Rán*," muttered one of the Norsemen. "We're not at sea, but she would pull us into the depths and to our death. She is the sea goddess come to kill us."

Tyra's grin spread as she licked her lips again and bit her bottom lip. She had been unable to avoid the rumors ever since she was a child, and she had hated them. Not only did they discount her real parents, they were not kind gods.

Rán and her husband *Ægir* drew sailors to their death. *Ægir* was responsible for the storms that pulled men from their boats, and *Rán* captured them only to drag the sailors to their feasting hall at the bottom of the seas. It was the opposite of Valhalla.

Tyra was aware people spoke of her natural ability when they mentioned the two sea gods, but until that moment, she despised them. Now, she intended to make the most of it. "Perhaps I am. Perhaps you have caught me and my husband *Ægir*. Do you trust us not to kill you?"

"Ridiculous," Grímr grunted. "We are nowhere near the sea."

"And that make you think there's a limit to a goddess's power? Perhaps I am Loki."

"You are a woman," called another Norseman.

"So you say. Has that ever stopped me before? Did Odin and I not bear and suckle babes?" Tyra referred to a tale that told the story of how both Odin and Loki shapeshifted into women to not only bear babes, but to also nurse them. The tale also said Loki shapeshifted into a mare to bear Odin's steed, which became the fastest horse to ever live. Tyra would play upon their superstitions, even if her mind considered the tales to be ridiculous exaggerations.

Bjorn tried not to laugh as he watched the Norsemen become more and more uncomfortable as Tyra spun her story. He did not enjoy her arousing smiles and taunts, but he understood what she was doing. Bjorn wished she reserved them for him alone, but pettiness and jealousy would not keep them alive. He admired her creativity and quick thinking even though she did not appreciate the comparisons to the sea god and goddess, and he did not want to be likened to *Ægir*, but Tyra shrugged as she continued goading the men. She turned her attention to the Highlanders.

Bjorn realized it was their turn to receive her trickery and manipulation. He listened as she wondered aloud if she might be a kelpie, some other shapeshifting creature from the sea that the Highlanders believed in. She pointed to her eyes which blended blue and green into a beautiful hazel, but she used it to insinuate it was the mark of the fae. Bjorn noticed the superstitions did not affect the Highlanders as much as the threat of vengeful gods did the Norsemen, but several were growing restless and looking around. He caught himself before he choked when he watched Tyra turn her attention back to Grímr and ask him if he would like to learn how he would die.

"Sigrid told me. Aren't you just a bit curious to find out what the runes told her? Perhaps you could better prepare. It is rather messy."

"I don't fear death."

"Is that why you hide like a little girl whenever you must fight us?" She asked, innocence dripping from her words. "Or has a seer already told you when you will die, and you don't want to alter fate?"

"We all die when *Nornir* decides it is our time. The day I was born predestined by fate. I have no reason to fear death."

Tyra nodded, looking speculatively at Grímr. "Very well. If you say so, but I would decide which of these men will take over from you before tomorrow." A ripple of whispers spread through the men who continued to watch Tyra and Bjorn.

"Haven't you told the men who'll lead them after you die?" She swept her gaze across them. "I suppose that means any of you might be the next leader. The conqueror who gets all the spoils. But then, if Grímr hasn't told you who to follow, what will you do if someone tries to usurp your power?"

Tyra looked at each man, making him feel as if she spoke to only him. If attempting to scare them with threats of the gods' wrath or devious faeries did not work, then she would plant seeds of malcontent.

"What if Grímr dies before he pays you? Has he told you where he keeps the gold he promised you? Do any of you know? What if the man he intends to lead after him decides not share the wealth?" She looked back at Grímr as if she hoped to sink the last of his ships. "If he dies, and you don't get paid, do you have a reason to fight? I wouldn't go another day without getting the last of my promised pay. Otherwise you might never get it."

Bjorn snickered as he watched Tyra's tactic stir every man until they were buzzing like a hive of angry hornets. She had appealed to or scared every man who stood behind Grímr. She had created dissent, and Grímr snapped at them, but he failed to silence them.

"Bind and gag them!" Grímr ordered the men who still surrounded them. Tyra slashed at the men who attempted to seize her, but three of them overpowered her, forcing her to the ground. The other four men struggled until they pushed Bjorn to the ground beside Tyra. They held knives at the ready when they ordered Bjorn to put his shirt and boots back on. They had a rope coiled around them and their feet bound before they had an opportunity to struggle to their feet. Bjorn kicked one man in the groin who dared rub his cock in front of Tyra.

Their captors were quick to get them gagged and pinned down. The men hurried to back away from the hissing and snarling couple, but they forgot to bind either of their wrists. Bjorn slid his hand over Tyra's and squeezed it. She rested her head against Bjorn's back. She did not dare close her eyes for longer than a blink, but she relaxed a little when his solid frame propped her up. His other hand reached back to entwine their fingers. Tyra knew the angle must have been a strain on him, but the comfort he offered was too dear to give up. She shifted to make them both more comfortable. Bjorn's thumbs swept over her hands as she squeezed them back.

They stayed that way for hours until a Norseman braved their snapping teeth and removed their gags. He tossed dried beef at them, but neither of them were able to reach it from their laps. The man cackled like an old woman, amused with his own antics.

"I need to relieve myself," Tyra muttered. She had drunk nothing in hours, but she wanted to give their escape another attempt.

"Good thing you're a woman. You can pish where you sit." The man walked away, and the camp began to settle for the night. Tyra waited until no one had moved for half an hour before she dared whisper to Bjorn.

"I still have another knife in my boot. They never checked even after I pulled the first one out. If I can get to it, then I can try to cut us loose."

"If you can get to it, give it to me. I'll be able to cut through the rope faster."

"All right."

Bjorn pretended to stretch his back and find a better position as Tyra pulled her knees in as far as she could and slid her foot back. She fumbled with the end of the hilt. She almost reached but not quite. She tried again and almost had it when a guard moved toward them. She pretended to scratch her leg as Bjorn straightened up. Tyra laid her head back against Bjorn and let her eyes close, except she kept them open just a crack. She would not make herself any more vulnerable than she already was. When she was sure the man left, she turned her head toward Bjorn's ear.

"I almost had it. I touched the end of the han-dle, but I didn't manage to grasp it. I can try again."

This time Bjorn acted as if he was if he was leaning to one side then the other to stretch. It was enough for Tyra to wrap her fingers around the hilt. She jerked it free and slid it beneath her legs which she stretched out.

"Got it," she murmured.

"Wait a few minutes before you pass it to me. They were watching us as I moved around. Let them relax again."

"I think I can get my feet free once it's safe to move again."

"Be careful. You'll do it from beneath. Don't cut yourself."

"I don't intend to."

"Does anyone?" Tyra huffed. "I love you," Bjorn whispered.

"I love you more."

"Not possible." They both smiled before remem-bering where they were.

"I'm going to find the nearest bed and keep you in it for a sennight while I make love to you every way we can both come up with," Tyra teased.

"Promise?"

"I shall tie you up if I must."

"I wouldn't mind it if you were worshipping my body," Bjorn teased back.

"Worship? Mighty big opinion of yourself."

"I will show you what is mighty and big."

"You already have. And I intend to keep you in that bed, so you can remind me over and over."

"And if I should like to tie you up and worship your body, Ty?"

"Who am I to argue with what my man wants?"

"You shall get us caught if you make me laugh."

They fell silent as they watched the camp, certain few people were still paying attention to them. Tyra pulled her legs in again and leaned as far forward as the ropes allowed. She rested her cheek against her knees as if she were falling asleep. She grasped the rope from behind her legs and opened her knees just enough to spy down and ensure she did not sever her hand instead of the rope.

When it gave way, Tyra tapped Bjorn's arm. She covered the hilt with her palm and slid it along the ground until Bjorn's hand once again covered hers. He squeezed it before doing the same as she did, cutting his legs free. Then he set to work on the coils that kept them pressed together. He remained leaned over with his knees apart as he sawed the rope from beneath. He made hard and fast strokes, careful not to impale his chin or throat. It was awkward, but it was the least obvious maneuver. It took several minutes before the rope frayed and broke apart. Bjorn remained bent over to keep the rope in place.

"It's done," he whispered.

"Which way do we go? Did you see which way we came from?"

"I did, but we can't go back that way. They will track us too easily."

"Which direction will they least expect?"

"Grímr will send men in all directions, but if we

can slip into the trees where he stepped out, that's the direction he will least expect. Why would we go toward where he hid? It does not have the densest tree cover, but it's enough to hide us or give us places to climb into."

"Agreed. We should wait a little longer. I can't tell if our movement caught anyone's eye. They might be waiting us out. Did you spot where the guards posted?"

"Yes. There is one straight in front of you, which is the way we need to go. I'm sure he's looking out rather than in, so he won't see us coming."

Another hour passed as Tyra and Bjorn waited for the darkest hours of night to blanket them. The guard changed once, but no one else stirred. They sat far enough from the dying fire that they struggled to find their own hand in front of their faces.

"It's time. Don't let go of my shirt." Bjorn rose to a crouching position and helped Tyra to her feet. He pulled his shirt loose and pushed it into Tyra's fingers. "Tell me if you can't go on. Don't wait until you can't keep up or fall."

Tyra tugged once in agreement.

"Now," Bjorn breathed.

They darted toward the tree line. When they were a few feet away, they spotted the guard. Bjorn pressed Tyra behind him as they slowed to a walk. He covered the man's mouth and slid the knife across the man's throat. He dropped to the ground without a sound, and Bjorn pulled Tyra back to his side. They dashed into the trees and continued to run, each with a hand held out in front of them. Tyra could not tell how long they ran. She forced herself to breathe in through her nose and out through her mouth. She matched Bjorn's stride, knowing he was going slower to accommodate her shorter legs. Once she had her breathing under control, she nudged Bjorn and picked up their pace. They were both trained to run long distances, and even though Tyra did not enjoy it as much as Bjorn, she would last as long as he did.

Bjorn was sure they had run for an hour before they broke free of the trees and entered an unprotected glen. He wanted to curse as he scanned the little that was visible ahead of them. He knew Tyra was trying to listen for anyone who followed them. He thought he had heard pursuers a few times, but no one ever caught up. Bjorn also knew they did not dare stand there much longer in case someone was on their heels. He pulled Tyra toward tall grass, but she hung back.

"Bog," Tyra whispered. "Tall grass means bog." She was right. He remembered coming close to being sucked under by one the first time he raided along the Scottish coast.

Bjorn led them through the shorter grass until the outline of more trees came into view. Bjorn thanked the gods that Scotland had as many forests as the Trondelag, if not more. They entered the woods just as the sky began to lighten, making it possible to see a few feet in front of them, but it was still impossible to tell where they were going. Bjorn looked to his left and spotted what he was sure was a large oak. He took Tyra by the wrist and led her to it. They stood below it as they looked at the low hanging branches.

Tyra understood what Bjorn intended, so she jumped up and wrapped an elbow over the branch. She was prepared to pull herself up until Bjorn's boost just about sent her flying over it. She pulled up her legs until she coiled herself around it. She sat up and reached for the next branch. It was spindly and snapped. She inched closer to the trunk and brought her feet under her, reaching up again to find an even sturdier branch than she stood on.

Tyra hoisted herself, discovering another thick branch beside it that formed a vee where they met at the trunk. She moved onto the second branch and waited for Bjorn to join her. He was only seconds behind her. While she panted from climbing, he was still breathing as smoothly as when they finished running. Bjorn reached out for Tyra, glad he held her against his side despite their precarious balancing act.

"We can wait here until there's more light. Then we'll have to climb higher." Tyra's voice was so quiet, Bjorn strained to make out the words.

"Are you all right?" he pushed her hair aside, putting his lips near her ear. His breath sent a shiver along her spine and desire spiked deep within her belly.

"I'd be better if being so close to you didn't do such funny things to my insides."

Bjorn's chuckle was soundless, but his side moved beneath her. He took her hand and placed it against the ridge in his pants. "It's not one sided."

They sat in silence as Tyra leaned against Bjorn, his body heat keeping her from shivering when her perspiration dried and chilled her. They held their breath as they listened to something rustle the leaves behind the tree where they hid. Bjorn turned his head and let the air whoosh from his lungs when he realized it was a stag and doe not far away. The stag was rubbing his antlers against the bark of a nearby tree.

"Deer," Bjorn whispered.

Tyra nodded and pointed higher into the branches. Bjorn waited while Tyra rose, bracing herself against the trunk. There was enough light during the predawn hour for her to see more of the tree.

She spotted the limb she wanted to climb to. It would be high enough in the foliage that no one would spot them from the ground. She was grateful for the days of training and hours of swinging her sword that strengthened the muscles the axe tore when it sank into her chest. She would not have had the strength to climb otherwise.

Tyra continued until she sat on the branch she wanted. Bjorn followed her up, climbing more like a squirrel than a man. She marveled at how nimble he was for being so large. He moved through the leaves, hardly stirring them, even though he looked like a bear approaching. She reached out her hand and tugged, helping him to the final limb. He slid onto it behind her and pressed her back against his chest. He wrapped his arms around her and kissed her temple.

Bjorn relished the freedom to shower Tyra with affection. Finally. He had waited half a score of years to sit as they were now. He never imagined it would be in a tree evading captors, but it would not diminish his glee. He was smiling despite their circumstances as he replayed in his head each time she said she loved him, and he wanted to bellow it from the treetop they sat in.

Instead, Bjorn pulled Freya closer and sighed as she sank into his embrace. One of her hands rested on top of his folded ones over her belly while her other hand rested on his thigh. She found a snag in the leather and fiddled with it. She inhaled the pine and musk that clung to Bjorn and the fresh air that wafted through the leaves. Tyra's body relaxed little by little as her breathing deepened. Her body twitched twice, making Bjorn grin as he leaned his cheek against the crown of her head.

"Sleep, my love. I will watch over you," he murmured. He wanted to shut his eyes too and drift off, but he would not risk them falling or being found. He was just as exhausted, but he remained alert. Dawn broke with bright pink and purple hues splashing the sky as the fiery ball rose behind a thin cloud cover. It temped Bjorn wake Tyra to share the beauty with her, but she had curled into him even more, and light snores escaped between her lips, sounding more like a purring kitten.

Bjorn fought to keep his eyes open, but the warmth from Tyra's body was such a comfort, that his need for sleep almost overcame him. He jerked, and for a moment, he feared his body had twitched like Tyra's as he slipped toward sleep. But then he heard it. His mind was telling his body to stay awake. The sound was distant, but in the open meadow it carried. He was certain voices were moving toward them.

"Ty, wake up," he nudged her. "You have to wake up now."

Tyra tried to twist away and batted at his hand as she burrowed further into his chest.

"Tyra," he said with more force to his tone. He hated what he had to do, but he covered her mouth and pinched her nose. Tyra came awake in a panic. Her arms were pinned to her side, and someone covered her mouth to keep her from screaming. Within an instant, the hand squeezing her nose disappeared. "Ty, it's me. I'm sorry, my love, but you must wake up. Silently."

Tyra looked at Bjorn, her eyes wide in fear and disoriented. Her gaze shifted as she took in their situation. It came rushing back to her, and she nodded her head. Bjorn dropped his hand from her mouth and eased his hold on her. She reached out and found his nipple, twisting as hard as she could. Bjorn stifled his yelp and glared at her when she smirked.

Tyra recognized his look meant he would get his retribution, but it was only fair turnaround.

Bjorn gestured with his fingers that someone was walking toward them from behind. Tyra froze and strained to hear what Bjorn had. She tapped his hand once to assure him she caught the sounds, too. They sat motionless as the voices drew closer with each breath.

"Where the bluidy bleeding hell are they? How far can that eejit and his whore have gotten?"

"I dinna ken, but I'm bluidy tired of traipsing around after them. The bitch was right when she said Grímr should pay us before we continue on. I dinna want to wander aboot in the dark, risk falling into a bluidy bog, to nae get paid."

"Haud yer wheest. Ye whine more than a bairn with wet raggies. Ye'll tell them we're coming if ye dinna pipe down."

The third voice was authoritative and put an end to the other two men's conversation. Bjorn wanted to grumble since the men talking helped him gauge how close they were drawing. They were beneath the branches on the other side from where Tyra and Bjorn sat when they spoke again.

"I'm certain we heard them," a fourth voice spoke. This one was a Norseman. "They were in front of us through the woods, but it's as though they disappeared once they got to the clearing. We have searched all of the meadow and not come across them. Where do these woods lead to?"

Bjorn looked at Tyra, and they both prayed the Norseman would get an answer that helped them.

"Back to the Ross keep," said the first man who spoke. "It isnae that far past the end of the forest. They will be in a right pickle if that's where they've gone." The man with the strident voice snickered, but the lack of mirth grated on Tyra's nerves.

"Then do we continue that way?" asked the Norseman. "Or assume that if they walked that way, the scouts caught them?"

"We carry on. Grímr was clear he wanted them back. He doesnae care who finds them as long as he gets them back. And it's the Ross laird who will pay us tonight if we bring them to him," reasoned the Highlander again.

"Perhaps a wee beastie got them during the night, and we shall find what's left of them," said the man who'd complained earlier. "Nay prisoners to wrestle and bring back. I dinna trust that mon. I witnessed what he did to Donal's face before he crushed ma brother's windpipe."

"Aye, and nay one should underestimate the woman," said the Highlander who'd remained quiet. "She cut off a man's cock and grinned while doing it. She isnae right in the head, that one. Barmy as the day is long. I like ma meat and potatoes where they are."

Tyra turned her face into Bjorn's chest to smother her laugh. Her movement shook some of the leaves, and they both froze.

"Did ye catch that?"

"Aye, in the branches. A squirrel or a bird. Let's move on. I dinna want shite landing on ma head. I dinna care what ma mother said. It isnae good luck to have anything shite on ye," said the authoritative Highlander. The men passed below the branch Tyra and Bjorn sat on and continued through the trees. Their voices faded as they discussed the meal they hoped awaited them at the Ross keep.

Tyra and Bjorn looked at each other as the same thought ran through both of their minds. The three Highlanders carried on a conversation, but the Norseman said nothing since he asked whether they should continue on. They did not have long to wait before an arrow sailed into the leaves and landed with a thunk into a branch several feet below them. Another whizzed past them, but when it failed to meet a mark, it dropped back to the ground.

"Come out now or risk my arrow finding you," called the gruff Norse voice. Tyra and Bjorn did not move. "Very well. Your funeral."

Several other arrows soared into the leaves, a few coming too close for comfort.

"I shall just wait down here. You can't stay up there forever. You must come down, and I'll be here to greet you."

Bjorn gestured to himself and then pointed down. Tyra glared at him and fisted his shirt. She mouthed the word "no."

"Stay," Bjorn mouthed. Tyra tugged on his shirt, but he kissed her. He whispered in her ear, "I love you. You will always come first. I will die before I stop protecting you."

Tyra's face crumpled as she tried to keep Bjorn from shifting to stand on the branch below them. She watched Bjorn grip the hilt of her knife between his teeth as he moved toward to the ground. He stayed close to the trunk where the branches were sturdier and kept him hidden, his tan clothes blending with the bark.

"Good choice," called the man from the ground.

Bjorn spotted the veritable giant looking at him, bow and arrow pointing toward him. The man had the arrow notched and the string drawn back. Bjorn glanced up at Tyra once more before swinging from one branch to another, making it difficult for their pursuer to maintain his aim.

Bjorn moved along a branch, his hands holding the one above him as his feet slid over the notches and bark. He was as close as he dared get without the man having a clear shot. He took a deep breath before jumping toward the giant Norseman. Bjorn was already drawing his fist back as he tackled the other man. He slammed it into the man's face, using his own substantial weight to keep the man from drawing enough air back into his lungs after the fall knocked it from him.

Bjorn's mind would not shake the image of Tyra's face before he left her above. He pummeled the man until he would never stand again, would never threaten Tyra again. He reached for the knife he let fall from his mouth as he left the tree. He slid it across the man's throat just to be sure. Bjorn would not leave any man alive who might harm Tyra.

Tyra scrambled down the tree, and she launched herself as he reached up to help her down. She wrapped her arms and legs around him as she buried her face into the crook of his neck. Her sobs rattled her slim frame. She squeezed her legs tighter as though she feared he might try to put her down. He stroked her hair and rubbed her back until she leaned back and cupped his face.

Tyra looked into Bjorn's eyes, searching for something she could not name. The love and tenderness she found reassured her. There was a fearlessness and steadfastness that was always present in Bjorn, but it somehow meant so much more now. She pressed her mouth to his as she poured all the love she possessed into that kiss. She did not cry often, but she had been so afraid Bjorn would not live to hold her, kiss her, love her again.

Tyra experienced rage unlike anything she had ever known before grow within her chest as she watched her fellow Norseman aim his bow at Bjorn, willing to betray them for money from a Scotsman, the one willing to supply Grímr with warriors. She had been ready to avenge Bjorn's death. She had seen the man's face before hurtling herself into

Bjorn's arms. The damage Bjorn had done paled in comparison to what she was prepared to do had the man killed Bjorn. Tyra had been angry before and recognized the sensation of bloodlust coursing through her, a sensation she discovered when she entered her first fight. But what happened moments ago made her understand the trance-like state a berserker entered. She was sure she was there until Bjorn drew the knife across the dead man's throat.

Tyra pulled back from Bjorn and brushed his hair back before laying her forehead against his. Neither had words, and there was no need. When Tyra's confidence in her ability to stand without collapsing returned, she dropped to the ground. She stepped around Bjorn to look once more at the dead man. She spat on his face before drawing her booted foot back and kicking his head.

"*Níðingr*," Disgraced, honorless man. Tyra's lips curled in disgust as she hurled the insult. Bjorn stood behind her and placed his hands on her shoulders. "I am glad you knocked his bow from his hands. Let him rot for eternity. He deserved to die with no weapon in his hand."

They both stood staring at the man as blood pooled around his head. Bjorn understood Tyra's anger. He experienced the same emotion when he pictured her being in danger, and he was just as disgusted at the man below him. Had the dead Norseman been fighting for only Grímr, even on foreign soil, they would have respected him as a warrior, but Bjorn overheard what Tyra had. The man fought for money from a Christian, supported a Christian. That was unforgivable.

"Come. We have to leave before the other three wonder why he isn't following them," Bjorn whispered.

Tyra nodded. She grabbed the bow and quiver

before rounding up the arrows that had fallen back to the ground. Bjorn pulled the man's sword loose and checked for more knives. He strapped the sword on and gave Tyra a knife he found along with the one she lent him. He tucked two more into his belt.

Tyra faced the direction the men headed then turned to her right, pointing in front of her. It was the general direction they traveled from the day before, but it was far enough from the trail that both Bjorn and Tyra were confident they would not run into Grímr's men without warning.

<h1 style="text-align:center">ELEVEN</h1>

Tyra and Bjorn moved through the forest on silent feet, listening for any disturbances, even ones that were animals. They strained their ears for any warning the woodland critters would offer. They walked with enough space between them to fight off an attack from any direction or run without tripping over each other. The sun was moving overhead, but the tight leaf canopy kept the heat from pounding onto them. It was dim, but far more was visible than during the midnight dash. Their heads were on a swivel as they stayed alert, never letting their guard down.

By midmorning, they came to the edge of the forest. The land dropped into a steep but narrow ridge, and the crag they stood on threatened to break off with their weight. Across from them was a mountain that had little foliage growing on it and seemed to be made from loose rocks and dirt. They stepped back and looked around.

To their distant right was the trail their captors had used, and to their far left was the Ross keep. Neither found the trail nor the castle. Bjorn and Tyra had no way to estimate distance, so they were unsure whether either posed an immediate threat. They found where the crag ended, and a solid land bridge led to the foot of the mountain.

"What now?" Tyra asked.

"I haven't a clue."

They looked over the ledge again as stones skidded down until they landed in the stream that ran through the base of the ridge. Tyra tried to remember if Lorna had described anything like this when she helped Tyra make the maps.

"I think the woods led us to the Ben Wyvis Lorna told me about. She only mentioned and pointed to where they would be on the map. She didn't tell me they were actual mountains."

"I doubt she imagined we would ever come near them. Do you remember where they are in relation to where we entered Ross land?"

Tyra tried to recall, but Lorna had not given her many details. "I remember she said there was a forest at its base, so that must be what we passed through if we are now looking at the mountains. Regardless of which direction we take, it will be a long way to traverse."

"What's on the other side?"

"Lochs, I think, and then eventually the wrong coast."

"So what do we do? Climb up and survey what surrounds us, or do we try to orient ourselves based on what you remember?"

"Climb. Lorna only mentioned it in passing. I'm not even sure this is Ben Wyvis." Bjorn looked at Tyra, proud of her tenacity but concerned about her endurance. He cupped her jaw. "Don't worry about me, Bjorn. I can make it."

"I always worry about you. Don't you know that yet?"

"Worse than an old woman."

"And you're stuck with me."

"Hurry, and you can show me how you stick to me." Tyra laughed as she turned toward the end of the ridge. They walked hand in hand, almost like a regular couple not trying to avoid recapture. When they came to the base of the mountain, they realized it was feasible to scramble up it, but it would leave them exposed to anyone looking in their direction.

"We use caution while we climb. Anyone looking this direction will spot us before we do them. We'll have to keep an eye out even before we get to the summit," Bjorn continued to look around. Being out in the open made him uncomfortable, but they had few choices left to them. "We have several hours of climbing, and it may be dark by the time we reach the summit. Are you prepared to spend the night in the open?"

"We haven't much choice. It'll be safer for us at the summit even if it's going to be cold."

"You go up first. If you slip, I'll catch you."

"And if you slip?" Tyra glared at him. "Why do you think I would accept you being in danger any more than you're willing to accept it for me?"

"Because I'm bigger than you, my wee beastie. I rather like that. Suits you." Bjorn grinned before lifting her off her feet and hoisting her onto the mountainside where she began to climb. She kicked loose shale onto Bjorn.

"Whoopsie."

Bjorn growled playfully. "You'd better reach the top before I catch up."

"Perhaps I want you to catch me."

Bjorn opened his mouth to say, "about time," but he snapped it shut before he ruined the moment. Instead, he looked around now that they were several feet from the ground. "I don't see anything. Do you?"

"No."

They continued to climb, stopping every couple

hundred feet to look at their surroundings. They observed nothing until they were higher than the tree line of the forest where they had hid. Once they were above the trees, they had a clear view well into the distance. Bjorn and Tyra discovered small lochs scattered around the far side of the mountain. They did not notice any movement, smoke, or metal glinting in the sun, reassuring them that they were alone, as best they could tell. They walked and scrambled for the rest of the morning and all of the afternoon.

Tyra estimated it took them six hours to reach the summit even though it was not a remarkably high mountain. The uneven terrain meant they had to use caution when they chose their footing and inch along parts of the mountain until they found more even paths. When they reached the summit, they had the clear view they needed, but they were both thirsty and hungry. Neither had eaten or drunk anything in over a day. Tyra became lightheaded from dehydration and the altitude. She was sure there was movement on the far side of the mountain, but she rubbed her eyes to find there was nothing there.

"I thought I saw it, too." Bjorn stood beside her.

"We'll have to wait to learn if there is anyone's there, and if so, whether they are friend or foe. But I suspect it's the altitude and hunger."

Bjorn pulled his shirt over his head and put it on Tyra despite her protests. "You're cold," he whittled.

"And you will be, too."

"I'm fine."

"So am I."

"Tyra," he warned.

"Bjorn," she snapped before closing her eyes. When she opened them, her sense of calm had returned. "You are always taking care of me. You've kept me alive. Please let me do the same for you. It bothers me that I'll be comfortable when you're at risk of freezing. I can't accept that."

Bjorn saw the pleading in her eyes as much as he heard it in her voice. He nodded once and took his shirt back. "Then let's find a spot furthest out of the wind until we figure out what to do next."

The mountaintop was flat, more like a plateau, so they did not have to worry about slipping to their deaths. There was little to keep them from being exposed to the elements, so they traveled down the far side of the mountain until they came to aspen, birch, and rowan trees scattered about. They cut low branches from the aspen trees, and while they did not provide as good protection as evergreens, they would build a lean-to of sorts. They picked berries from the rowan tree even though they would be tart. It was that or go hungry for at least another day. When they returned to the summit, they worked together to prop the branches they carried into an overlapping mat. They lifted it together and slid below it, using their backs to keep it up. The branches were just long enough to reach over their heads if they huddled. It had been a struggle to drag them to the top even though it had not been a far walk down. When the wind whipped across the plateau that night, they would be glad to have the meager shelter.

Bjorn and Tyra watched a spectacular sunset from their vantage point upon the mountain. They wrapped their arms around one another as they shared their body heat. It surprised Bjorn how much heat Tyra exuded once he held her close to him. She was almost overheated, and he was comfortable. As Bjorn relaxed next to Tyra, his mind wandered, and he wished it had not. Questions rattled around as he contemplated why it took them so long to admit they loved one another.

"What are you contemplating?" Tyra murmured. "I can tell you're trying to work through something."

"How can you tell?"

"I don't know. I just sense it. You seem relaxed but unsettled at the same time, if that's possible."

Bjorn tried to make the muscles in his back release the tension he held, but all he ended up doing was shifting about. "I can't seem to get certain questions out of my head."

Tyra stilled. "I'm guessing those questions are not about how we're going to find the others."

"No. They're not."

Tyra tilted her head back to look at Bjorn and found trepidation rather than curiosity. She offered him a peck before tucking her head against his chest. She tightened her hold around his waist and snuggled as close as possible, lest she climb into his lap. Bjorn assumed this was her assent to him discussing their past.

"It seems natural to hold you now, and to kiss you whenever I want. I wasn't confident we would get to this point. I understand why the misunderstanding happened; I just don't know why you remained angry for so long."

It was a fair thing for Bjorn to question, but she did not have an answer that seemed reasonable anymore.

"At first, I was so hurt and disappointed and angry. I was convinced I meant nothing to you. I could not stand looking at you or being near you. It hurt so much. Then I was forced to watch you with other women, and that seemed to confirm my impressions. I meant nothing to you. I decided you were selfish and self-centered. At least where it concerned me. I struggled to reconcile the man I love and know you to be, with the man I was so sure you were with me, or toward me. So I grew angrier. When you didn't approach me again, I couldn't get past that hurt, so my grudge continued on until it just became normal. I was jealous, as well. Consumed with jealousy every time you were with another woman or one talked about you. Then two years ago, when the rumors trailed off, I was relieved, but a crueler side rejoiced, imagining that women no longer wanted you. I look back now, and I realize how patient you were with me when I can't imagine any other man being like that."

"I was patient because I could tell you were hurting and angry. I just never imagined it was only over me. You seemed to move on, perhaps not with many men, but you smiled and laughed when I wanted to crawl into a hole. That same consuming jealousy burned in me whenever a man flirted with you, and I was miserable those years you were with Knud. I wanted you to find happiness, but gods, how I wanted to kill him. I wanted to rip him apart for being the man who got to hold you, to talk to you, to just look at you every day. I was so miserable that I no longer wanted to pretend. I couldn't. I didn't want anyone if it wasn't you. I gave up hoping I would ever win you over, but I also gave up wanting to find someone to replace you. Substitutes just didn't work. It was only when I was drunk and lonely, or at feasts when I was sure I was the only one who didn't have someone, that I give in and bedded a woman. But you heard them. It was always you who I wanted, who consumed my mind and my heart. It was your name I called out. It was you in the dark."

"What about after our talk on the dock? You went to Gunnhild." Tyra's hushed tones carried hurt Bjorn wished he had never caused.

"I didn't go to her. We passed each other, and I

followed her. It was one of those times where I was so alone. I failed you, as a friend and certainly as anything more. Then you swam out to me, and we seemed to make progress. When I said I didn't want to make the same mistake twice, I meant I wasn't going to make love to you outside where anyone might find us. I wanted to be somewhere you deserved. You didn't give me the chance to say that, and that rejection was more than I could take that day." Bjorn scrubbed his hands over his face. "I didn't bed her. She touched me and holding you against me already had me aroused. It had been so long that it didn't take much. I tried to stop her, but my body was already three steps ahead of my mind. She was well aware I had you on my mind. We fought about it. I knew after that that I would rather be celibate than live with the guilt."

Tyra ran her hand over Bjorn's chest as she listened to him. It made sense. All of it. She had not considered bedding a man since she broke things off with Knud. Fritjof would have been the first man in well over a year.

"But Tyra, I sense there is more. You were sure I was self-centered and that my ego was too big, but that doesn't explain why you were convinced I was selfish. What did I take from others that I wasn't willing to give back?"

"Some of it was my selfishness. When I noticed a woman you favored, who I feared would be more than a passing interest, I was angry that you found that first. That you would fall in love and marry before I did. I also know what you preferred."

"Someone I pretended was you."

Tyra laughed and shook her head. "That was not what I thought. I know those women were the ones who spoke of settling down and getting married. That they accepted giving up being a shieldmaiden and being left behind. I thought you were selfish to expect someone to do that. To leave them behind."

Bjorn tilted his head back as understanding took hold. He shifted his position and lifted Tyra onto his lap. The branches fell, but he did not care. He needed to be closer to her, and short of stripping away her clothes and making love to her outside, once again, this was the best he would get.

"You feared I would abandon you to go on great adventures. You feared I would leave you behind like your father did when he sailed away but did not return."

Tyra sniffled as she fought back tears. It would be the second time that day she cried, and it seemed illogical to cry if her reason for being angry was not wanting to give up being a shieldmaiden. She despised being weak. Bjorn tucked hair behind her ear and lifted her chin.

"I understand your fear. It's been the same way with everyone I have cared about my entire life. At least as long as I can remember. My father came here, and while he returned, I was never with him again. He and my mother died while I stayed with Ivar and Lena. I've battled the guilt that I didn't die along with them."

"Bjorn, you were just a child. What could you have done? You have suffered more than any of us realized. I figured out that the risks you took were not to show off or prove yourself, but a hope that you might join your parents. I didn't like that risk taking either. I understand now why you were doing it, but it came across as selfish to me that you would leave us, me, behind."

"Ty, I had no intention of asking you, or expecting you, to remain behind. Just the opposite. I've always wanted you by my side. To consider sailing without you makes me sick with fear. When I feared you might die, I wanted to give up. The only thing that kept me going was the possibility that you might live, and I would miss being near you. I can't leave you behind. I can't imagine how we will ever have a family because I don't want to travel without you, but I would never let you travel while you're carrying, and someone would have to stay home with our children. I also wouldn't let you go without me because I'm terrified no one would protect you well enough."

"I suppose it's a good thing that I don't want children yet." Tyra tilted her head. "Do you?"

"When the gods bless me to be a father, then I will be ready." He leaned in for a deep kiss. "Ty, I will be a farmer when it comes time to have a family. I won't leave my wife and children behind."

"Your wife? You didn't say 'you.' You said 'my wife.'"

Bjorn caught the doubt in her voice and wanted to laugh that she would still wonder who he wanted to spend his life with. "I did say 'my wife.' I didn't say 'a wife.' Ty, you will be my wife."

"Is that a proposal?"

"If you believe it to be. I believe it's fact. I won't let go of you. I've been in love with you since I was seven. Seven. Now that you have told me you love me, twenty years later no less, there is no chance I will let you get away. I meant what I said the other night, that making love to you changes everything. I am yours as much as you are mine."

"Just don't die on me," Tyra whispered. It was an unreasonable request to put before a warrior, but she had to say it.

"I told you. I'm not going anywhere without you, and I'll be damned if I let you let die."

"I feel so foolish and so guilty. This time we lost. It's my fault."

"Shh. No, it isn't. I could have, should have,

worked harder for us to have these conversations sooner. I was too scared and still licking my wounds from ten years ago. I was a coward," his voice trailed off. Bjorn was not expecting the fist to his gut or for her to cinch the neckline of his shirt closed in her hand.

"Don't you ever, ever say that again," Tyra growled. "You are not, and never have been, a coward. I refuse to hear those words from you again. You will not take on a shame that is not yours to bear. I would kill anyone who said that about you, so I damn well won't hear it from you."

She shoved his chest away as she scowled at him. Bjorn laughed as he kissed her furrowed brow, her pinkening cheeks, her nose, and her downturned mouth. His kiss was slow as he coaxed her into opening for him. He swept his tongue across her lips before plunging in. He took his time to build her need into a raging inferno. Tyra pulled at his shirt until she slid her hands beneath. She hummed in appreciation as her hands glided over the chiseled muscles of his chest and stomach. She slid her fingers to his nipples and circled them with the tip of her index finger, then pinched them, eliciting a growl as he moved along her jaw to her neck.

He kissed a fiery path to her collarbone as he pushed her shirt down over her shoulder. He nipped with his teeth then swept his tongue over each spot to sooth it. His lips inched along until he found the spot behind her ear that made her shiver. Tyra's nipples hardened as Bjorn's breath tickled her ear. He turned his head to flick her earlobe with his tongue, then sucked lightly. His tongue found the whorl of her ear, and his breath made her shiver again.

"I'm still hungry. This little snack wasn't nearly enough" Bjorn purred.

The air was not as cool as they feared since it was

still early evening, and the wind died down. Bjorn pushed the branches off him and cradled Tyra's head as he laid her on the ground. His hands traveled over her body as he kneeled between her legs. As he brought them back to her waist, his fingers found their way beneath her shirt. His mind roared that he had surely been plucked from earth by a Valkyrie when his hands found her pert breasts.

Tyra arched her back to fill his hands as she pulled him toward her. When he lowered himself to his elbows, she squeezed her knees against his hips as her hands caressed his backside then grabbed it not so gently. Bjorn thrust his hips against her mons, and Tyra lifted her hips to meet him. He pulled away and unlaced her leather pants. He tugged them to her ankles before he yanked her boots off and pulled her pants all the way off. The last of the sunset had already faded, and he cursed the gods for depriving him once again of the sight of Tyra's body as he pleasured her. His touch along her inner thigh was like a feather, and she pulled at his shoulders as her need grew.

"I told you I'm hungry. Would you deny a starving man his feast?"

"And if my hunger gnaws at me and won't subside?" She was as aroused as he was, and his cock strained against the uncomfortable tightness of his own leather pants.

"I'm not giving up on tasting you, but we can compromise." Bjorn wondered if she would understand his implications. "Take your clothes off and turn around."

Bjorn came close to climaxing just from hearing Tyra agree to what he had not dared put into words. He was quick to strip off his boots and pants before lying on the ground. Tyra was the one to turn around as she straddled his hips, but she found what she was searching for in the dark. His iron length jutting from his body made it easy. She wrapped her hand around his cock at the first dip of his tongue into her sheath. She did not bother to not contain the moan that escaped, nor did she want to.

Tyra wanted Bjorn to understand she craved his ministrations as much as she was about to enjoy offering him hers. She flattened her tongue at the base of Bjorn's rod as she bathed it with sweeping licks until she came to the tip. She flicked the ridge below the head of his cock and smiled when he twitched. His groan was followed by his lips drawing in her bud as he sucked and made her entire body shake. She lowered her mouth and took him in, inch by inch, as she teased him. She relished the spank he gave her, and she wiggled her hips in response. His length sunk into her mouth as she began to apply pressure, and he gripped her backside.

Bjorn was sure their tryst would be over in a matter of seconds. Tyra's mouth on his cock was beyond anything he had ever experienced, and far beyond what his imagination had conjured countless times over the years. He dragged in deep breaths and blew the alternating cool and warm air onto Tyra's sensitive skin. His fingers dug into her hips as he drew her back closer to him. He ran one hand over her back and bottom while the other investigated her nether lips before dipping two fingers into her sheath as he continued to work her pleasure nub with his lips and tongue.

Tyra's elbows tried to give out as her body responded to Bjorn's touch. He found a spot along the wall of her womb that she as sure no man had ever discovered. It was almost too distracting to remember she was in the midst of pleasuring him, too. Her hips undulated to the rhythm he set as her mind evoked images of their bodies joining in ecstasy. She increased the pace of her hand and mouth as her arousal soared with her thoughts and Bjorn's touch. She cupped his bollocks and rolled them in her palm as he added a third finger. Tyra was unable to withstand the need that enveloped her as her body raced toward release. She lifted and pulled away as Bjorn reached to bring her back.

"No," she growled as she faced him and straddled his hips again. She lowered herself onto him, not muffling her moan as her body took him in. She rocked her hips as her climax rose from the depths of her belly as wave after wave of pleasure tightened all of her muscles. Bjorn felt robbed of watching Tyra's face as she climaxed around him. He rolled her onto her back and came onto his forearms. Bjorn thrust into her with long, slow strokes as she writhed beneath him. If he thrust any faster, he would spill his seed. He refused to end things that soon. He would draw out her need until he pushed her over the edge several more times.

"More," she whispered.

"More what, my love?"

"More of everything. More pressure, more speed. Harder, Bjorn." Each sentence drawn out as she pressed her feet into the ground to meet his thrusts. "Show me."

Bjorn understood what she meant, and he had no reservations about showing her just how much he craved her. He pulled back and lifted her hips as he surged into her harder with each thrust. He was not convinced the night's darkness made his vision black. Tyra on him and around him was bliss he never would have conceived as possible until that moment. Her muscles spasmed around him as she pleaded for more. Bjorn continued to hammer his sword into her sheath as she cried out his name. Hearing it on her lips was the point of no return for Bjorn. He thrust once more before pulling out. He scooped Tyra into his arms as he leaned back. He kneeled as she wrapped herself around him. He stroked her back as she panted, trying to catch her breath. She clung to him as though afraid he would put her down.

It was only once they both controlled their breathing that they fused their lips in a tender kiss that was the opposite of their heated and aggressive joining.

"I love you," Tyra murmured against his lips.

"I love you too, wife." Bjorn whispered.

"I'm not your wife."

"Maybe not yet to everyone else, but you are to me."

"I will gladly be your wife, husband." His breath hitched at her words. She ran her fingers through his hair as he settled. "What is it?" She wondered.

"I never thought to hear you call me that. I've prayed and asked the gods over and over, but I didn't think they would ever grant me that. Once Sigrid arrived, I was too scared to ask her in case she didn't see us together. I shall never forget hearing you call me husband for the first time."

"You are rather sentimental. You're a softie underneath all those slabs of muscle."

"Slabs of muscle, huh?"

"You know it."

"But I like hearing it. Ty, you are the most beautiful woman I have ever seen. To know you desire me —" he broke off as his head sank. She pressed a kiss against his forehead.

"And don't you realize you're the most handsome man I have ever seen? I've always been in awe of your body. Now I can touch it."

"Whenever and however you want."

Tyra laughed, "You may change your mind when

I won't let go. I shall have my hand wrapped around your cock as you try to spar with Leif and Erik."

"Your hand, your mouth, your sheath. Anything, anytime."

"I'm ready. Are you?"

Bjorn growled as he laid her back onto the ground. It shocked him that he was ready to make love to her again, but he was. He slipped into her entrance and groaned.

"Bjorn, it's so good, that moment when you first enter me. It's as if everything is right again after waiting so impatiently."

"I know what you mean."

This time, they moved slower as they explored each other's bodies. They discovered more of each other and how their bodies moved in sync. Once they finished and their skin grew clammy with the brisk air, it forced them to dress again. The temperature had plummeted since they began making love, and they appreciated the branches as they settled for the night.

"Sleep, little one."

"I'm not so little," Tyra yawned.

"You are compared to me, and you're tired. Sleep, little one."

Tyra burrowed into Bjorn's chest. "You take the first watch, but don't try to avoid waking me for my turn. You need to sleep too."

She was breathing deeply before Bjorn could argue. He rested his cheek against her head as he looked into the darkness, his eyes peeled for danger.

TWELVE

Tyra nudged Bjorn awake as the sun peeked over the horizon. He attempted to let her sleep through the night, but she awoke a few hours later and pinched him for not waking her. She had colorful words when he tried to insist she go back to sleep. Bjorn relented with a laugh and drifted to sleep as quickly as she had. Now the sun was coming up, it was time for them to decide what to do next.

Once more they looked out at the breathtaking vista. While the Trondelag had steep mountains and gushing waterfalls that were awe inspiring, the greenness of the fertile lands in the distance were a marvel to them both.

"That is why we should journey here. For that land, not for men, not so we can fight ourselves," Bjorn wondered aloud.

"Do you think this might be where we build that farm you spoke of last night?"

Bjorn wrapped his arm around Tyra's waist as he looked into her upturned face, her eyes earnest. "If this is where you would like to live, then I will happily farm here. If there is somewhere else, then I shall follow you."

"I can't stop wanting to say I love you."

"I won't stop you. I've never heard anything better," Bjorn grinned at her. "I love you, too."

She stood on her toes as she kissed him, but she pulled away just as Bjorn tried to deepen it. He grumbled as he reached for her. He would not be satisfied until he had kissed her properly and thoroughly. Tyra licked her lips as if to savor the taste, and Bjorn was ready to pounce.

"Don't do that, Ty. You are temptation come to life."

"Do what?" she licked her lips again.

"If you ever want to get off this mountain, you will stop teasing me."

She pouted but looked toward the direction which they traveled two nights ago.

"I don't like having responsibilities," she muttered to which Bjorn laughed.

"But your belly rumbled, so you must be hungry. For something other than me."

"I see your arrogance is back," she mused.

"Only because you have made me feel better about myself than I have in years." His low tones wrapped Tyra in a different warmth. After their feuding, knowing she made him happy warmed her in a way even his lovemaking did not.

"I feel the same, Bjorn."

———

They spent the next fifteen minutes assessing their choices, and they agreed they needed to travel in the direction they came when Grímr took them hostage. They supposed he would have moved on by now, either in continued search for them or to find the others, if not to continue his recruitment and training. Tyra and Bjorn set off and made their way down the mountain face. The terrain was rough, and they slid in several places. Bjorn grew so anxious that he would not take another step until Tyra walked behind him and held the corner of his shirt, just as she had when they fled in the dark. Rather than argue, Tyra agreed. In part, she appreciated the help and it made her worry less, but she was aware it made Bjorn less anxious, too. She admitted to herself that she enjoyed knowing she made Bjorn happy. It was a better, more genuine sense of accomplishment than when she used to make him miserable on purpose.

It took them less time to hike to the base than it did to climb, but it was still several hours later when they walked away from what Tyra was convinced was Ben Wyvis. They alternated walking and jogging as they tried to make up the distance they had to travel without exhausting themselves, since they still had not eaten more than the rowan berries. It was early afternoon when they reached the base of the mountain, and sunset approached by the time they had to stop. Both of them weaved and stumbled as they walked.

"Do you hear that?" Tyra murmured.

They had only spoken when necessary to maintain stealth in case they stumbled upon Grímr or any of the Rosses. Bjorn shook his head. He strained, but nothing came to his ears except for the soft rustle of trees beside the path they found.

"It's water. It's soft, but I am certain." Tyra pointed to their right. They found a well-worn path several hours earlier and walked closely along the tree line. It had been used enough for them to know it led somewhere of significance. They hoped it would either take them somewhere useful or give them information to orient themselves.

Tyra pulled an arrow from the quiver she had taken from the Norseman Bjorn killed. Bjorn drew his sword in one hand and a knife in the other. Bjorn nodded for Tyra to go first, knowing an arrow would reach an attacker much sooner than his sword. He stayed close without being in the way. She crept through a gap in the trees until she spotted the stream. Beside it was a group of men in plaids. Tyra's eyes opened as she looked over her shoulder at Bjorn. He had seen them, too. They tried to fade back into the woods, but a squirrel chattered angrily at them. The sound made a couple of them laugh.

"The wee beastie sounds fit to be tied. I wonder what has him chattering away. Rabbit or another squirrel," one man chuckled as he looked over his shoulder. It was an instant later that he was on his feet drawing his sword. "Norsemen!"

"Shite," Tyra muttered.

The five men lounging beside the water only moments ago were now irate Highlanders charging after Bjorn and Tyra. Bjorn stepped aside as Tyra rapidly fired arrows, striking one in the throat and shoulder. He fell to his knees as Tyra launched three more arrows, one finding a home in a man's arm. He roared and snapped the arrow where it entered his skin. Despite it being his sword arm, he raised it over his head as he raced forward.

"Back and to the left," Bjorn called as they moved into an opening that would give them more room to fight.

Tyra shot two more arrows into the man she had already hit. He only seemed to grow stronger as his injuries worsened. She was out of time to use her bow. She flung it to the ground before pulling two knives from her belt. She and Bjorn backed into each other to protect themselves. It would be the two of them against three angry warriors and one enraged monster who ran with arrows sticking out of him. They were willing to take those odds. The first man lunged at Tyra as she sliced his arm with her knife.

She twisted away as Bjorn swung his sword at the man he faced off with.

Tyra slipped under her opponent's arm and came up just below his chin with her blade pointed up. It sunk into the man's throat, and blood splattered her face. She did not even flinch. Tyra pushed him away as she yanked his shield from his arm. She swung the shield at the next man who came from her right. Bjorn had already felled the first man he fought. Now he defended himself against the warrior who resembled a porcupine as well as the man's friend. He sliced through the leg of the first to approach. He attempted to sever it, but the man jumped back just in time.

Bjorn lunged again and again as he drove the man back, moving them both away from Tyra as she wielded the shield like a sword, hacking and slicing with it. She crashed it into her opponent's head as he stumbled, surprised at the viciousness and ferocity of her moves. Tyra kicked the man in the groin before bashing him in the head twice with the shield. Freya's near-fatal mistake years ago taught Tyra to never assume an enemy was dead. She drew her knife across his throat and watched with satisfaction as blood bubbled from his throat and mouth.

Bjorn continued to fight the two men as he maneuvered them further from Tyra. It also meant it left his back exposed. The pincushion warrior circled around, forcing Bjorn to fight men on both his left and right. He parried and thrust, alternating his attention as his opponents drew closer. Tyra spun around and found Bjorn being cornered. She dashed toward him and launched herself at the man she had already shot. She knocked him off balance and scrambled back in time to kick the back of his knees. When his legs gave out, she jumped on him again, pushing his belly to the ground. Her weight forced the arrows deeper into his body. He tried to twist and fight, but his energy was draining from him. Tyra reared back and drove her knife through his back and pressed all her weight into the hilt, ensuring the blade sank into her enemy's heart. By the time she looked up, Bjorn had dispatched the other man.

"Three to two. My average is still better than yours," Tyra panted as she rose to her feet. "I hope you can keep up better in bed."

Bjorn grinned as he wiped away blood and whatever else stuck to his forehead and cheeks. He looked Tyra over as she smirked at him. He walked to her and grabbed a fistful of her shirt as he pulled her toward him, lifting her onto her toes. His kiss was fierce and passionate but playful too. "I look forward to you testing me."

Tyra kissed him back just as hard before spanking his backside. "I'm thirsty and now dirty. Let's go to the stream before anyone else shows up."

They wiped their blades on the grass and made their way to the stream. They walked without making a sound out of habit, even though the recent battle would have alerted anyone nearby. When they reached the banks, they watched fish swimming below the surface of the swift moving water.

"Shall I show you how I'm a better fisher than you, too?" Tyra teased, knowing this was one thing she would never best him at. Bjorn seemed to only have to look at fish, and they would jump into his net or swallow his line.

"You can try. But why not settle on your win? I'll only show you up."

Tyra grunted as she bent over the water and scrubbed her face, refreshed from the chilly water. Once she no longer had blood on her hands, she cupped water into them, drinking greedily. She looked over to find Bjorn doing the same but looking at her and laughing.

"What?"

"You are the least feminine woman when you fight, but only moments later you look like a dainty water nymph. You are a bundle of contradictions, and I'm drawn to every one of them." Tyra laughed as she splashed water at Bjorn. "Nice. I try to say something flowery, and you scoff at me."

"There's one of those contradictions."

Bjorn growled as he splashed a wave at Tyra, soaking the front of her. She stood up and backed away from the water as she stuck her tongue out at him. She acted as though she was looking for berries, so Bjorn was unprepared for the shove he received when he bent over to scrub his face. His arms flailed as he tipped into the water. He caught himself before going all the way in.

"That's it." Bjorn pounced on Tyra and lifted her his shoulder. He trudged into the water and dumped her in as he sank down to hold onto her. They both came up sputtering but laughing.

"We both needed the bath. If only we had soap," Tyra mused.

"Indeed. I've never seen you so playful after coming so close to dying."

"I'm relieved we both lived to be playful. I'm too tired to pretend I don't love your attention and company. I intend to enjoy my time with you nowadays. We fought. We won. We move on."

"Your practicality is alluring."

"Alluring? That's not a word I would think describes me."

"Alluring. Seductive. Ravishing. I can think of plenty."

"Well, don't use them all up today." Tyra scrubbed her shirt as the blood leached from her clothes. "But would you hurry? This water is freezing, and I'm even hungrier than I was before. And this time I want real food."

Bjorn finished scrubbing his own clothes before using his shirt to capture one fish after another. Once he had five laying on the shore still flopping about, he climbed out and looked around.

"We can't stay here. Not with their bodies still laying near the path. We have to move before we can make camp."

"Agreed. Perhaps we cross over to the other bank and continue in the direction we were going."

Bjorn nodded as he scooped the now-lifeless fish back into his shirt. They waded across and walked for another hour before deciding to make camp near the water. With the water to their backs, they had one natural defense. Anyone who tried to cross it would make enough noise to alert them, but there was little likelihood anyone would in the dark.

"Do we dare a fire?" Tyra looked around.

"A small one. Just long enough to help our clothes dry faster and to cook the fish."

"Do we eat and move on, away from the wood smoke?"

"I don't think so. Anyone who smells our fire will be here before it's out. The breeze is strong enough that the smoke shouldn't linger into the night."

Tyra nodded and began looking for sticks as Bjorn scaled and deboned the fish. She had a fire started by the time Bjorn had their meal on skewers. That sat in silence as their food cooked. Both enjoyed the companionable silence as they remained alert but began to settle in for the night. Once they ate, they arranged several evergreen branches to make a ground covering and blanket of sorts. They had already let the fire die down, so they smothered the flames before they settled in for

Tyra to take the first watch. She sat beside where Bjorn lay. Her bow and arrows at her side, a knife in her lap, and the sword in her hand. With only two of them to defend themselves, she would not risk anyone drawing too near before she began fighting back.

The cool air chilled Tyra as she sat in her damp clothes, but the shivering kept her awake when her eyes wanted to droop. She recited in her head every sailing song she remembered as she scanned the woods around them. Every so often, her gazed landed on Bjorn, who slept. He looked relaxed and boyish. She did not bother resisting the temptation to brush away a lock that fell across his forehead. She was just about to sit back up when he captured her hand and brought it to his lips.

"I enjoy awakening to your touch," his voice groggy. By mutual silent agreement, they had not touched each other that night. They did not have the natural privacy or defense of the mountain plateau, nor did they want a repeat of how Grímr's men caught them.

"I didn't intend to wake you. You still have time before your watch."

"I'm up now. You sleep."

Before Tyra had the opportunity to argue, they froze at the sound of someone, more than someone, as they listened. It came from the woods around them.

"We'll break our bluidy necks before we find them. We are better off waiting until we can see one foot in front of the other."

"We saw—"

"No. I'm not waiting until daylight to see if my best friend stumbled to her death. There was too much blood back there."

Bjorn and Tyra were on their feet as they listened

to Strian suggest they stop, Erik get cut off by Freya, and Freya's irritated and impatient order.

"Frey," Tyra called out.

"Ty?" Bjorn and Tyra turned as one to witness Freya burst through the tree line before hurdling the smoldering fire embers and tackling Tyra. Bjorn caught them as they tumbled backwards. He looked around to find Strian and Erik running after Freya but skidding to a halt when they spotted Freya and Tyra hugging one another until both struggled to breathe.

Once Bjorn was sure the women would not knock each other over, he walked to Erik and Strian. Erik pulled him in for an embrace, and Strian shook his forearm.

"What happened to you?" Freya demanded. "One moment, you were drowning your sorrows in some of Alex's whisky, the next you and Bjorn disappeared."

Freya struggled to make out Tyra's face in the dark, so she would not let go of her friend's hands. Bjorn moved closer to Tyra, but he did not speak for her. Strian and Erik crowded behind Freya as more men filtered into the small camp. A few men began rebuilding the fire. Tyra watched the men at work, and it was not long before a spark took hold. She pointed to the tree boughs she and Bjorn had been using.

"I'm getting impatient, Tyra," Freya warned.

"Shocking," Erik murmured, but clamped his mouth shut when glared at him.

Tyra sat and pulled Freya down next to her. Bjorn once again stayed close, but he was unsure whether Tyra would want him to give away their newly formed relationship before she had a chance to tell Freya. He should not have worried.

"You and Bjorn finally made love," Freya looked past Tyra to Bjorn.

"Freya," Tyra hissed as she glanced at Strian and Erik.

"Don't bother telling us that part. We figured it out when we found your vest and Bjorn's cloak and sword."

Now that there were no secrets, Bjorn scooted closer to Tyra as she reached back to him. He wrapped his arm around her waist, but it was not enough for Tyra. She moved to sit between his legs as he pulled her flush to him.

"Since you already figured that out, you know we didn't just wander off. Grímr's men found us. They took us before they even gave Bjorn a chance to get dressed."

"They stole you naked as a babe," Strian hooted.

Bjorn shot a glare at him before breaking into a grin and nodding his head. "Killed a man with my bare hands with my bare arse on display. Very freeing not having clothes restraining me. It seemed to shock the Highlanders. Tossed me my clothes and told me to get dressed. Tyra then scared them out of their wits, making both the Norsemen and the High-landers fear she was some magical spirit that would have her revenge. They bound us and gagged us until one of them removed the gag and threw dried beef at us."

"But they didn't check me for weapons." Tyra picked up the story. "I'd had a chance to put my boots back on before they took us. They didn't find the knife I keep there. Bjorn and I waited until it was well into the night before we cut the ropes and snuck into the forest that Grímr had appeared from. We ran until we passed through a clearing and then trav-eled back into a forest. We spent the night in a tree, then Bjorn killed a Norseman who tried to shoot us. That's how I ended up with a bow and quiver."

"Once that happened, it was impossible to stay. I guess the Ross keep was not far past the end of the woods. We traveled in a different direction and came to a flat-top mountain." Bjorn's brow furrowed as he looked around. "Where are Lorna and Rangvald?"

Tyra froze when she realized Bjorn was right. The older couple was not with their friends. She tensed as she looked at Freya. She caught her friend's forearm as she feared the worst. Freya patted her hand before prying off the fingers that bit into her arm.

"They are on guard. We found the men you must have killed, and it was Lorna who said you crossed the stream to move away from them before making camp. She and Rangvald had some of their people fan out to sweep the area further from the stream. They remained as a midpoint between the others and us. The Sutherlands are tending to the bodies."

Tyra relaxed and let go of Freya once she learned Lorna and Rangvald would join them. Her fear that they had died while looking for her and Bjorn was numbing. He sensed her anxiety and held her closer.

"Shh, they're all right, and we are now, too," Bjorn murmured against her ear. He looked up at the rest of the group and continued their story. "We came down the mountain and headed in the direction we came with Grímr, but far from his path. Tyra and I walked for most of the day before Tyra stopped us because she heard water. We went in search and found the stream and the Highlanders. There was a fight. They lost, we won. We crossed the stream like Lorna predicted and made camp here."

Freya had sat without speaking through her friends' story, and now she would have her questions answered. "So, you're finally made up. Have you told

each other you love one another, or are we going to
have to wait for that? You do realize this is more than
just coupling. Are you going to marry, or do we have
to wait another ten years for you to get to that? How
did you admit it to one another?"

Freya's rapid-fire questions had everyone
laughing but her. "Wife," Erik scolded. "There may
be things they would like to keep private."

"Horse shite. She wouldn't relent until I admitted
I love you. Now I want to know. She only had to wait
a couple months. I've waited a damn lifetime."

Erik put his hands up in surrender.

"We talked before the men took us, then we had
time to talk more over the past two days," Tyra relented. "There were a lot of needless misunderstandings, mostly my fault, but now we understand one
another."

"Misunderstandings? I suppose you'd call them
that," Freya scoffed.

"They weren't mostly your fault. I was just as
guilty." Bjorn broke in. "We are both guilty for our
own misery. But either way, we have moved on."

"Onto each other," Erik teased.

Tyra ducked her head, not from embarrassment
but to hide her laughter. Bjorn growled but then attacked Tyra's neck as he nuzzled and nipped. She
giggled, and Erik and Freya froze.

"You giggled," Freya accused.

"I did. You've been there when I've giggled
countless times."

"Not when Bjorn is around. Not unless it's at his
expense."

"Well, he's still the cause. I just like this reason
better." She twisted to kiss Bjorn's lips.

"Praise Freyja," Erik teased.

Tyra turned back to Erik. "Your wife had nothing
to do with this, no matter what she might say."

"Not that Freya," Erik laughed.

"Oh," Tyra nodded. "Yes, I thank the goddess Freyja, too."

"Anyway," Freya interjected. "When will you wed?"

"You're very presumptuous," Tyra raised an eyebrow at her friend.

"Then I shall have my father arrange it," Freya crossed her arms and raised an eyebrow in response.

Bjorn watched the women stare off at one another. Tyra was extracting her pound of flesh for what he was sure she had endured for years, as Freya gave unsolicited advice she undoubtedly had not followed when she and Erik chased one another.

"She's already my wife, as far as I'm concerned. We will deal with the rituals when we arrive home, but I've declared it." Bjorn ended the standoff and received a sharp pinch on the thigh for it.

"Thank you, husband. You might've let her simmer a little longer."

"I'm not in the mood to be on the receiving end of her ire, so thank you, Bjorn." Erik dodged his wife.

Freya laid a hand on Tyra's arm, "I'm overjoyed for you. I'm so glad you have the love you've always deserved."

Freya and Tyra embraced once more. "Sisters," they whispered to one another just as they had since childhood.

"Aboot bluidy time. I'm done traipsing aboot these woods looking for ye weans." Lorna's voice carried across the camp as she, Rangvald, and Andrew Sutherland trudged toward the others. She ran to Tyra and pulled her to her feet, squeezing her in a motherly embrace.

"Someone mentioned ye were on a mountain.

Was it dirt and loose rocks with aspens and birch growing on it? Flat on top?" Andrew inquired.

"Yes."

"Ben Wyvis," Andrew confirmed.

"That's what Tyra figured. She remembered Lorna saying something about it." Bjorn added.

"You were right all along. I should have followed your advice sooner." Tyra leaned into the embrace as Lorna stroked her hair. Lena had been the only other woman in her life who hugged her like a mother. Her aunt never had.

"Aye, lass. But ye have, and despite being chased by a mad mon, ye are happier than I've seen ye in the moons I've kenned ye."

"I am," Tyra beamed.

"That's wonderful," Rangvald boomed, "But it's the middle of the night, and I'm too old to be up at this time."

Lorna snorted. "Ye are up at this time every night." She waggled her eyebrows at her husband. The others stifled their laughter as Rangvald hoisted his wife over his shoulder and carried her to a spot on the other side of the fire. Erik looked away as his parents kissed.

"We told you what happened to us. What about you?" Bjorn asked.

"Searching for you. We haven't seen Grímr once. We ran into some Ross men, but Andrew wasn't able to get anything from them," Erik explained.

"And dead men don't talk, so they won't be telling Grímr where we are," Freya added.

"Andrew, how far are we from the Ross castle?" Tyra asked. She wondered how much distance she and Bjorn had put between themselves and another potential captor.

"Aboot three days hard ride. The mon ye heard exaggerated a tad. The Ross keep is a day's ride past the edge of the forest. I'd wager he didna want the Norseman to ken. They were likely to catch ye, kill him, and keep all the money for themselves. Ross wouldnae have turned ye over to Grímr. Ye're too bonnie," he jutted his chin toward Tyra then looked at Bjorn. "And he would have had too much fun torturing ye. Cruel bastard, he is."

"He wouldn't have had time to torture me. I'd be dead before I let anyone near Tyra."

Tyra patted his arm. "And dead men don't help their women escape."

Tyra had returned to his lap after Rangvald carried Lorna away. She twisted and rested her head on his shoulder, shivering when she pictured being captured again, knowing Bjorn would get himself killed trying to protect her. He had already proved his willingness to put himself first. The tremors began as Tyra tried to burrow deeper into Bjorn's chest. He ran his hands over her back as her fingers clutched his shirt. He looked over her head at the others and shook his head.

"Tyra, you've had your turn at watch. It's mine now. Why don't you get some rest?" He said gently, but she would not release her hold.

"You've both taken enough turns at watch, I'm sure. There are plenty of us to do it. You both need some sleep and food. I bet you're starving," Freya stood and marched to the horses. She brought back some dried beef and handed it to Bjorn.

"We had fish earlier, but nothing but rowan berries before that. Thank you." Bjorn handed a strip to Tyra, and she chewed as her eyes drifted closed as his own exhaustion began taking over. When they had both eaten two strips, he tucked Tyra against his chest as he spooned her. They both slept until well after the first rays of sun poked over the horizon.

THIRTEEN

Tyra awoke to a rock beneath her head except it rose and fell as if she were on her ship. She laid still and realized she was propped against Bjorn's side, her head on his chest. His hand caressed her arm which draped across his belly.

"I think I will insist we sleep this way every night." Bjorn twirled a strand of her hair around his finger.

"And when we each have a ship to captain?"

"I won't."

Tyra propped herself on Bjorn's chest and look up at him. "What?"

"I'll be your first mate."

"That's ridiculous."

"What's ridiculous is thinking I'm not sleeping with my wife or that I'd cross from my boat to yours each night."

"And if I offered to come to yours some nights?"

Bjorn grinned wolfishly, "I don't think you want my crew to witness how I will ravish you each night. Remember, you and Freya are the only ones with cabins. Besides, I may love sailing, but you are the better captain. I'd be honored stand as your first mate."

Tyra searched Bjorn's eyes for any hint he was jesting, but all she found was tenderness.

"You would give up your ship for me?" Tyra struggled to say as the lump in her throat threatened to choke her. After her, Bjorn was the best captain in Ivar's fleet.

"I'd give up everything for you."

She pulled herself until she was level with Bjorn and cupped his jaw. "If you want to farm, then when we get home, let's speak to Ivar."

Bjorn tucked hair behind Tyra's ear. "We shall save that for when we are ready to have a family. Till then, we will sail on your ship."

"Aren't you worried the men will mock you?"

"Are you kidding? They will be beyond jealous knowing I'm bedding you every night when they have naught but their hand unless they want everyone to watch them tupping a woman against the rail. What woman would agree to that?"

"And I shall be envied for finding a husband willing to give up his ship for me."

Once again, Bjorn flashed a wicked smile. "I doubt that's what they'll envy."

She smacked his chest, and he rolled them over, so Tyra's back rested on the ground. "Shall we test that theory?"

"No," came Erik's voice.

Bjorn groaned as he laid back on his side of the pine branches. "You couldn't give me five more minutes?"

"If five is all you need, then I'll save Tyra the disappointment." Erik's needling sparked laughter as warriors broke down the camp. Tyra scrambled to her feet and reached out her hand to Bjorn. She grasped his extended one and pulled him to his feet, just as she had done countless times after knocking him down when they spared. This time she strained to kiss him as she tapped his backside. "Five minutes would have been enough for me," she whispered.

Bjorn growled as he snagged her around the waist when she spun away. He pulled her back against him. "You ride with me, wife. Be sure to get your furs back from Freya. We don't want you to catch a chill."

Tyra glanced back over her shoulder as she dashed to Freya's side. The two women whispered before Freya pulled a bedroll and furs from beside her own. The happiness on Tyra's face shone so brightly Bjorn was sure it would blind him. He intended to prepare his horse but found Strian, Andrew, Rangvald, and Erik discussing their plans for the day.

"Are the women aware you're conspiring?" Bjorn cast a wary glance over his shoulder, aware the women would be furious if they assumed the men excluded them. Ivar made it clear to him that while Erik might lead Ivar's warriors in battle, both Erik *and* Freya were to lead Ivar's people during the expedition. Erik and Rangvald had the decency to look sheepish, but Strian gloated. Andrew looked around still getting used to the dynamics among the foreigners.

"They were just telling us what their wives decided this morning. They were informing us of the plans," Strian held his belly as he cackled.

"You sound like an old woman," Erik muttered.

"But I'm not the one being led around by the bollocks by a woman." Strian gloated.

"And who kept you warm last night? It was my woman who kept me toasty," Rangvald chortled.

Strian pursed his mouth as he shook his head. "It's a fine thing they are smarter than either of you."

"We know," father and son returned as Rangvald clapped his son on the shoulder.

"Mount up," Lorna called as she walked past the men.

Tyra was waiting beside Bjorn's horse with the reins to her own mount in her hand. "I want to ride with you, but what if we have to fight? And it'll tire your mount faster than the others," she worried.

Bjorn pulled her lip loose from her teeth with the pad of his thumb. He took the reins from her hands and fastened them to his horse's saddle. "Your horse will be next to us if you need to mount. Otherwise, your horse will be more rested than the others, so we can trade off if need be."

"You have an answer for everything." Tyra found herself being lifted onto Bjorn's horse and him swinging up behind her before she considered mounting hers.

"Wrap the furs around you, Ty," he breathed next to her ear, and spurred his horse to follow the others.

The morning passed without event. Bjorn held Tyra in his arms as they plodded along behind Freya, Erik, and Strian. Rangvald and Lorna rode at the front of their warriors. Bjorn's hand roamed over Tyra's body as he stared straight ahead. Her furs were thick enough that his hand's movements did not show. He tortured himself as Tyra's breathing deepened each time he brought her to the brink. His hand kneaded her breasts, tweaked her nipples, and cupped her mound as the horse's swaying gait edged her closer to release. His cock strained against her backside.

By the time they stopped in the early afternoon to water their horses, they were in such a state of arousal that Bjorn dragged Tyra into the trees after casting a knowing look at Erik and Strian. Bjorn was desperate to have Tyra, but he would not put her in jeopardy again. Erik and Strian surreptitiously slipped into the woods on either side of the couple, giving them enough space for privacy but close enough no one slipped past them.

Tyra was impatient after spending the morning being tormented by Bjorn's questing hand. She picked up the pace and towed him behind her. She found a large trunk and stepped up to it. She looked over her shoulder as she unlaced her pants and pushed them down over her hips. Bjorn stood stunned at the sight of Tyra's bare backside as she held her shirt above her waist.

"Bjorn, you can look another time. We have to hurry," she hissed. She braced herself with one arm extended and pushed her hips back in invitation. Bjorn feared he might die on the spot as the blood drained from his head and pooled in his groin. He unlaced his pants as he stepped forward. His hands grasped Tyra's hips as he thrust into her. Tyra feared she would swallow her tongue as she tried to muffle her moan. She pressed back against Bjorn as he surged into her over and over.

"Tyra, I won't last long. You're so damn tight. You'll milk me dry before I can make you climax."

"So close," she groaned. "Harder. This isn't about making love, Bjorn. Fuck me."

Bjorn growled as his hand grasped her breast. He squeezed hard as Tyra met each of his thrusts as she pressed back against him. His other hand slid to the apex of her thighs and found the button that would trigger her release. He circled it as he pounded into her over and over. There was no finesse or tenderness in this coupling. It was need born of repressed feelings held inside for far too long, and an awareness that the others would deduce what they were doing if they stayed away too long.

"Bjorn, I'm there. So close. Don't stop." Tyra panted.

Bjorn drove into her and rocked his hips, pushing him ever deeper and pushing Tyra over the edge. He tilted her chin, so he had a clear view of her face as she came apart in his arms. It was even more glorious than the first time they made love all those years ago. He had been certain nothing exceeded the beauty he witnessed that day by the fjord, but watching Tyra climax now that they both admitted their feelings far surpassed what he imagined was possible. His body began to shudder, signaling his release, so he pulled free as he kissed her, pouring his love into the kiss. Tyra twisted and pulled him into her embrace as she sagged against the tree trunk. They pressed short, hard kisses against each other's lips.

"One of these days, I'm going to bed you in a bed." Tyra grinned as she kissed him.

"And one of these days, I'm going to keep you in that bed for a sennight."

"Promise?"

"On my ring." They exchanged one more kiss before they both heard an owl hoot. Tyra's eyes bulged from her face.

"They know?" she hissed as she pulled her pants back into place.

"You didn't think I would take you into the woods again without someone keeping watch."

Tyra huffed, but he was right. A raven caw sounded from the other side of the tree, and Tyra hung her head.

"You told Freya," Bjorn accused.

"No more than you told Erik. She caught us, and I'm sure she followed."

They were laughing when they stepped around the tree to find Freya standing with her arms crossed.

"If you're both done, which from the sounds of it you are, we need to ride out."

Erik and Strian stepped forward and did little to hide their mirth.

"Five minutes really was all you needed," Erik taunted.

"I suppose that's because he knows what he's doing," Tyra tossed at her best friend's husband as she smirked and pulled Freya back toward the horse.

Bjorn strutted past his friends as he shook his head. Tyra still surprised him with the things she said. She grew up around three wild boys and a girl as equally suited to besting those three boys as she was. Bjorn should have known by now. She would always give as good as she got.

As the warband rode out, Tyra rode her own horse. They both accepted that they were incapable of withstanding the torment of riding together again. The leaders decided that morning that they would ride toward the Ross keep. Bjorn and Tyra had recounted what they remembered from their brief time in Grímr's temporary camp. There had not been that many men, so it was reasonable to assume the rest of Grímr's men were still with their allies, the Rosses.

It took the rest of the day and all of the next for them to approach the keep at Allanfearn. They had traveled close to the coast of the Firth of Moray. No one said it aloud, but they all wished they had known this would be their destination. Both the Norsemen and the Highlanders could have sailed rather than ride over hill and dale. It was after sunset when Andrew called a halt as they came to the last hill that would keep them out of sight from the guards on the Ross keep's battlements.

"Remember, they dinna fight with any honor. I'm sure they have seen us by now, so dinna underestimate their being prepared. Just because we havenae seen them doesnae mean they havenae seen us. We'll send scouts out in the Ross plaids we took from the men Bjorn and Tyra killed. As long as ma men dinna get too close, they may pass for another sentry. Ma hope is they can get close enough to learn where this Grímr character camps. I imagine he's within the walls, but I dinna trust Ross's hospitality, and I doubt Ross trusts Grímr. This means he'd camp in the glen on the other side of this hill. There isnae much land between the keep and the coast. They dinna have any cliffs to protect them. Daft buggers to have built at such a low point, but their reputation keeps most away from them, and the rest dinna want their boggy stretch of land. It also means there is little space for us to hide. We make camp here, but no fires tonight."

It was with reluctance that the Norsemen handed control of the mission over to the Sutherland heir after Lorna pointed out that Andrew was the only one who knew where they were. Lorna had never travelled this far into Ross territory and had moved away more than a score and a half years ago. When she and Rangvald raided, they sailed to the Hebrides or further south toward England.

As they made camp, Andrew selected the men who would scout for him. There was little to do once they assigned the watch. The Norsemen and the remaining Highlanders ate in silence and settled down early. With no fire to see by, there was little to do but go to sleep.

"Sutherland," came an urgent call that woke Bjorn. The voice was nearby but quiet. It surprised Bjorn that it woke him, until he realized Tyra was already standing and strapping her sword on. It was Tyra's movement that actually woke him.

"Sutherland," the call came again as horses approached. Tyra and Bjorn joined the others as the scouts rode back into camp.

"Where's Donald?" Andrew asked as he caught the bridle of the lead horse.

"Dead," his scout responded. "They arenae alone. The Munros are there, too."

"Which ones?"

"Both. Our neighbors and the ones from the Black Isle."

"Bluidy hell." Andrew rattled off several more oaths Tyra had heard Lorna use but did not understand. When she heard Lorna add a few more she recognized but did not understand either, she realized the situation was dire.

"How many?" Lorna asked as she came to stand next to Andrew.

"Easily five score Munros along with the Rosses and aboot three score Norsemen. There's so many that they're camped outside the walls. Fires blazing and whisky flowing. I would think ye could hear them all the way here. We didna have to get that close to see what was what," the young man recounted.

"Well done, Cormac. Ye and the others find something to eat and wet yer whistle."

"But that's nae all." Andrew gestured for the man to continue speaking. "There are Welshmen there. Bowmen."

Andrew turned to look at the Norsemen. Rangvald stepped forward. "The Norse have raided as far south as Wales and taken islands along their coast. Grímr must have recruited from there too, or perhaps Hakin before he died."

Andrew scowled but nodded. "This will make approaching the keep far more difficult. The reach of their longbows exceeds anything yers or ma archers can do."

"That means we can't wait until daylight to attack. They'll just pick us off if they spot us," Freya ruminated aloud. "We have to go soon. If we can be in position before the sun rises, we can breach the walls and be inside the keep before Grímr or the Welsh figure what is happening. If we can sweep the castle, we can fight Grímr and the Welsh with the benefit of the keep's battlements to put an end to Grímr. Can we make it to the coast without alerting Grímr or the Ross scouts? If we can, we swim around and take the keep from the water."

"Aye, ye can ride aboot an hour south and come back along the coast. Ye will have a rough time in the waves, but ye can do it." Andrew looked skeptical, but Freya knew what the other Norsemen did. They would not need to swim far if they made it to the coast. They need only make it look like they came from the sea to wreak fear and havoc. Once the Ross clan realized there were Norsemen near the water, they would assume the worst and prepare for a large-scale attack. They would not be ready for only a score or so. "If ye do that, we will draw attention away from the postern and sea walls."

Within minutes, Norsemen from Rangvald's and Ivar's armies mounted and rode out. The majority left for the coast, but a significant number stayed to aid the Sutherlands. Rangvald also used it as insurance that the Sutherlands did not develop a patriotic need to side with the Rosses.

Tyra, Bjorn, and the others rode the hour south as Andrew suggested before turning to proceed up the coast. The tide was low, so they rode through the packed sand, making little sound as the horses galloped along the water's edge. When the keep came into sight, the warriors dismounted and left their horses with five warriors assigned to guard them. The rest of the force crept forward until they reached a marshy area that separated them from the keep.

They would have to wade out, since none of them dared trying to walk through it. They stopped to slather dark mud onto their faces, leaving only the whites of their eyes as ghoulish warnings of their approach. They entered the water resembling an army of apparitions rather than mortal men and women. The water was frigid, but it was not unlike what they were used to. It burned their skin and made their blood pound as it forced them to swim against the current.

Bjorn led since he was the best swimmer of all of them, followed by Tyra and Freya. The three of them had raced often as children, and the chill bothered them the least. As they turned toward the shore, they let the waves drive them in, conserving their energy for when they were soaked and trying to scale walls. The warband emerged with knives clenched between their teeth. They waited until they were within earshot of the battlement guards before they drew their swords.

The sound of metal rang through the air, and it was only a moment later that the first alarm went up. Their peals of laughter matched their ghoulish appearance. They clanked their swords and knives together, creating a screeching cacophony. Bjorn pointed his sword and bellowed a war cry as the Norsemen raced to the battlements. Freya was on Erik's shoulders as Tyra received a boost from Bjorn.

Both women threw the ropes they carried; their aim precise. The grappling hooks sunk into the masonry, and the women began climbing. Other ropes hung down the side of the keep as more Norsemen scrambled up the wall. Tyra and Freya led the charge once they pulled themselves onto the wall walk.

The Ross guards were unprepared not only for the Norse but for women. They stumbled backwards as they looked around. Women streamed over the wall as the first wave, since they were light enough to stand on shoulders while the grappling hooks were being thrown. By the time the men began to join them, the women stood looking at one another with no one left to fight.

Freya and Erik led Ivar's warriors in one direction as Rangvald and Lorna headed in the other. As the hoard rushed in each direction, the bailey filled with Ross clansmen. Some had weapons while others had workmen's tools like shovels, pitchforks, and blacksmith tongs Tyra had forsaken the bow and arrow for the rope and the ability to swim. Now she wished she had it. She scanned the men running toward them. She eyed the ones she would aim for first. She struck without mercy as she hacked through one after another until she pulled a bow from one man's arm and found a quiver propped against a wall.

Tyra was sure Freya was doing the same. Once both women had arrows, they moved to the side overlooking the bailey. They began picking off men who were unable to find their attackers, since they blended in with the night sky.

Bjorn watched as Tyra and Freya fought several feet in front of him. He watched both women gather bows and arrows before taking aim at the people on the ground. He and Erik pushed through the melee to get to their women. They stood with their backs to the women and fended off any man who attempted to cut them down. One pointed his bow at Tyra and received Bjorn's sword blade through his eye for casting his glance in the wrong direction.

It was not long before the Sutherlands were streaming through the gate having sent several of their men over the wall to raise the portcullis. The

Sutherlands flooded the bailey and overwhelmed those the Norse archers had not shot. Laird Ross roared as he stormed through the keep doors onto the steps. Andrew was there waiting and ran the older Highlander through before he swung his sword.

"Ye should have listened to yer priest, auld mon," Andrew spat out as he looked at the dying man. "Pride goeth before destruction, and a haughty spirit before a fall."

A man slipped from the shadows and dashed toward the corner of the steps pointing toward the gate. Bjorn was certain his eyes were deceiving him.

"Sutherland! There he goes! Grímr, we shall hunt you down and leave your bowels for the carrion. May Odin's ravens, Hugin and Munin, carry the word of your disgrace back to Valhalla." Bjorn leaned as far over the wall as he dared, and Tyra pushed him out of the way seconds before an arrow sailed over where his head had just been. She landed her fist in his gut.

"You promised not to die. Don't be an idiot." She kissed him before getting to her feet and running toward the stairs.

"See what you've been missing," Erik jested as he took off after Freya.

Bjorn looked again, but Andrew was fighting another Ross, and Grímr was nowhere in sight. Bjorn scanned the bailey but was sure he would not find the man there. He ran to the other side of the wall near the portcullis. He would wager Grímr was fleeing, but it was too dark to tell.

The battle in the bailey was over within half an hour. With the Sutherlands present, the Norsemen allowed the Rosses to keep their lives. The Norsemen raided the keep but were not willing to fight the Sutherlands over the kirk. There was grumbling from many, but Lorna silenced it with one loud whistle. They bound and gagged the remaining Ross warriors while women huddled in groups as they shielded the eyes of their children.

"And that is why they grow into weak men and women. They shield their children from death when no one can escape it," Tyra sneered as she and Freya wiped their swords clean. "We are victorious because we accept it and do not fear it. We mourn those we lose, but we know we shall meet again in glory while we feast with the gods."

"Blasphemous heathen," one woman screamed. "Savages."

Tyra turned to find the woman sobbing as her friends tried to silence her.

"We're savages?" Tyra mused as she walked closer to the woman. "And just what are your men who whore themselves to our enemy, a pagan at that? Your jarl, or laird, whatever you call him, sold your men's sword arms to a Norseman. We aren't the savages when it was your leader who invited us to your table."

"The good Lord will smite ye and have his vengeance." The other women failed to silence her.

Tyra spread her arms wide and looked around. "Then you will not want me to stand too near when your White Christ shoots his bolts of lightning at me. Ah, but wait, that would be my mighty god, Thor, who commands the lightning."

Tyra laughed as the woman cowered. She looked at the woman in disgust. "Stop your sniveling. We are not Grímr or his forsaken brother. We do not wage war on unarmed women and children. You will live to see another sunrise, but your voice grates on my nerves. You cower before your children and cause them to fear what is no longer a threat to them. Show some courage and teach your children to be stronger than you ever will be."

Tyra watched as the woman shrank back into the

shadows and pulled her children into her arms. She shook her head as she moved to stand with Freya once more as Lorna walked toward them.

"Lorna Mackay!" The same woman's voice screeched.

Lorna looked up confused. "Aye?"

The woman screamed again, "Ye traitor. Ye whore. Ye brought the Devil's men to our door."

She brandished a knife as she ran toward Lorna, rage disfiguring the woman's face. Tyra took a step forward, ready to block the woman's path. She drew back her sword, but Freya's arm flew out to stop her. The Ross woman charged Lorna and ran into Lorna's fist. The impact made the woman's head snap back before she collapsed to the ground.

"'We do not wage war on unarmed women and children.' Remember?" Freya whispered.

"I dinna ken who she is, but she kenned me. Then again, there arenae many Highland women who run off with a braw Norseman and return to fight alongside the mon whose brother killed ma family. I suppose I stick out a bit." Lorna shook out her fist and checked for broken skin. "Bluidy hard head. I may have broken ma wee finger."

"You told her to have courage," Bjorn said as he stepped behind Tyra. She spun around and jabbed her finger into his chest. He wrapped his hand around it and grinned at her.

"And I told you not to get yourself killed. That wasn't courage up there. That was arrogance," Tyra's voice broke.

"Come here, my wee beastie."

"Don't tease me." Tyra's bloodlust dissolved as she let Bjorn pull her into his embrace. "I'm not ready to lose you."

"Good thing because I'll insist upon being found."

"Not funny," she murmured as she wrapped her arms around his waist. "Are you all right? Did you get hurt?"

"No. You?"

Tyra shook her head. She breathed in his scent. Beneath the grime, sweat, and blood, she still smelled pine from the needles they slept on. She did not understand how it was possible after their dip in the firth, but it soothed her.

"Grímr got away." Bjorn spoke over her head to the others. He looked down at Tyra, and his heart slowed, reassured she was unharmed and in his arms.

"We know. Andrew was ready to go after him, but he had to fight off the blacksmith who came at him with a red-hot poker. He's being treated for a burn," Rangvald informed them as he pulled his wife to his side. They whispered as they reassured one another that they were hale.

"So, what now?" Freya asked.

"I suppose we rest and wait for daylight. Grímr knows we're here. We have guards posted on the walls to make sure he doesn't attempt what we did or tries to sneak off in the night. We'll fight tomorrow as we planned," Erik shrugged.

Tyra looked at the women and children who still huddled in the dark. She found a young woman who seemed more in awe than in fear of her. She approached the girl but stopped a healthy distance in case she might try to follow the example set by the clanswoman who called out Lorna's name. When the young woman neither moved nor flinched, Tyra spoke to her.

"Take the women and children into the keep. Get them blankets and fed. They can use the laird's family's chambers for the night. They'll not be harmed up there. No one will disturb them." The young woman nodded and started to usher the others toward the keep steps. Tyra warned, "Paint me a fool for my mercy, and I will make an example of you."

The young woman only nodded as she herded the others toward the keep. Tyra turned back around and discovered the others watching her.

"What? My mother died when other Norsemen raided our homestead. No one offered her any mercy, and I have lived with the guilt of her hiding me and protecting me. I may not respect them, but I won't be the cause of a child's suffering. I'm not a monster," she trailed off.

Strian stepped forward and embraced her. Had it been any other man, Bjorn would have ripped his limbs from his body. "No one offered my mother mercy either during that raid. I live with the guilt of being on my first raid while my mother was being attacked and killed."

No more was said on the matter as the conversation moved on to the upcoming battle.

FOURTEEN

The remainder of the night crept by as they did little but wait for sunrise and Grímr's inevitable attack. Andrew tasked his men with finding vats of lard and tar. Once they gleaned information from the surviving Ross clan members, warriors from all three groups moved the vats onto the battlements and set logs below and tinder spread around them. They already raided armory, so fresh swords and arrows were on hand. Warriors spread additions shields on the battlements. It took less than two hours to complete these preparations, so they sat and waited.

As the sky pinkened with the first hints of the sunrise, Bjorn made his way to the battlements to check on the boiling cauldrons. They set the fires, and the mixture of grease and tar was already releasing a pungent odor. Bjorn wondered why the noxious fumes were never enough to warn away attackers. The scalding brew had splashed him more than once over the years, and he had burn scars as evidence. Tyra and Freya moved into place with their bows and several quivers nearby.

Andrew, Rangvald, Strian, and Erik worked to reinforce both the portcullis and the postern gates. There were warriors positioned facing out toward the surrounding fields and the bailey in case the Rosses attempted to raise a defense.

Bjorn scanned the tents pitched beyond the castle wall and tried to find Grímr. Even though Grímr recovered from the leg wound he sustained months earlier, he still walked with a slight limp. Bjorn struggled to find him, but he told himself he should not be surprised, since Grímr never fought on the front line. Their nemesis claimed to stay toward the rear to cover the backs of the advancing fighters and to encourage the subsequent waves of warriors. It did not fool anyone. He remained in the rear to stay alive. He was far more ambitious than his older brother, Hakin, gave him credit for.

Had Freya not already killed Hakin, Grímr would have done so after his brother put forth the effort to capture Rangvald's and Ivar's settlements. Greed and deviousness drove Grímr and made him a legitimate threat, where his brother preferred brute force to make his point.

Movement caught his eye as men exited three tents. He was unprepared for how many fit in each, but each man carried the distinct Welsh longbow. Bjorn swore under his breath and was glad they found the extra shields. The archers could fire their arrows from where they stood in the field and strike down warriors standing on the battlements.

"Freya, dip your arrows into the tar." Tyra rushed to get through her quivers. Their archers would light them and then fire them as the enemy approached. They would also use them to set ablaze the men attempting to scale the walls. The archers were close to done as orders were barked as men climbed the steps to the wall walk. Erik led a group of men while

Strian brought up the rear as they carried a fence made from spears tied together. They would raise it as the first men came over the wall, impaling them before they got their feet on the battlements. Tyra looked down at the bailey and recognized something similar at the portcullis and the postern gate. She turned around in time for the first flaming arrow to sail toward the keep.

"Shield wall," she called as she dove for hers. The shields banged together as they protected themselves from the onslaught of arrows. Tyra crept to her embrasure and thrust an arrowhead into the cauldron fire next to her.

"Open," she called, and the two shields in front of her separated enough for her to release a flaming arrow as the first warning to Grímr that they were prepared to fight. More arrows sailed over their heads, and the warriors maintained their shield wall.

"We wait them out. Don't waste any arrows when we can't yet reach them. Let them use up their arrows before we even use ours." Freya's orders traveled through the still morning air. She looked to Tyra, who nodded. It was a toss-up on any given day as to which of the women had the better aim. They were both among the best in their tribe, taking quick aim but having the patience to hit their mark.

Hundreds of arrows landed on the wall walk, and they heard screams of agony when one broke through the shield wall. The warriors were quick to close the gap when an arrow felled a warrior. Bjorn crouched low as he moved toward the barbican where Erik kept watch. The gatehouse was more elevated and gave a clearer view of the area behind Grímr's camp.

"Do you see aught?" Bjorn asked.

"Nothing. Only their camp. It isn't as large as we supposed last night."

"They are sleeping tight in their tents. I watched Welshmen stream out of three tents. They must have sat up to sleep."

"Then perhaps they will be too tired to put up a fight." Erik's jest made Bjorn smile, but they had gotten little more sleep than their enemies. Bjorn followed Erik's finger as he pointed to the right side of the camp. "There. That's Grímr. I'm sure I saw him limp toward one of his men."

Bjorn and Erik ceased talking as they strained to see across the expanse to where two men conversed.

"You're right. That is him, and it looks like he's just given the order for them to attack."

The two men watched as a hoard of Norsemen stampeded toward the castle, banging their sword hilts against their shields. Tyra's voice rang out.

"Hold!" Tyra counted to five. "Hold!"

She poked her nose into the embrasure to watch as the Norsemen drew closer.

"Hold!" She bellowed once more. This time counting to twenty before drawing her own bowstring back. "Fire!"

The shield wall parted as archers lurched into their openings and launched their blazing missiles at the enemy. The shields clanked back together as the archers reloaded. Each archer called out to their shield guards when they were ready to fire once more. Tyra and Freya picked off one man after another, pausing only long enough to light their arrowheads. The bellows of pain coming from the ground far exceeded the ones the women heard when the Welshmen took aim. The shield wall remained intact as the Welsh continued to rain down their own flaming arrows. When one of the Norse archers fell on the wall, another took their place.

"Ready the tar!"

Bjorn's voice surprised Tyra when it came from

behind her, but she did not dare turn to look. More men pushed forward into the shield wall as they lifted the handles of the cauldrons. It would take at least four men to lift each one.

Bjorn slid between two warriors to get a closer look at the approaching army. The first wave of fighters who survived the arrow barrage were hurtling toward the wall, and ladders hit the masonry as he looked to his left. They did not stay propped very long, the Norsemen waiting until the climbers were just high enough to be maimed or killed when they fell. However, some of the ladders were remaining where they butted against the wall as men and women tried to scramble up them.

"On your mark!" Bjorn called. He watched as the cauldrons began to dump the boiling mixture onto the attackers, each group of men deciding for themselves the right moment to pour. The contents of the vat between Tyra and Freya streamed down and splashed across the heads of a score of Norsemen and women. Freya was the first to release a flaming arrow, and the greasy tar erupted in flames. Tyra pointed her arrow further down the wall toward the vat that tipped over on her other side. She, too, fired an arrowhead that burned bright red. The howls of agony grew as more and more of Grímr's fighters fell victim to the aggressive defense of the keep.

"Look." Erik pointed his sword through an opening. "The next group comes."

With most of the grease and tar already spilled over the wall, they would rely on the fire that spread between the keep and their onslaught of fighters. It made it difficult—but not impossible—for the ladders to thud against the wall as Grímr's forces swarmed the base of the keep. The archers continued to shoot those who came within range. Despite the flames, tar, and arrows, some were reaching the top of the ladders.

"Spears," Strian called from near the barbican. Bjorn and Erik helped the others raise the spears and push them over the heads of the shield wall that broke apart for the new defense to take their place.

"Stay down," Bjorn said over Tyra's shoulder. "If you must, get off the wall and go to the bailey."

"And leave you here? No."

"If I'm dead."

"Then I shall be a berserker."

That was all there was time to say before Bjorn and the other warriors thrust the spear fence into the enemy who survived long enough to scale the wall. As more fell from the ladders, they knocked down many who were climbing behind them. The landing killed some and injured others enough that they were no longer a threat. Freya and Tyra drove arrows into the chests and backs of those who moved. They might not be a threat again that day, but neither would they live to be a threat another day.

In the bailey, Rangvald, Lorna, and Andrew led the Highlanders and Rangvald's warriors. A tree trunk pounded into the gate. "They must have chopped the tree when we arrived," Andrew mused. "Too bad it didna land on them."

The wooden gate rattled but held tight with the planks of wood wedged against it, the metal rivets doing their job to keep the wood from splintering.

"We need more archers on the barbicans," Lorna cut in. "We need these men dead nae slamming their pole into us." She walked to where Tyra and Freya were stationed and called up to them. "We need ye above the gate. They're battering the portcullis."

"We're coming," Tyra called down. She looked to Freya who nodded and grabbed her own quivers. The women crawled out of the shield wall and remained hunched over as the ran to the gatehouse. Bjorn watched Tyra, torn between going as her shield guard and remaining with the spear wall. He chided himself for not giving Tyra or Freya enough credit. They fought alongside one another for years, protecting each other with a savage determination. It was only since Hakin began causing trouble that Bjorn began to partner with Tyra. He needed to remember the women were a team, but it did not make it any easier to watch the distance grow between them.

"It's a struggle, and I will let you know if I ever reconcile myself to watching her walk away," Erik consoled him. "You're not alone in your protectiveness, but it's been the two of them since long before we joined in."

Bjorn nodded as he forced himself to concentrate. If being distracted got him injured, Tyra might finish him off.

Freya peered over the wall at the team of Highlanders who rammed the tree trunk into the gate. She turned back and called down to Lorna. "Do they have one at the postern gate?"

"No. They dinna seem interested in that one since it's too narrow to let many men in at once. The archers would get them."

"Good because they're bringing another battering ram. I just saw it."

"Bluidy bleeding hell," Lorna looked at her husband. "If the girls canna get them, they will be through the gate in minutes."

"I know, my love. I need you to gather your shieldmaidens while Andrew gets our men and his. We will be ready to greet our guests."

Lorna and Andrew split up to go their separate directions while Rangvald remained to call out commands. Tyra and Freya had no way to light their arrows as the fires on the barbican were only smoldering now they no longer boiled the grease. They fired in rapid succession, but they failed not stop the second tree trunk's arrival. The Highlanders and Norsemen positioned themselves so they could batter the gate with alternating thrusts. The power and force was enough to splinter the wood. Rangvald issued commands, but Tyra was too focused to interpret what he said.

"Freya, I'm almost out of arrows," she hissed at her friend.

"Me, too."

"Take mine and continue shooting while I go back for more," Tyra offered.

"There aren't more. At least not ones the others won't be using. Mine are hitting their mark, but there are so many down there that we can't get them all."

"We have to tell the jarl," hissed Tyra as she peeked over the wall.

"I know. I'll do it. Then we join them below." Freya crawled to the back of the gatehouse and looked down at the bailey. She spotted Lorna gathering her warriors as Andrew ordered his into formation. "Rangvald, we're out of arrows. There aren't any more for us. The others need the rest elsewhere. Tyra and I are coming down."

Tyra followed Freya to the bailey where they drew their swords, having left their bows behind. They fell in with the mixture of Norse and Highland fighters who stood waiting for the gate to give way. Their wait was not long; the gate swung open as shards of wood flew toward them. The attackers dropped the battering rams, and the warriors flooded the bailey. Freya and Tyra positioned themselves to protect each other's blind spots. They swung and sliced as Highlanders sneered, underestimating the power of the two trained shieldmaidens. They fought their way forward as Grímr's Norse warriors now joined the melee. Shields clashed together as they served as both a weapon and a defense. Tyra jammed her shield into the face of her opponent, obscuring his sight, before plunging her sword into his belly.

"Ty!" Tyra spun to discover Freya fighting off two men as a third approached. Tyra ran toward the new assailant, her shield blocking her body as she raised her sword high above her shoulder, taking aim at the man's chest. Tyra was slim and agile, so men did not consider how much force she transferred from her lithe frame into her attack. She slammed into the man and made him stagger back several steps. She was relentless as she drove her sword into his shoulder then swiped it across his thigh until she got a clear path to his belly.

"Thanks," Freya said as she stepped over the body of a man she slayed. "He came out of nowhere."

The sound of a war cry neither of them understood drew their attention to the gate as Welsh longbowmen rode into the bailey on their ponies. They took aim at anyone who appeared Norse, killing several of Grímr's men in their pursuit of Rangvald and Ivar's forces. Freya and Tyra rushed toward a corner of the keep that gave them shelter from the new attackers.

"Now what?" Tyra panted.

"I've haven't a clue. I never considered they would ride into the bailey. They'll pick us off like chickens roosting."

Tyra slid toward the edge of the wall to peek at the archers who guided their horses with their knees and continued to shoot bolt after bolt at close range. Tyra looked up at the battlements where she last saw Bjorn, but she could not spot him. She prayed he was just too far away and not lying dead. She scanned the bailey and watched Norsemen and Sutherlands falling like autumn leaves. They had the advantage until the Welshmen entered the fray. Now the tide was turning, and it was not in their favor.

"Have you seen Grímr?" Freya whispered.

"No. I doubt he's even here. Maybe one of our archers riddled him with arrows, and he never made it to the keep."

"I would venture to guess he never made it here, but not because any of us stopped him," Freya responded.

"You're most likely right. The bailey is being overtaken by Grímr's forces, but the Welshmen are struggling to use their bows now that they're in close quarters. It's not to their advantage after all. We need them to dismount."

Freya tapped on Tyra's shoulder, and they switched places. "Their ponies seem a bit high strung. A good spooking, and they may throw their riders."

The women looked at one another before darting away from the wall. They ran wide of the first rider, but Freya let out a high-pitched screech while Tyra banged the hilt of her sword against her shield from behind the animal's right flank. It danced about as its rider tried to control it. Freya dared get closer and continued to wail as Tyra added a piercing whistle to the noise.

Many of the horses were becoming more and more agitated despite being trained for battle. Several other shieldmaidens recognized what Tyra and Freya were attempting and lent their voices to the bedlam. With more whistles and screeches coming from multiple directions, several ponies reared, unseating their riders. Norsemen and Sutherlands pounced. In no time, the Welsh were killed or subdued, but Tyra became confused when another wave of Highlanders tore through the gates.

"How many of them are there?" Tyra muttered.

"I don't—" Freya did not finish as the men running into the bailey appeared to be running from something rather than toward the fight.

"The hounds of hell are on us!"

"The Devil rides."

"Nay, it's God's avenging angels."

Tyra and Freya looked at one another with furrowed brows not understanding what the men meant. Then they heard it. A great war whoop went up from just beyond the gate. More of the enemy forces ran into the bailey searching for shelter. Tyra and Freya charged to the steps leading to the battlements and found Erik, Bjorn, and Strian grinning.

Strian pointed, and the women looked out to discover a wave of Highlanders on horseback galloping toward them. Their faces were painted with blue woad and their horses wore metal-studded chaffrons over their heads. The horses also wore metal peytrals to protect their barrel chests, the metal links ringing as they collided with each hoofbeat. Lorna and Rangvald raced to the top of the steps, and Lorna hung over the top of the wall before her husband pulled her back.

"*Bratach bhan chlann aoidh!*" "The White Banner of Mackay," Lorna called as Alex and his men galloped closer to the keep.

"*Manu forti!*" With a strong hand came his responding bellow.

"Hold fast!" Came a deep, booming voice.

"The MacLeods are here, too," Lorna cheered.

"*Tulach Àrd,*" came another baritone as the horsemen drew closer.

"Bluidy hell," Lorna whispered. "The Mackenzies came."

A tidal wave of warriors on horseback and foot flowed toward the keep as more and more men appeared. They divided on Alex's call. It resembled the Red Sea parting as echelons, staggered lines moving diagonally, broke apart as the MacLeods and Mackays set their sights on the keep. The Mackenzies took a path to the camp.

Alex and Kenneth rode into the bailey as their men swarmed the Welsh, Norse, and Highland mercenaries that still stood. Rangvald whistled, and Bjorn and their forces fell back so the new arrivals did not confuse them with the enemy. Once the MacLeods and Mackays recognized which shield patterns belonged to the enemy, Rangvald's and Ivar's warriors rejoined the fight. The Sutherlands remained fighting since the Mackays and MacLeods recognized their plaids. Tyra led the charge back down the battlement steps as she and Freya moved into position. Both women blinked rapidly as Bjorn and Erik pushed them and took their places defending their backs.

"Now we fight," Bjorn growled.

FIFTEEN

With the added support of the Mackays and MacLeods, the tide turned once more in their favor. The fight ended soon after as bodies draped with the Ross plaid or clutching Norse shields littered the ground. Nervous Welsh ponies continued to dance about, still agitated from the distraction Tyra and Freya caused.

"Cousin, it is good to see ye, ye auld goat. Where's Erik?" Alex gripped Rangvald's forearm as he pulled Lorna in for an embrace with the other. Andrew Sutherland stood to the side.

They looked around to find Erik taking Freya to task for the risks she took with the horses. Bjorn was near to the couple as he chastised Tyra for the same thing. Both women stood with their arms akimbo with their sword hilt resting against their hip. It was comical to watch how the two couples' movements mirrored one another. Once Freya and Tyra listened to all they were willing to, they each grabbed an ear attached to the man they loved and twisted. They pulled the men toward them before diving in for a passionate kiss. It almost seemed like they competed for the longest kiss.

"Our son takes after ye, Rang," Lorna teased. "He's worn off on Bjorn, poor lad."

"And those young women must have been listening to your stories." Rangvald swiped away Lorna's hand as she reached for him. He pulled her in for a quick, hard kiss and a tap on the backside.

"If all of ye tender hearted couples are through fornicating," Alex failed to keep the laughter from his voice, "Perhaps we'll discover whether the Mackenzies nabbed that toad. He's slipperier than an eel."

Tyra and Bjorn walked over to the rest of the group with Freya and Erik following not far behind.

"Good of you to show up," Erik teased his cousin. "We thought you might have gotten lost."

"Just gathering a few friends to join the *ceilidh*."

"Hardly a party, but I will dance a jig over the mon's grave," Lorna growled.

Rangvald and Alex left the group to issue orders before they all headed to the castle gate, which hung off its hinges. They only made it a couple hundred feet past the castle when a young man with a mop of flaming red hair rode up. He nodded to the men and grinned at each of the women. He was handsome in a boyish and charming way that had Rangvald, Erik, and Bjorn pulling their women against their sides. Strian and Andrew laughed.

"It's wise ye men keep yer women from the bastard before he has them chasing after him." Kenneth MacLeod walked up behind them.

"MacLeod, thought ye were dead. Always late to everything except for every meal," goaded the Mackenzie warrior.

"Tormod, still wanting everything ye canna have." Andrew laughed.

Tormod Mackenzie dismounted and stepped toe-to-toe with Andrew. The two men remained at a standoff until they burst with laughter. Tormod slung his arm around Andrew's shoulder as he drew his horse behind him, and they all moved back into the bailey.

"I worried aboot ye," Tormod grinned. "Ma sister would have ma bollocks in haggis if aught happened to you."

"She likes ma pretty face."

Tormod snorted, "I doubt that is the only part of ye she likes."

Andrew blushed despite puffing out his chest. Tormod turned toward the foreigners.

"Tormod Mackenzie," The redheaded man extended his arm to Rangvald.

"Are ye Angus's lad? Ye look like him," Lorna asked. "How is he?"

Tormod reached for Lorna's hand and bent over it. No one had offered her such a courtesy since she left Scotland with Rangvald.

"He is with ma mother," Tormod murmured.

"Ach, lad. I'm sorry to hear that. How long have ye been laird?"

"Eight years."

"Ye were but a wean," Lorna sounded saddened at the news.

"It is as the Lord planned, ma lady."

"Aye, it is. Being with your mama is where he wanted to be."

Lorna stepped back, and Tormod looked at Freya and Tyra, eliciting glares from Erik and Bjorn. Both women looked at their men before smiling prettily at Tormod.

"I wouldnae, if I were ye," Alex warned. "I didna ken what Freya meant to Erik when they arrived the first time. I learned fast; I feared I'd lose ma life for staring."

"You came close," Erik grumbled, but he stepped

forward to shake the younger man's forearm. "I'm Erik Rangvaldson, and this is my wife, Freya Ivarsdóttir."

"I am Bjorn Jansson, and Tyra Vigosdóttir is my bride." Tyra's blinding smile made him realize he had not referred to that way yet. He had told her and the others she was as good as his wife, had even called her that, but she discovered a new joy at the promise of their future together. She leaned into his embrace and rested her head against his shoulder.

"And last but not least, I am Strian Eindrideson."

A gasp sounded over Strian's shoulder making him spin around. A pair of sapphire eyes stared back at him before melting into the shadows of the keep. Strian made a strangled sound and raced after the small figure. The others watched him disappear around a corner. Bjorn shrugged.

"I gave up trying to understand him when we were children. He's not secretive, but he only reveals what he wants others to know. We'll find out when he's ready. Onto what matters, Mackenzie, did you find Grímr?" Bjorn brought the conversation back to the reason they stood together in the enemy's bailey.

The young laird shook his head with disgust. "I laid eyes on the bastard, but it was as if he disappeared into thin air. By the time I got across the camp, he'd disappeared. I didn't see him run or ride in any direction. He just wasn't there."

"He makes a habit of that," Erik interjected.

"So, what now?" Freya looked at her husband then her father-in-law.

"We spend the night. Say our farewells to our dead, then we deal with their dead in the morning," Erik shrugged.

Alex shook his head, "We'll tend to the Christian burials while you send your warriors to Valhalla."

His voice was soft, ensuring it did not float beyond their immediate gathering. Lorna reached out her hand and gave his arm a squeeze. "Thank you, lad."

Burying and cremating the dead would consume the rest of the day and well into the night. They looked around and began calling orders to their various groups.

***

Strian was sure he was seeing things. He did not dare trust the eyes he looked into belonged to the woman he remembered. He kept the slight figure in his sights as she dashed toward the postern gate. Rather than try to pass through, she leaped as she reached the wall and began scaling it. Strian was on her in a moment, grasping her around the waist and pulling her to the ground. She spun around swinging, but Strian's much larger body was no match. He pressed her back against the wall and pulled the woolen hat from her head. Waves of deep brown hair tumbled to her waist.

"Gressa," Strian choked out.

"Hello, Strian."

"You ran from me." The agony in Strian's voice made Gressa flinch. They stood staring at one another until Strian made a sound similar to a wounded animal. His mouth descended, but he paused before bringing his lips down to hers. Silvery-gray eyes stared into sparkling blue ones. Strian pressed his mouth to Gressa's as memories flooded both their minds. When they parted, Strian brushed a tear from her cheek. Gressa tried to duck under his arm, but he pressed her back against the wall.

"You ran from me," Strian repeated. "Do you know how long I searched for you? And now you try to escape."

"That was a long, long time ago, Strian."

"It feels like yesterday. I think about it every day as though it was only a moment ago."

Gressa's spine stiffened as she pushed at his chest. "Well, you shouldn't. There's no point."

"There is every point. Where have you been for the past ten years?"

"Where the hell do you think?"

Strian's eyes widened. "Are you a Christian now?"

"I'm many things now, most of which you wouldn't understand."

Strian looked down at the most beautiful face he had ever seen, the one that haunted his nightmares. "Are you another man's wife?"

"You have no right to ask that."

"I disagree." They stood staring at one another once more, tension rippling across and between them. "Gressa, where have you been?" Strian's voice was little more than a whisper as he beseeched her to give him answers he had searched for over the past ten years.

"Wales," she admitted.

Strian staggered back. "Everyone told me you were dead, but I knew you weren't. I would have felt it."

"I was close to dead when you left me behind."

"I did not leave you behind! I searched and searched. I wouldn't board my boat, but Ivar and Leif carried me kicking and screaming back to it. I went over the side the moment they let go. I swam back, but Ivar had me shackled to the mast since I refused to follow his orders."

Tears welled in Strian's eyes for the first time since he watched his father's pyre drift away during that same voyage. He had lost everything by the time Ivar's fleet sailed away from the Welsh island off the coast of Anglesey. He bracketed Gressa with a hand on each side of her head. He turned his face into his arm as he tried to control the sob rising within him.

"I didn't know that," Gressa whispered, her voice hoarse from her own tears.

"I lost my mother just before we sailed, then my father on that voyage. I only learned a few moons ago that my uncle was responsible for my father's death. I lost you, too."

"That was a long time ago, Strian." Gressa pressed him away, and he let her step away. "Too much has happened since then."

"What are you doing here? How did you get from Wales to here? That's the other side of this blasted island."

"They sent here me with the other archers. They recruited us."

Strian head snapped back. "Did you know who you would fight? Did you know it was our people?"

"No, and they're not my people anymore."

"Yes, we are. We will always be your people."

Gressa shook her head. "Strian, my home is with my people in Gwynedd."

Strian was certain someone struck him with a battle axe as he tried to take in what Gressa said.

"What is there that is more important?" he sneered. "What man warms your bed so well you would rather stay with Christians?"

Gressa's hand flew across his face. "And what women have you pleasured since you thought I was dead?"

"I never thought you were dead."

"But you never denied bedding other women."

"What did you want from me? You made a better life for yourself in Wales. Did you even try to return?"

Gressa's silence was more than Strian could bear. He gripped the sides of his head. He forced himself to breathe, and when he looked back at Gressa, she staggered away from the venom that filled his eyes.

"If you liked Wales so fucking much, you shouldn't have left. Like it or not, you are going home. To the Trondelag." He grabbed her arm and dragged her back toward the bailey. "As my thrall."

———

Tyra was exhausted by the time the last of their people were floating into the firth as their souls traveled on to their final resting place. She prayed they were each standing before the doors of the great feasting hall. She had seen that the women and children she sent into the keep the day before found protection and were well cared for. She longed for a bath and a bed. Her back and shoulders ached, and she had bruises all over her body. She squealed when Bjorn swept her off her feet. He hooked one arm beneath her knees while the other pressed her against his chest.

Tyra rested against him as he carried her into the keep and was falling asleep by the time Bjorn carried her into a chamber. She smelled rosemary and thyme, making her curious enough to open her eyes. She noticed steam rising from a tub before a hearth. Tyra wrapped her arms around Bjorn's neck until he pretended to splutter. Once she was on her feet again, she wasted no time peeling the filthy clothes from her even filthier body.

"I would burn these if they weren't my only clothes."

"And I would keep you naked if you wouldn't have to appear before anyone else."

She turned back to grin at Bjorn, but snapped her hands over her chest, not hiding her breasts but her scar. It was the first time since they reconciled that he had a clear view of the damage the axe did. It had been dark the other times. Bjorn shook his head and pulled her hands away.

"Bare those marks with pride, Tyra. You saved my life when you received those. You put your life before mine, and I will be grateful until the end of time." Bjorn kissed along the worst of the scar. "There is naught that will convince me you aren't the most beautiful woman alive. Don't hide from me. You never have to hide aught from me."

Bjorn shed his clothes, too, and walked with Tyra to the bath. He stepped in, then helped her over the side. The settled with Bjorn's back against the tub, and Tyra draped across his chest. They soaked, both too tired to do more.

When Tyra caught herself drooling on Bjorn's chest and felt the rumble of his laughter beneath her cheek, she forced herself to sit up. The tub was cramped, so she had to turn and sit between his legs. She moaned as Bjorn ran a lathered wash linen over her arms and back, massaging the knots as he went.

He passed the cloth over her breasts, and her body responded despite her fatigue. She was aware of how Bjorn's body reacted while hers pressed against him. He washed everywhere he was able to reach, having to leave her legs to Tyra since his arms were not long enough. He poured water over her head then lathered soap into her hair. She moaned over and over as he massaged her scalp, his powerful hands cradling it. He once more poured water over her head and washed away the suds.

"Go warm yourself beside the fire while I finish." Bjorn pushed Tyra to her feet.

"But I don't want to." She sounded petulant, but

she did not want to miss the opportunity to touch Bjorn as he had touched her. She stepped from the tub, but instead of doing as Bjorn said. She wrapped a drying linen around herself, pulled a stool next to the tub, and ran a soapy linen over his body, her hands burning a trail as Bjorn gripped the sides of the tub. Her hand wrapped around his cock, and he scrunched his eyes closed as the sensations coursed through his entire body.

"Ty," his hushed tones did not hide the need.

"How do you think I felt moments ago?"

Bjorn scrubbed his own head as Tyra finished the rest of his body. Once he was clean, he stepped from the tub, not caring that he was creating a puddle. He helped Tyra to her feet once more and pulled the towel from her body. He took in the stunning sight of her magnificent body. He had not seen her bare since the first time they made love all those years ago.

The times they had made love on this voyage had been in the dark, and their rushed tryst in the woods had only afforded him a view of her delectable backside. He feasted on her body until he looked up and noticed her lick her lips. She gorged on the sight of his aroused staff. She wrapped her hand around it again and stroked him as her head fell back. Bjorn growled and dragged her to the hearth. He snatched a plaid from the foot of the bed and snapped it open before easing Tyra to the floor. He followed her down until his body rested between her thighs.

"I thought I was too tired to do aught but fall sound asleep. Now that is the last thing I want to do." Tyra caressed his back as she drew her fingertips across it.

Bjorn slid into her body, and they both closed their eyes as they savored the bliss of their bodies becoming one. They held one another for a long time until need overtook them, and sentimentality fell away. Their pace was slow as Bjorn thrust as deeply as he could, and Tyra's muscled clenched, keeping him in place until they both needed him to thrust again. They flew over the edge into ecstasy together. Neither of them made an effort for Bjorn to pull out. As they floated back down to Earth, Bjorn kissed Tyra's temple.

"Ty," he breathed beside her ear. "You never had time to get that herb from Freya, did you?"

She shook her head. She stared into Bjorn's eyes. "I don't know that I want to anymore."

"And I don't know that I want to go into battle again knowing you are there, possibly carrying our babe."

"Where does that leave us?"

"Looking for a farm when we return home."

Tyra grinned as she cupped his cheeks. She lifted her head to kiss him, their eyes locking, both growing serious. "I'll ask her for it in the morning."

"I won't mention the farm to anyone until after we settle this business with Grímr." They both understood their duty, and they were willing to accept it.

"We have plenty of time, my love," Tyra kissed him once more.

"The rest of our lives." Bjorn returned her kiss and rolled onto his back, bringing her with him. He threw the plaid over them.

They both fell asleep as their eyes drifted closed, and neither moved until the sun poured into their chamber.

A pounding at their chamber door awoke Tyra and Bjorn.

"What?" Bjorn bellowed.

"We're all needed in the bailey," Freya called back. "Tyra, let me in."

Tyra looked at Bjorn and shrugged. She wrapped the plaid around her as Bjorn swiped a damp drying linen from the ground. Tyra looked back to be sure Bjorn was covered and only shook her head when Bjorn held the linen in front of his groin but did little to hide the rest of him.

"She's your cousin," Tyra hissed.

"So? I know she isn't looking."

Tyra opened the door and watched as Freya scowled when she noticed Bjorn. "It's one thing to know you're mauling my best friend, it's another to find the evidence."

"I'm sure I said something similar to Erik about you, cousin," Bjorn teased.

Freya turned back to Tyra. "I brought this for you. I imagine you will need some, too." Freya handed over a small oilskin wrapped package. "Pennyroyal. I haven't that much to spare, but we can look for more before we leave. If you hurry."

"Thank you. I was going to ask you about it this morning."

"Figured at much. Ty, don't wait much longer to make the tea. If you already have need of it, it'll incapacitate you for at least a day. It'll only be worse if you wait longer."

"I know. Thank you."

Freya stepped back through the door, and Tyra pushed it closed as she walked back to the pile of dirty clothes she had no desire to put back on. She wished she had washed them last night and spread them out to dry. She chided herself for letting Bjorn distract her once more.

"What did she mean if you already have need of it? And that it'd incapacitate you. Will it make you ill? I was under the impression it was safe to use."

Bjorn pulled her into his embrace, and she could not miss the worry etched in the lines around his eyes and between his brows.

"It is safe. She meant that if I'm already carrying a babe, it will make me lose it. It hasn't been that long, so if it flushes my body of a babe, it wouldn't be much worse than having my courses. If I wait, and I'm carrying, it will be far worse. I would bleed more and be in far greater pain."

Bjorn froze, uncertain of what sounded the worst from what Tyra just explained. "And if you might be carrying our babe? You would still drink the tea?"

"It's far too soon for me to know. It would be at least a fortnight before I might have a clue. Even then, I wouldn't be convinced for at least another moon. If I knew for sure, I wouldn't even consider it, but I don't know. I'd rather not wait but consider this as prevention instead."

"But we would know then before the fortnight is up. We would know if you had been carrying."

"Yes." Tyra watched Bjorn try to work through what she was struggling with, too. She was not sure if she could withstand the outcome, the guilt or the disappointment. Either would overwhelm her while still conflicted over whether she was ready to begin a family with Bjorn. "If I don't start using the tea, then I might end up with child, if I'm not already."

"I know," Bjorn swallowed. "Tyra, it's your choice. I will support whatever you decide."

"But what do you want?"

"I don't know. That's why I trust your decision."

Tyra found the responsibility to be far heavier than anything else she had ever expected. "I will save the tea until my courses are due. I will drink it then. I won't know if it's the tea or nature that brings on the bleeding."

Bjorn held Tyra as they both reconciled themselves to the decision.

"We have to meet the others," Bjorn whispered, and Tyra nodded. "Ty."

Tyra looked up as she stepped back. Bjorn cupped her cheek and said, "We haven't talked about it, but I want to marry as soon as we get home."

"I want that, too."

"But what if that takes several more moons? Are you all right with waiting?"

"I don't know that we have much choice." Tyra grinned, "Unless you want to be wed in the White Christ's church."

"Hardly," Bjorn growled then chuckled.

"Me neither. And they call us heathens. They put their god on a cross and stuck nails in him. Hardly sounds civilized."

"I'd rather celebrate Odin's life than the death of some man from a far-off land. Bah." Bjorn handed Tyra her clothes, then looked for his. "I don't like thinking of you only being my companion. I don't want anyone wondering if there's any chance that either of us is not committed to this relationship."

Tyra could not help but laugh. It started as a tiny bubble and erupted into gales. "Bjorn, do you really imagine anyone in our tribe will doubt that? After how long it's taken for us to admit how we feel? I suspect there is no one within Ivar's homestead who doesn't know we've been in love with each other since we were children. The only two who didn't was us."

Bjorn pulled on his clothes, and as his head popped through his collar, he shook his head. "They might, but Rangvald's men and these Highlanders don't."

"Worried someone might try to woo me away?" Tyra teased.

"No. I just don't want you to beat some poor woman who makes the mistake of smiling at me." Bjorn sauntered over to her.

Tyra tugged him to her, and just before she kissed him, she breathed, "I wouldn't just beat her. I'd kill her. You're mine."

SIXTEEN

The bailey was busy as the Mackenzies, MacLeods, Mackays, and Sutherlands gathered to decide how they would deal with their rogue neighbors the Rosses. Rangvald and Lorna stood with their own people, and Freya, Erik, and Strian mingled with their tribe members. Tyra watched how Erik blended in with their tribe, even though his own family stood feet away. He had not abandoned his tribe or his parents, but for the sake of the mission, he stood beside Freya and supported her as the leader of Ivar's forces. Bjorn may have led the warriors in battle, but Freya was Ivar's representative when they made decisions. Strian was the voice of reason whenever they needed it, and she led their fleet. They had each matured into the role they were meant to play within their tribe. A wave of gratitude crested within her chest as Bjorn wove his fingers with hers.

"We have to follow him," Freya's voice carried as she argued.

"And if we have to track him across Scotland?" Erik asked.

"Then you better be ready for a sore arse, because you will be in the saddle for a long time," Freya quipped.

"Do we have any idea where he went?" Bjorn asked as they joined the conversation.

"No," Freya shook her head.

"I can find out," Strian cut in. All heads whipped toward him, but he was looking at a group of captives who huddled together awaiting their fate. Men tried to be brave, while women whimpered. They were all aware of the tales of what became of Norsemen's thralls. They feared being sold to the east, and it was a justified fear. Some of them might be, but many would become servants in Ivar's and Rangvald's households. Strian looked at the faces turned toward him and shrugged. "I'll let you know what I discover."

He walked away before anyone asked him what he meant. Tyra and Freya exchanged a glance, but he left Bjorn and Erik confused.

"If he learns nothing, do we send scouts? I'd rather not ride all over this island if we can sail wherever we need to go. How do we know Grímr doesn't try somewhere else? England? Francia?" Bjorn brought them back to the topic.

"I'd love it if he tried to recruit in Francia. They'd cut off his bollocks and serve them with sauce," Erik quipped.

"We should talk to the Highlanders and discover what they think. They'd be better informed if there are any other clans near here who might harbor or support him. If they don't think so, we should sail wherever we go next," Tyra reasoned. Rangvald and Lorna joined them as Tyra finished speaking.

"We agree with Tyra," Rangvald chimed in. "We suspect he will try to recruit from England. If that's the case, then we should return to our ships and sail."

"Do we continue with this voyage or do we return home for more warriors?" Freya asked. "We lost much of our forces, but not so many that we can't still win if Grímr's recruitment remains slow. My concern is more battles like we have fought will leave us underpowered if he succeeds in finding more warriors. Do we wait till that happens and risk going home with our tails between our legs, or do we regroup then return with an even larger fleet?"

"Wales," Strian stated quietly. Faces swung toward him, having not noticed he slipped back into the group. "He's going to Wales. The archers impressed him, and he wants more longbowmen. But he intends to sink our ships first. He wants us trapped."

Strian's taut jaw and hard stare told the rest not to questions how he knew. Strian would not make a suggestion unless he was sure it was reasonable and judicious.

"Then we return to our ships," Lorna stated.

They spent the rest of the early morning making plans. There were arguments over whether they ride back to Mackay land and hope to capture Grímr and his forces as they headed north or should they use the Ross birlinns to sail to Sutherland, where Andrew's clan would provide more boats to get them back to Tongue and Castle Varrich.

"There are not enough boats here to carry all of us to Sutherland. Even if the Mackenzies and MacLeods rode home, we still can't get everyone to Sutherland," Rangvald argued.

"Then we prioritize who sails to Sutherland, and we send back boats for the others," Lorna responded.

"Doesn't that defeat the point of the boats offering us speed? If we have to wait for them to ferry back and forth, then we don't gain any time," Rangvald looked down at his wife, who stood with her hands on her hips, not at all intimidated by a husband who was twice her size.

"Nae when I ken the currents will still move us faster than a horse. Once we are all on Sutherland, they will have birlinns to join the ones we take from here." Lorna swung around to look at Andrew. "How many do ye have we can borrow?"

"If we sail to Crumbathyn, we might pick up a dozen or so from the keep and neighboring fishermen. But I dinna think that's the best way to go. We are better off riding. It'll take us far longer than to just go on horseback."

Rangvald gloated as he looked at Lorna, whose eyes shot daggers at him. "Vera well," she conceded.

By midmorning, they were ready to ride out. They had rounded the Welsh archers who survived, along with several young Ross men and women. They left behind the married women and children with the wounded. The ones who survived the journey on foot would become servants once they returned to the Trondelag. The Highlanders bit their tongues despite being adamantly opposed to the practice. It was the price of peace and keeping the alliance between the Mackays and Rangvald's tribe, which meant the Sutherlands, Mackenzies, and MacLeods would benefit by extension.

Alex Mackay, Andrew Sutherland, Kenneth MacLeod, and Tormod Mackenzie rode together, refusing to discuss what happened behind them as the Norsemen rode out with their line of captives bound at the wrists.

"We canna ignore the Munros who joined in with the Rosses and this bluidy Norsemen. They fled like the wee cowards they are, but they willna remain quiet if they can rally against the rest of us," Tormod looked at his companions. They were not always on good terms, but they had a common enemy now, and that made them the best of friends.

"I suspect we can track them to Castle Foulis rather than Castle Varrich," Alex scowled when he pictured anyone making their way to his home other than him. "It may be worth the detour to check."

"Nay. Let me go," Andrew spoke up. "It's closer to ma home. Ye need to get to Varrich before anyone else does. If Grímr goes to Foulis, too, then we will get him there. But if he doesnae, ye canna risk falling too far behind. If we find him there, then we do away with him, and I'll send messengers to each of ye. If I dinna find him there, I return home for more men. I'll meet ye again where Grímr's boats sit on the Mackenzies' shore."

"Vera well," Alex spoke with authority as the oldest in the group.

Andrew signaled for the Sutherlands to break off, and they turned north to return to their territory, which neighbored both the Rosses and the Munros.

"Where are they going?" Rangvald called out.

"Ye must deal with Grímr, and we must deal with the Munros. We canna allow them to go unpunished for siding with the Norseman. They may be allied with the Rosses, but they put their own heads in the nooses by coming along." Alex looked over his shoulder as Rangvald drew closer. "We suspect they may head to Castle Foulis, which is closer to the Rosses' and Munros' border. If they aren't there, then we will all meet on the Mackenzies' shore. Rang, if we don't pick up their trail, then I must take ma men back to Varrich. I'm sure Grímr kens ye came ashore there. I have to check on ma people."

"And us? Do we go back to Varrich when we already agreed to go search for them on the coast?" Rangvald demanded.

"Nay. Ye can ride on with the MacLeods and the Mackenzies. Ye will be in good hands with them. None of them want to end up as the Rosses did." Alex gave a pointed look over his shoulder to where the line of captives trudged, struggling to keep up with those on horseback. "Ye could send yer captives with me, so ye dinna have to drag them along."

"Can we trust you to not turn them loose?" Freya asked as she rode closer. She and Erik now rode behind Alex since Rangvald and Lorna joined their cousin. The other two Highland leaders rode ahead but kept their ears on the conversation. Tyra and Bjorn were not far behind, and Strian rode in the rear, keeping an eye on the prisoners.

"They are captives from a clan that sought to destroy ma ally and would harm to ma other allies. Why would I show them mercy?"

"Because isn't that what your White Christ teaches? Turn the other cheek. That is not how we live," Freya continued.

"I'm well aware," Alex's comment had some bite.

"Then we have reason to wonder."

"Cousin, ye are new to the family, so I ken ye dinna realize that ma honor means everything. I dinna lie, and I dinna play people—ma family— false."

Erik reached out a hand to keep Freya from responding. She snapped her mouth shut and glared at her husband. The group fell into silence as each person retreated into their own thoughts until scouts returned in the early afternoon.

"Ma laird, the tracks break off. One set, the larger group, is going north, but there is another group that is now traveling southwest. I dinna ken where they are going. If it's to Mackenzie land, they should go northwest," one of the Mackay scouts reported.

Strian joined the group when they spotted the scouts. He was sure where the smaller group was going.

"The smaller group is headed back to Wales in anticipation of when Grímr joins them. I suspect he intends to race us to Varrich so he can destroy our fleet. He knows if he does that, then we can't leave. We'll be stuck here with no choice but to enter the skirmishes he arranges. If the Munros do not head where Sutherland suspects, then they are still with Grímr." Strian looked at the Highlanders who were just as attentive as his friends. "I'd wager he will use the Munros to recruit for him. He will have the Munros convince other clans that they must side with them to protect themselves from the invading Norsemen, us. If I were Grímr, and I had a clan willing to ally with me, I would retreat and let them do the dirty work."

The others listened to his logic and knew it was sound.

"You are quite the strategist. If you were not on our side, I would worry about how your mind works." Bjorn grinned as he gripped Strian's shoulder. "Did someone give you some insight?" he whispered the last part.

"Not willingly." Strian's hushed tones did not carry beyond Bjorn.

"But you're sure?"

"As I can be."

"Good enough for now, I suppose."

"This changes things." Erik looked at the other Norsemen. "If what Strian suggests is true, and I have to agree with him, then we need to make our way to our ships, not Grímr's. If he traps us here, then we can't stop him."

"And if Strian is wrong?" Tyra finally spoke up. Her glance was apologetic, but they were used to her being the voice of dissent, not because she disagreed, but because they always needed to consider their plans from every angle.

"If ye dinna mind ma suggestions," interjected Tormod Mackenzie, beaming at Tyra and Freya. "We all must head north regardless of whether we follow Mackay to his land, or we return to ours. We continue that way, and if the tracks lead elsewhere, we follow them. If they lead to Mackay land, and Alex says ye dinna need us, then ma men and the MacLeods go to Grímr's boats. I dinna have any qualms burning his boats, or better yet, breaking them apart for firewood."

"He's right," Freya smiled back but yelped when Erik lifted her from her saddle and dumped her in front of him.

"Ride with me wife. I've missed you," grumbled Erik.

"About time. I was wondering when you'd invite me." Freya's smile to her husband was pure seduction.

"Then we find somewhere to water the horses and ride north." Kenneth MacLeod had remained silent during all the negotiations. He was like Strian and often the voice of reason, but he preferred to observe then act on his decisions rather than blindly trusting the decision making of others.

SEVENTEEN

They made steady progress north after watering the horses at a stream the scouts found. Erik and Freya whispered to one another, taking turns blushing. Tyra watched them and wondered if she and Bjorn would ever be that affectionate in public. She dared sneak peeks from the corner of her eyes, but Bjorn was paying keen attention to their surroundings. She tried not to sigh aloud. Tyra respected Bjorn's commitment to their safety and how seriously he took his role as the leader of their warriors, but she was unable to quell the envy that tickled her gut when she watched Freya and Erik together. She and Bjorn had made progress unlike any she imagined, but there was still much for them to learn about one another when it came to being in a romantic relationship.

They stopped for the night when they became unable to travel with such a large force in the dark and because it was impossible for the captives to trudge behind them for any longer. Tyra maneuvered her horse into line with the others as one of the shieldmaidens and her husband hobbled the horses together. She was about to swing her leg over her saddle when large, firm hands grasped her waist.

Bjorn plucked her from her horse as though she weighed little more than a child. As he lowered her to the ground, he pressed their bodies together, his arousal pressing against her.

"Do you have any idea how uncomfortable it has been for me to ride like this all day?"

Tyra's brow furrowed with confusion. "Does that happen when you are in the saddle that long?"

Bjorn chuckled and shook his head. "Only when I ride near you. I've just never been able to tell you before."

"I don't understand why. You spent the day focused on scouting our surroundings."

Bjorn lifted her chin and looked into her luminescent eyes. "Can you guess why I couldn't stop looking around, checking for any signs of danger? Because contemplating us being attacked, of you being taken or injured, is unbearable to me. It doesn't mean I paid any less attention to you. There wasn't a moment when I wasn't aware of exactly where you were or what you were doing. After the battle, I realized riding double only puts you in danger."

Tyra leaned in to kiss him, and it was a soft brushing of their lips, a testimony to the love and tenderness they shared. It was not only desire, but love. "Thank you."

"You're not angry? You won't tell me you can fend for yourself?"

"I know you know I can. I enjoy knowing you care enough to still try to protect me."

"Ty, Erik might be comfortable holding Freya while they ride, but if they ambush us, neither of them can fight properly riding double. It's not a risk I'm willing to take when we're in pursuit of our enemy. It doesn't mean I want to hold you any less than Erik wants to hold Freya."

"Will you hold me tonight?"

"I hadn't planned on letting go."

They walked arm-in-arm to the campsite where fires were already being built. Tyra looked around and spotted Freya with her bow. Her friend looked at her and gestured toward the trees that surrounded their campsite.

"Bjorn, Freya and I are going to hunt." Bjorn tensed but smiled then nodded. It made him uneasy to let her go. She understood it was not him being controlling, but it was a fear born out of what they already endured.

"Do you want to come with us?" She rested her hand on his arm.

Bjorn shook his head and forced a smile. "No. I will set up our bedrolls while you go."

Tyra leaned in for a kiss before grinning, "You shall make me a good little wife one day."

She danced away, but not fast enough to avoid a firm spank. Bjorn watched as she walked into the trees with Freya and several other women. He turned back and unsaddled their horses, bringing their saddles closer to the fire to use as pillows. He laid out their bedrolls, overlapping them. When he finished, he joined Erik and Strian at the fire and welcomed the mead horn they passed. The air had a chill, and the mead warmed his belly. The three men chatted until Freya and Tyra stepped out of the woods with the other women. Bjorn and Erik released audible sighs then broke into laughter. However, Bjorn's dried up when Tormod walked in front of Tyra. His pose was not intimidating but flirtatious.

"Don't," Strian spoke under his breath. Bjorn looked at him, but Strian shook his head. "Don't go over there, charging like an angered bull. You can't keep being so possessive. She isn't interested in anyone but you. If you're overly protective, you will make her look weak. As though she can no longer defend herself. Best case, she politely declines. Worst case, she cuts off his cock and hands it to him. Either way, she will be at your side soon enough."

———————

Tyra watched as Freya grinned and walked away when Tormod stopped her. She would admit he was a handsome man with his fiery red hair and charming smile, but she liked Bjorn's brooding more and blond hair. She smiled and dipped her head before trying to step around him.

"What is he to you?"

Tyra did not misunderstand, but she was not interested in answering anyone's demands, least of which came from a man she did not know.

"Who is the blond man?" Tormod tried again.

"You have to be more specific than that. We're all blond." Tyra was not about to give in.

"Bjorn. Who is he to you?"

"My husband."

"That isn't what I was told."

"And you've been asking? I wouldn't let Bjorn find out. We have an arrangement much like what your people call a handfast."

"Then it is only a trial and can end."

"No. It is only until our priestess can perform the rituals. We have already declared our commitment to one another. He's my husband." She tried to step around him, but he shifted once more.

"I don't believe that. I know your people don't always marry. You are companions who may leave and move on whenever you want."

"We may not believe in marriage as your White Christ teaches you, but our pledges are just as sacred. Bjorn is my husband." Tyra's voice hardened like the shards of ice from the glaciers near her home. "I think you want the novelty of bedding a Norse-woman to then brag how you tamed a savage. I'm not interested. If you want a good poke, there are plenty of other women who would enjoy obliging. We don't lock away our virginity like something to be scared off. Find one of them. You're bound to learn something."

Tyra was done being polite. She walked forward, her shoulder landing in Tormod's hard enough to make him step back. Tyra gave the rabbits she killed to the men skinning and preparing the meal. She joined Bjorn by the fire and was glad to accept the mead he handed her.

"Is everything all right?" Bjorn wrapped his arm around Tyra's waist as she wrapped both of hers around him and leaned into his shoulder.

"Yes. I just realized how much I appreciate you, and how much I prefer you over any other man."

Bjorn kissed her forehead. "Who would've dared imagine you would say those things to me?"

"I didn't." Tyra leaned back. "I told Tormod you're my husband. We've said we're husband and wife already, but is that true?"

"Tyra, you are not my companion or my mistress. I am not your lover. Those are relationships that can end, that either of us can walk away from. You may have every right to divorce me whenever you want, but ours is a marriage the gods created. It has been our fate since we were children. I'm sure if Sigrid were here, she would tell you the same. No priestess has blessed us, but we are married." Bjorn kissed her forehead again. "If I have to, I shall claim we handfasted and are learning to accept the way of the Scots."

"You wouldn't."

"I would if it laid to rest anyone's doubts that you're my wife."

Tyra's hand slid up Bjorn's belly as his muscles rippled under her fingers. She placed it over his heart. Bjorn pulled her against his body more and cupped her jaw. They rested their foreheads together.

"I love you," they said as one before melting into a kiss that left them both looking for privacy.

"We can't," Bjorn sighed. "I'm not having a repeat of last time."

"Others will make love tonight. We will just be quieter." Bjorn looked doubtful. "You look as though you've never done that before."

Bjorn's face heated as red creeped from his neck to his ears. Tyra covered her mouth as she giggled. His face glowed in the firelight.

"We both have pasts," Tyra reminded him.

"Doesn't mean I want to revisit them. With you."

"You're mine now, so what does it matter if we talk about it?"

"Because when I think about your past, I want to rip Knud's limbs from his body then spit down his throat."

"But you know how things stood between us."

"I do. But I didn't then. And he isn't the only man I want to bludgeon. I don't like being reminded of you with someone else. Not when I could have avoided it."

"You don't know that. Perhaps the gods didn't want us together yet. Perhaps we tampered with fate that day, and we shouldn't have made love."

"Ty, don't say that," his voice rough. "I never want to look back at those moments with regret. I have enough for everything that happened afterwards."

"I don't regret it either. Not now. I was angry for too long, and I robbed myself of a happy memory because of it."

"No more talk of the past."

"What is done is done."

By the time they finished talking, the meal was ready. Tyra's belly growled, and Bjorn teased her that he would be careful not to lose any fingers eating near her. It had been a long day, and the next day would be the same. People found their places around the fires. The Highland men grouped together while the Norsemen found their spots, couples choosing places away from the glow of the fires. Bjorn chose a place close enough that they would not grow cold overnight, but he had already wanted privacy before Tyra suggested they make love.

Tyra laid down and held the covers open until Bjorn slid in behind her. He wrapped his arm around her waist and pulled her back against him. His rod rubbed against her backside as she gripped his thigh. The arm beneath her neck reached until his hand slipped inside the neckline of her linen shirt. He brushed his fingertips over her nipples, making them contract into tight beads. His other hand moved to between her thighs. He pressed the heel of his hand to her mound, and Tyra arched her back. She reached further behind her and cupped his cock, eliciting a hiss from Bjorn as she squeezed. She fumbled with the laces at his waist as he undid the ones to her leather pants. When he had untied hers, he made short work of opening his. His stiff length jutted from his thatch of curls.

Tyra wiggled until she pushed her pants below her knees. Bjorn's fingers bit into her hip as she lifted her knee. He guided himself into her sheath, and they both paused as the savored the pleasure. Bjorn licked and nipped at her nape as the hand that played with her breast came free of her shirt to entwine fingers with Tyra. Once they were one, Bjorn's hand went on a quest to find the hidden pearl that would make her find her release. He rocked his hips as she continued to press back against him, her lush bottom rubbing against his hips. Bjorn pressed his finger to the apex of her thighs and found his treasure. He created slow circles as her breath become short and unsteady. She squeezed his fingers as he thrust harder.

"Bjorn," she breathed.

"Mmm."

She stifled her moan as her body rockeed toward completion.

"I can't wait much longer," she whispered.

"Don't."

She pulled his thigh closer to her hip as his entire body encompassed her in warmth and security. Her release built from low in her belly as she squeezed her eyes shut. The pleasure ricocheted throughout her middle until she curled her toes within her boots. Bjorn buried his face in her hair as his hand slid back to her hip, and his fingers sank into her flesh. He thrust once more before pulling out.

They were both breathless, their chests heaving as they tried to draw air into their straining lungs. When Tyra finally moved, she inched her pants over her hips, but before she tied them, Bjorn rolled her to face him. He slipped his hand down the leather until he cupped her backside. Despite the snug fit, he stroked and squeezed as he kissed her over and over.

"Neither of us likes it, but until you start drinking the pennyroyal, it would be better if I pulled out."

"I know," Tyra said around a yawn. She kissed his collarbone and snuggled closer to his chest. He held her as she fell into a deep sleep. He followed her soon after.

Morning came all too soon, and Tyra was stiff when she woke up. She slept better than usual, and it was from having Bjorn beside her, but the ground was still hard. People were moving around the camp just as she and Bjorn rose. She followed some of the other women into the trees for privacy. She was ready to step out from the woods but hung back when she heard her name and Bjorn's.

"I doubt Bjorn will keep Tyra. He will tire of her now that he has her. She has nothing to offer him. He is the nephew of the jarl, and she is a penniless orphan."

"A penniless orphan he's been in love with since we were all children."

"Bah. His pride stung that he couldn't have her. Now that he has, what's there left to want?"

"And I suppose it'll be you he turns to."

"Me or anyone else with a nice pair of tits."

"He hasn't exactly been making his rounds the last few years."

"And who is the only one he comes to? Me."

"And whose name does he call out? Hers. Gunnhild, I would be careful. You're more likely to get a blade across your neck than Bjorn back in your bed."

Tyra inched closer and peered around a tree to find Gunnhild and Solvi speaking. Two other women were there, but they had said nothing yet.

"I, for one, would be happy if he came back to my bed. He's bigger than any other man. And talented, too," Gala, a petite woman with light brown hair, grinned as she looked toward the camp.

"Do you want to be with a man who refuses to use your name? He only says Tyra's name. No pet names either. Just hers." Astrid added. She was a tall and slender woman aptly named for the beautiful goddess.

Tyra wanted to hurtle herself forward and rail against each of them for talking about her behind her back and for considering Bjorn available. There was little for her to do that would not make her look insecure, and Bjorn straying did not worry her. He was steadfast like a loyal dog. Now that they were together, she did not worry about him choosing another woman. She worried constantly about his death and being left behind, but not about his fidelity. She straightened up, but a hand came around her waist and hand over her mouth. She bucked and tried to scream.

"Shh, little one. It's only me. I came to find out what you're spying on."

Tyra relaxed when she recognized Bjorn's voice but kicked her heel back into his shins for frightening her. She turned and tried to push him back the way he came, but he was as sturdy as a mountain and about as immovable.

"Tyra is fooling herself if she thinks Bjorn will be satisfied with her. He's never been satisfied with just one of us. Even two of us," Gunnhild cackled.

"That may have been true in the past, but have you seen them together? Since they returned from Grímr's camp? Why do you think we weren't enough?" Astrid gave Gunnhild a pointed look. "The man's besotted with her, always has been, and now shows everyone."

"She can't do what any of us can. I heard Knud stopped bedding her less than a year into their relationship. He let her stay with him because he pitied her. Even her family doesn't want her," Gala spoke up as she nodded to Gunnhild. "Who else has she been with? She can't know how to please a man with appetites like Bjorn's."

"I'll say it again, since you don't seem to be listening. He's only ever wanted her. He's warned us never to speak of it, but we all know he only thinks of her when he's bedding us. I'm tired of that. I want a man who wants me, not one imagining I'm someone else," Astrid turned away. "I wish them well. They deserve to be together, and I'm certain it is the gods will."

"Leaves more of him for us," Gunnhild called out.

Bjorn was shocked by what he was hearing. He was ashamed and embarrassed that Tyra had to listen to these women speak of his past with them. It disgusted him that anyone should speak about Tyra in such a diminishing and hateful way. But it enraged him that anyone would plot to get between Tyra and him. Bjorn stepped away from Tyra, but when she pulled on his arm, he shook it loose. He stormed toward the group of women who did not see nor hear him coming.

He wrenched Gunnhild's head back as he wrapped his hand in her ponytail. A blade was at her throat before she had the chance to defend herself. The other women drew their swords but were wise to keep their distance.

"You have run your uncivil tongue once too often, Gunnhild. I warned you before we left about speaking against Tyra. You have a high opinion of yourself for a woman I couldn't be bothered to look at while bedding. And we all know why that is. Your friends said as much. You have never been the one I want. Tyra is. You were just a quim or a mouth available when I was tired of my hand. For that, thank you. Anything else? Don't kid yourself. Be glad you are a woman because you'd be dead if you were a man. I don't strike women when I'm not in battle. However, Tyra is within her rights to fight you, if she wants."

Tyra wanted to groan. It would have satisfied her

to ignore the women, but now Bjorn made that impossible. The other women looked to where she stood, and their eyes widened in shock and unease. Tyra joined the group and tapped Bjorn's arm. He released Gunnhild with a shove that sent her sprawling across the forest floor.

"Gunnhild, I don't want to fight you because I respect you as a fellow shieldmaiden, but I will kill you if you try to take Bjorn from me." Tyra looked at the other two women who were noticeably uncomfortable and shifted where they stood. "I say the same to you. Don't test me. There's no doubt that the only two women who might beat me are Lorna and Freya, and they're more likely to kill you before I get to you."

Tyra took Bjorn's hand as they turned away, but they did not take a step before Gunnhild spoke again.

"If we're all the same in the dark, Bjorn, perhaps you will not notice when one of us slips in. Or rather you slip in. Tyra hasn't had the best of luck in the last few battles. Would you die a lonely old man?"

Tyra froze as the other two women backed away, no longer willing to associate with Gunnhild. She turned around, but before she looked at Gunnhild, she looked at Bjorn.

"This will be on your head if I end up charged for murder."

"She threatened you," Bjorn scowled. "We all heard her. Solvi and Gala are not stupid enough to lie for a dead woman. Are you?"

Bjorn cast his glance at the two women who shook their heads.

"Make this up to me," Tyra purred.

"That is a punishment I look forward to taking."

Tyra was on top of Gunnhild before anyone realized she intended to fight barefisted.

"You don't have your sword with you, so I will not draw mine. You can try to reach your knives, but I will only use them to cut you to bits," Tyra hissed as her fist landed in the woman's face once more. Blood geysered from her nose as Tyra's fist pounded into her eye next. She wrapped her hand around Gunnhild's throat, but the woman was as strong as Tyra. She bucked until she got her feet under her and pushed Tyra onto her back. Gunnhild straddled Tyra as she rained down her own punches. Tyra did not block them, instead reaching for the knife she kept in her boot. She jabbed it into Gunnhild's side, and when the woman reared back in pain, Tyra rolled so she was once more on top. She slid her blade across the woman's throat, but only enough to cause a trickle of blood.

"You have a choice. You leave Bjorn alone and never speak of either of us again, or you admit that you won't do it, and you die now. Choose."

"You would kill me either way."

"No. Not if you swear on your fealty ring. Pledge it as a vassal to Ivar."

Gunnhild spat on Tyra. ."You may be Freya's best friend, but Ivar will not countenance you committing murder. He'll try you then execute you."

"And who will wear witness against me?" Tyra's voice sounded innocent, but the pressure she placed on the blade on Gunnhild's neck was anything but. "Do you think Bjorn, the jarl's nephew, would speak out against me, his wife? The one who told us to solve this by fighting. Do you think Solvi and Gala are so loyal to you they will not testify to how you intended to kill me to steal my man? Would you like to test that luck and die with shame before our entire tribe, or would you rather die with some dignity?"

"What dignity is there in this?"

"The real reason will never be said aloud."

"And what reason would you give?"

"I will tell the truth that you challenged me for Bjorn, but I will not tell others how you threatened to kill me. You are no one's favorite. I am."

Gunnhild struggled once more as she tried to reach her knife. Tyra hopped up and stepped back. She allowed Gunnhild time to draw her knife. Once the other woman was fairly armed, she attacked. She charged forward, driving her head and shoulder into Gunnhild's middle. Gunnhild flew backwards as Tyra followed her to the ground. Tackled, then pinned, Gunnhild was unable to gain any leverage to swing her knife. Tyra pressed the blade against the other woman's neck and drew it across. She continued to straddle her as the light faded from Gunnhild's eyes. She looked at Solvi and Gala in challenge, but both women shook their heads.

"No man is worth dying over," Solvi muttered.

The two women looked down at Gunnhild.

"She should have known that," Gala looked at Tyra. "You must have listened to us. Bjorn is a desirable man, and I enjoyed the times I was with him. But he is yours. He always has been. I have no intention of seeking him out. And after this, I'm sure no other woman will either."

Tyra wiped her blade across Gunnhild's chest.

"Good." That was all Tyra had to say. She did not feel like saying more nor did she think more needed to be said. Bjorn pulled her into his arms, but she was too angry to embrace him back. She waited until Gala and Solvi left before she thrust her hand against his belly, pushing him away.

"I had no intention of letting them know I was listening. I know you aren't going anywhere. You should have let them talk because that's all it was. Now a good shieldmaiden is dead, and I might still face charges for murder. How could you be so reckless?"

"How do you know so little about women?"

Tyra staggered back but then lunged forward, her hand coming within inches of Bjorn's face before he grabbed it. "I suppose I should ask the expert."

"Stop, Tyra. I'm not an expert, but you can talk to any man, and he'll tell you the same thing. A jealous woman is a deadly woman. Gunnhild's threats weren't made in jest. She wanted what was not hers, and she would've tried to kill you for it. It had nothing to do with me. She's been jealous of you her entire life. She wanted to be Freya's friend when we were children, but she had nothing in common with Freya. Rather than accept that, she blamed you. She knew I was in love with you. She bedded me to spite you more than she did because she enjoyed me. The fact that I called your name, and she knew I was thinking of you, only made her more spiteful."

"And you fed that fire by going back over and over."

"No. Realizing that a couple years ago is part of why I didn't want to be with other women. I may have slept with her when I was drunk, but you were still with Knud."

"And just before we left?"

"I explained that already." Tyra begrudgingly had to admit she understood why that tryst happened. "Tyra, she wasn't going relent. I didn't trust her not to kill you or get you killed in battle. I didn't trust her not to cause problems between us. And I definitely didn't trust her not to gossip. She would've destroyed your reputation and questioned your honor. What then? Ivar and Lena would stand by you, but would others trust you on the battlefield? Would others come to your defense? There was no way this wasn't going to end as it did."

Tyra closed her eyes and tilted her head back. She took several deep breaths as she tried to calm the anger and bloodlust that still surged through her veins.

"You might be right, but it wasn't your decision to make. You had no right to put me in that position."

Bjorn looked chagrined when he nodded. "That's true, but her conversation proved this fight was inevitable."

Tyra looked over at the dead women. A woman who she fought alongside only days ago, but Bjorn was not exaggerating Gunnhild's resentment toward her.

"What do we do with her?" Tyra looked at him.

"Tell Erik and Freya. They will be the ones to decide."

"Wonderful. Freya will leave her to the animals."

"That's my hope."

It was a terse conversation with Erik and Freya with far too many ears nearby, but Gala and Solvi corroborated their story, and Astrid stepped forward to tell the other things Gunnhild said before either Tyra or Bjorn arrived.

"Leave her to the wolves. She deserves no better," Freya's decree met with little resistance.

The Highlanders once again watched the Norse form of justice and only wondered how they ended up making a pact with the devil. They understood matters of honor, but they were not used to women fighting to the death. More than one Highlander looked at the Norsewomen with newfound respect, caution, and interest.

They rode away from the camp later than they

would have liked. They forced the captives to run behind the trail of horses and warriors on foot. The Highland scouts picked up the tracks, and they made progress even though they had to let the captives lag. Strian volunteered to oversee the team of Norse warriors who corralled and herded the thralls. Many were already growing weak and struggling to keep up. The taunts lobbed at them did little to help, but the threats kept them moving. Strian let none of his warriors carry out those threats, but they were an incentive. The day was almost over when the scouts once more returned with news no one expected.

"We are still a day's hard ride from Varrich, but we're on Mackay land. We came across some of our tenant farmers who had their home ransacked and burned by Munros. They said they didna kill anyone but stole what they could carry then set fire to the crofts and fields."

"Bluidy hell," Alex snapped.

"But that's nae all, laird. They said there were Norsemen with the Munros, and a man with a limp and an accent told Neill Munro they needed to hurry if they were going to meet their boats before we reached Varrich. They intend to sail there and sink your cousins' fleet."

"What? How is that even possible? How can they get to their boats that fast?" Alex bellowed.

"They must have left sailors behind with orders to meet them in a few days times."

The news put Tyra on edge. Any threat to her boat or the ones under her command made her anxious and angry. She looked at Bjorn who was already looking at her.

"I know, my love. We will get there as soon as we can."

"It won't be soon enough if his fleet is already on its way to sink ours."

Bjorn only shrugged. She was right, and there was little to do but ride hard the rest of the distance.

"Do we ride through the night and hope to overtake them or find them when the sun rises?" Bjorn wondered aloud.

"The road from here to Varrich is well worn and smooth. It wouldnae be impossible to ride in the dark," Kenneth MacLeod spoke up. Tyra looked at him and realized she had forgotten he was part of the warband. "It's possible if we ride through the night. If we can overtake Grímr and the Munros, then we stand a chance of fighting them and stopping his fleet. If we canna overtake them, then we meet them in the morning and fight. If we kill Grímr, then there will be no one to issue the order to attack yer fleet. If we dinna find him before we get to Varrich, we go after him once we ken yer fleet is safe?"

"And if he gave a standing order to attack when they are in range?" Freya chimed in.

"Doubtful. That mon is too prideful. It wouldnae satisfy him to have someone tell him about the destruction later. He will want to witness it," Kenneth explained. The others had to admit Kenneth had a good understanding of Grímr.

"What about Strian and the thralls?" Erik joined in.

"Yer friend and yer captives willna arrive until we've already fought any battle, land or sea. If ye're intent on taking those men and women home, then they shouldnae be near the fighting. They will either get killed or get rescued. The Munros willna let the Rosses go with ye without a fight. Yer Welsh archers willna give in without another fight unless they can escape first. They'll be in the trees and gone like a puff of wind before ye realize they're nae there." Kenneth shrugged. "Yer friend might nae like missing a battle, but he seemed very intent on those prisoners. Or at least one of them. He'd rather they stay alive than with you in battle."

Tyra was not sure what she made of Kenneth MacLeod's perceptiveness. She wondered what else he had deduced but not said. She had little more time to ruminate on it once they were galloping through the blackened night. They rode as quietly as possible for an army on horseback. The steeds' hooves churned up the dust and grass while they made the ground vibrate. They risked giving away their approach, but they were desperate to get ahead of Grímr either by strategy or by land.

EIGHTEEN

The sky was lightening, but they had yet to discover Grímr or the Munros. Tension was growing among the leaders of the combined forces.

"How'd he just disappear again?" Tyra asked Bjorn as they rode side by side. "We should have found them by now, unless they are traveling through the night, too."

"I would assume they are and may have been since they fled Allenfearn. That's why we haven't found them. They may be a day ahead of us."

"If that's the case, either they've already raided Alex's home, or our ships have sunk." Tyra was demoralized and frustrated. They had traveled throughout the Highlands to do little more than fight the same skirmishes they fought back home. They had accomplished little but lost several good men and women. They did not have Grímr to show for it, and she did not care about the thralls they collected. She had no need for any, and she did not involve herself in the slave trade. She was eager to discover what would happen next. Until that happened, she would remain unsettled.

"Tyra?" Bjorn spoke again as he tried to gaze at

her face in the dimming light of the moon. It was too early for the sun to cast any light.

"I'm all right. Just annoyed."

"We all are. It's as though this mission has been a failure."

Tyra looked at Bjorn. There was more in his voice than she was sure he intended. She leaned against her saddle horn as she twisted to look at his face.

"Bjorn, you did not fail any of us," she murmured, mindful that her voice did not carry. "You led us to victory in more than one battle. Grímr has a more elaborate network of mercenaries than any of us imagined. He's branched out into two countries now. The Norse haven't been to Wales in years. I never imagined they'd help him. I can't imagine how he's paying them after how Freya said they stole from him, and Inga is no longer alive to sell the women from her tribe. Either way, don't doubt yourself. You may lead us in battle, but don't forget Rangvald was there and so were four clans. None of them got Grímr either."

Bjorn reached out and pulled Tyra into his lap, taking her reins from her. He reached back and attached them to his saddle.

"What're you doing? I thought you didn't agree with me riding double with you."

"There is little likelihood we will meet up with Grímr soon from what the scouts said. Besides that, I was lonely."

"Lonely?" She snorted. "I was close enough for you to pick up."

"But you weren't in my arms."

"Where I belong." It was a statement not a question.

"Precisely."

Tyra leaned against Bjorn and rested her head on

his chest. She listened the steady beat of his heart, and she found her eyelids growing heavy. She pulled away and explained she dare not fall asleep, which is what would happen if she remained curled up against him. They rode together until they stopped to water the horses just after dawn.

"Castle Varrich is still more than half a day away," Alex announced to the Norse leaders. "Since we havenae caught up to them, they must be headed to meet their ships. If they were already at Varrich, ma sentries would have alerted me. I ken several have seen us pass through."

"So, what now?" Lorna asked.

"If they're meeting their boats, they're doing it at Lairg. Then they must sail to the Minch and then northeast to come around to the Kyle of Tongue."

"Can we beat them to Varrich?" Erik asked.

"Yes. There will be nay way yer captives will keep up though. Are you prepared to leave them behind?"

Erik, Freya, Bjorn, Tyra, Rangvald, and Lorna looked at one another. "Strian," Freya whispered.

"No," Bjorn was emphatic. "We can't leave Strian and the other Norsemen. The thralls are worthless in comparison."

"What do we do?" Tyra's frustration was clear. "We can't let Strian and the others get lost. Last they heard was to follow us to Varrich, but what happens if we get there more than a day ahead of them and don't stay? What if we go hying off after Grímr again?"

"I'll ride back for them," Lorna said. "I'll get Strian and the others. They can leave the thralls wherever I find them."

"Ye'd leave them to the wolves? They'd be unprotected and without aught to eat," Tormod was aghast.

"And why not? They were prepared to kill us only

a few days ago. They were prepared to send their men to an unknown land to fight an unknown enemy. If they're the rugged Highlanders you people like to claim to be, they'll find a way to survive." Tyra muttered before looking back at the road they traveled as if she expected Strian to come over the last rise.

"Ye people?" Tormod hissed.

Tyra turned back around and smirked. Tormod opened his mouth, but the threatening look on Bjorn's face made him think better than to argue with Tyra. Tormod crossed his arms and looked at Lorna instead.

"Ye canna ride back alone, and Rangvald is more likely to get ye killed than protected. Anyone sees ye with him, and they'll assume ye're the captive."

Lorna's peals of laughter had everyone looking at her as if she had gone mad. She covered her mouth but ended up snorting instead.

"What my elegant wife would say if she stopped cackling is, give anyone but a minute, and they'd discover it's more likely I'm her captive than the other way around. Bloodthirsty wench that she is." Rangvald pulled Lorna in for a quick kiss.

"Lady Lorna, it's been years since ye've been in this part of the county. I dinna disagree with Tormod offering his help," Kenneth's voice was soft, but his tone had steel.

Lorna looked at Rangvald before they both spun their horses around. "Keep up, lad," she called over her shoulder.

As Lorna, Rangvald, and Tormod faded into the distance with the Mackenzies following, the others looked at each other. "How much faster can we get to your home than Grímr if he sails?" Bjorn asked Alex.

"He must ride along, or even sail through, Loch

Sìn until he gets to the Minch. Then he must sail along the coast until he enters the North Sea and can turn east. Depending on the weather, it could be an easy sail to the North Sea, or it could be rough sailing into the waves. It's hard to tell. Ye can get every season in a day when ye're in the Highlands," Alex shrugged.

"And once he's in the North Sea, it's much the same," Kenneth noted. "It could be calm, or he could face a headwind that pushes him back."

"What I need to know is if there is time to wait for the others to return, or do we ride on without them?" Bjorn pressed.

Everyone looked at one another and settled their sights on Erik. He would now return to commanding his parents' warriors. It would be for him to decide what Rangvald's people did while Freya would decide for Ivar's. Neither wanted to make the choice.

Erik looked at Freya, and an unspoken conversation flowed between them before Erik turned back to Alex. "If we wait here for a couple hours, would it set us back too much? Would it give Grímr the advantage?"

"Nay. He has at least a full day's sailing ahead of him, and that's if the water cooperates." Alex's expression was speculative as he looked to the northwest. "We can remain here for a few hours, let the horses and men rest. If they arenae here before midday, we ride without them. I dinna want to ride through the night, but we may have to."

"Thank you, Alex." Erik's relief was palpable. He did not like his parents being separated from the group as they searched for a handful of Norsemen leading a group of angry prisoners.

They set up camp near a small loch close to the road. Alex and Kenneth posted scouts to watch for Lorna's and the others' return and a watch around the camp. It was a subdued group. Riding through the night exhausted both the Highlanders and Norsemen, but none would admit it. Hunting parties brought back rabbits and squirrels while some of the others fished. The benefit to waiting was everyone had a full belly, and some even caught a couple hours of sleep.

Tyra leaned back against Bjorn, but he was not as relaxed as his face would make one think. "What's worrying you the most?"

Bjorn absentmindedly ran his hand over Tyra's back and shoulder as he stared off in space. "I want to know how Grímr convinced the Rosses and Munros to help him if he has no money. I want to know whether the Munros continued on with Grímr and if they would sail to our home. I want to know how he recruited Welsh archers and why he plans to go there next when it's so far southwest. I want to know if he is going to Lairg or if we've made a monumental error in not continuing on. I want to know if Strian and the others will make it back here in time."

Tyra peered up at Bjorn as he rattled off all of her concerns. She felt calm and grounded while he held her, and she wished she offered him the same. She ran her hand over his chest, and he captured it before bringing her fingertips to his lips then returned it to his chest, some of the tension easing.

"I want to know those same things. I want to know how our ships fare. I want to know if we will reach them before Grímr, and I want to know if we will have to prepare to sail south or if we will return home."

"What do you want to have happen?"

Tyra shrugged. She knew what she wanted, but she knew saying it aloud would be selfish.

"Ty, it's me. Tell me," he cajoled.

Tyra closed her eyes and slid her hand into the neck opening of Bjorn's shirt. His warm skin was smooth against her cold fingers. He pretended to shiver, and the vibration of his chuckle was strong and reassuring.

"I want to go home and get married," she admitted.

"I do, too."

"But I also know that might be months from now."

"Are you worried things will change between us if we don't marry soon?" Bjorn was anxious about her response. He prayed things would only get better between them.

"No." Tyra's response was so even and unequivocal that Bjorn relaxed for the first time since sitting down. "I don't know how to explain it. We have already promised to marry one another, and I know that's as good as any vows we make before a priestess, but I want the rituals. I want to share those things with you. I want our parents' spirits to be there with us as we exchange rings. I don't want to miss out on that."

"Would we not have our wedding whenever we return?"

"Yes, I just—" Tyra stopped herself before she said what was on her mind. She did not want to cause Bjorn pain by saying any more about their parents.

"Tyra?"

She shook her head, but Bjorn was persistent. He pressed her forward, so she sat up and looked at him.

"I want you to find peace with your parents being gone, and I want you to know you'll never be alone again."

Bjorn blinked several times before he lifted Tyra into his lap. He buried his head against her shoulder as he took several shuddering breaths before he looked up.

"How is it you understand how I feel? That I feel that for you."

"I suppose because we are both orphans. We know what it is to be adrift, to watch others with their families and wish we had it, too. I want you to become my family."

They cupped one another's faces as they kissed. Bjorn's tongue swept across the seam of Tyra's lips, and she opened to him, the recesses of her mouth like warm satin. Bjorn groaned as her breasts pressed against his chest. His hand slid down her back until he palmed her backside. The tight leather did little to disguise the firm, round buttocks. Tyra shifted to straddle his hips, both uncaring that there were others around them. Tyra tunneled her fingers into his hair as she pressed her mound against the ridge in Bjorn's pants. Their clothes were an irritating barrier, but neither of them suggested they slip into the woods again.

"Ahem," Freya chortled. "If you two came up for air, you'd realize Strian and the others approach."

Tyra shot her friend a look of disgust. "Who came and told you? Last I saw, you were in much the same position with your husband."

Freya look unashamed and broke out into a wide grin. "Wonderful, isn't it?" She spun on her heels and moved toward the road where Tyra spotted the dust cloud approaching before any of the riders.

Bjorn and Tyra stood together as they watched a dozen riders approach with Rangvald and Lorna in the lead. Tyra craned her neck to catch a glimpse of Strian, but he was the last in line. His face was etched with a scowl unlike any Tyra had ever seen before, and he gave some of the dirtiest looks.

"What do you suppose has Strian looking like that?" Bjorn wondered.

"Are you serious? Look at who is riding in front of him."

"A woman," Bjorn shrugged.

"Gressa."

Bjorn's look of shock might have made Tyra giggle had it been a funny situation. "How long has it been?"

"At least five, ten years."

"Shite. No wonder he looks like someone pickled his mead."

"I wouldn't bring it up, if I were you. Let him tell us what he wants."

"I know. He's one to shut up when asked too many questions."

"Exactly. Let's go with the others."

They walked over to Freya and Erik, then met the incoming riders. Lorna and Rangvald were glad to find the group waited for them. Bjorn watched Strian yank the young woman from his horse, but he noticed a flash of remorse on Strian's face when she collapsed. Her legs gave out, and Strian pulled her against him. Bjorn watched them both flush before breaking apart. He caught himself shaking his head. His friend would not have an easy voyage with his new thrall. Strian marched over to the others with the woman in tow. She tried to slow him by digging in her heels, but he turned and picked her up over his shoulder.

"Plundering and pillaging again, Strain?" Freya taunted, but she snapped her mouth shut at his look of censure. He lowered the woman to her feet and spun her around.

"Hardly." He nudged his captive. "Speak. Tell

them what you told me." Her stare was mutinous, and she refused to say a word. "Speak, woman. I have no patience left for you. That expired long ago."

Her nose flared as she spat out her words. "I knew it. What will you do? Beat me get me to talk," she sneered. "I have naught else to say."

Strian struggled to remain in control. "Don't lie, Gressa. I haven't laid a hand on you to harm you. Tempt me as you might. Tell them. If not for me, then to help them. Help Tyra and Freya. Would you see them dead?"

Gressa's eyes opened wide as she looked over her shoulder at the two women she had known since she was a child. They both looked different than she remembered, but she supposed she did, too. Life's unpredictability had done that.

"Grímr sent Highlanders to the marches. He sailed in several months ago bringing chests of jewels, cloth, and gold. I assumed he raided or pirated the chest. The Highlanders paid a handsome price to the prince, so the prince sent a score of us north. They included me because of my past and knowledge of the language. I didn't have any choice, but I was careful to listen when Ivar's name came up more than once." She sent a pointed look at Strian. "I wondered what brought Ivar and Grímr together. I knew all of you would return."

"You knew," Strian growled, and Gressa forced herself not to step back when hurt flashed in Strian's eyes.

"Yes. That's why I didn't fight coming."

"So, you could help murder us, one by one?" Freya pushed her way forward. "You have changed. Not for the better. You have no honor left if you could kill us."

Freya pushed back through the group and stalked

off. Erik looked around, then followed Freya. Gressa continued as if Freya never spoke, but a tightness brought lines around her eyes and between her brows.

"Grímr is struggling to recruit more Scots. He doesn't have confidence in the Lowlanders, and the Highland clans are spreading the word to avoid him. He learned of the Welsh archers and decided that would be his newest plan."

"How did you learn all of this? Does he know you're Norse? Did he talk about this in front of you?" Tyra drilled her with questions.

Gressa looked at the ground and shook her head. "I overheard it."

"How?" Tyra demanded.

"I was in his tent." She looked up and dared anyone to say anything.

Strian made a sound like an injured animal. He lifted Gressa over his shoulder again and moved away from the others. "Why? How could you?"

"How could I not? Do you think they gave me a choice?"

Strian sucked in a breath that whistled. "He forced you?"

"He made it so I had very little choice. He threatened to torture someone important to me."

"Who? The man you're with? The man you've settled down with and made a cozy life with?"

Gressa's head swung forward and her forehead cracked into Strian's nose, causing blood to flow over his lips and chin.

"No, you arse. You. He threatened to torture you." Gressa shook with anger as she looked at Strian. "There. Are you satisfied?"

"No. Where is your man to protect you?"

"What man? You keep saying that. I never once

said I was with someone. You're the one who admitted to being with other women."

"And you said you've made a life in Wales you don't want to leave. By the by, I didn't say that."

"With my people. And I never said with a man."

Strian shook his head. "I don't believe you."

"Strian—" She did not get to finish before he was steering her back to the others.

"Finish telling them."

"He intends to sink your ships, then go to Wales for more men. He wants you trapped. The sea to the north and his mercenaries to the south. He plans to lay siege to the Mackay castle. If he doesn't catch you there, he believes he will before you can get more ships to sail back."

"Then he is after ma home," Alex spoke for the first time.

Gressa looked at the dark-haired man who resembled the blonde man who followed Freya.

"Are you Laird Mackay? Then yes, he is."

"We outnumber him. How does is he so sure he can keep getting away?" Kenneth MacLeod was suspicious of the woman whose wrists were still bound. "How can we be sure that's the truth?"

"At this point, why would I lie?" She raised her wrists to point out the obvious. "It's obvious you have more warriors. That's why he's going to Wales. He gets away because his son is with him. They're practically twins. You spot one then the other, but you don't realize the last time you were sure you glimpsed Grímr, it's his son. Grímr has already left wherever you're fighting. He would let his son die before he does."

Gressa's disgust was unmistakable, but Strian's look made her shake her head. He wondered if she had been with the son, too. She swayed toward Strian but caught herself.

"There is only one reason for him to return to the Trondelag. You kill his remaining sons. He will have no one to inherit Ivar's and Rangvald's settlements. The point of this was to create a legacy everyone would admire."

"They aren't even his real sons," Tyra muttered.

"But they are his only legacy," Gressa pointed out. "He would give up trying to take the settlements, but he wouldn't give up wanting revenge for their deaths."

Lorna glanced at her husband before announcing, "Then we have our plan. The sons are as good as dead. If he comes for Rang, let him. He will learn what mistake he has made setting his sights on my husband."

The others concurred. They needed to drive Grímr back to the Trondelag, where he would remain outnumbered. He might play cat-and-mouse there, but there were far more Norsemen to guard Rangvald and Ivar than there were warriors on this mission. Grímr stood no choice back home. They remounted their horses and galloped toward Castle Varrich and what they hoped would be their last standoff with Grímr.

NINETEEN

The ride turned out to be faster than Tyra expected, and even though they rode late into the night, they arrived at the base of the Kyle of Tongue before midmorning.

"It's two more hours ride, but we will reach Varrich before they do." Alex looked relieved to catch a glimpse of the body of water that was the last landmark before he was home. "Dinna dally. I need to be sure ma people are unharmed."

The force was still made up of Rangvald's and Ivar's Norsemen along with the Mackays, the Mac-Leods, and the Mackenzies. They made an impressive sight as they reached the last rise, and Castle Varrich came into sight. Alex's sentries met them and assured him that nothing unusual had happened during his absence, but he still wanted to verify that with his own eyes. Their numbers were far too large to accommodate all the warriors in the bailey, so camp was set up outside the wall while the leaders trudged into the Great Hall. Alex's chatelaine busied herself, ordering chambers readied and food brought to the exhausted and starving group. Alex sighed as he settled into his seat at the dais. He ran his hand over the table in front of him, relieved to be home.

No one spoke of Grímr or the inevitable battle while they sat at the table. Everyone needed a reprieve, if only for an hour. Once the servants cleared the meal away, it was inevitable that the conversation swung back to what would happen next.

"I need to check on the ships," Tyra cut in. The unknown made her anxious, and she would not rest until she was sure they were all still seaworthy.

"The sun will set soon. It'll be easier to see them in the morning," Lorna pointed out.

"No. I will see them now." Tyra rose and looked around. She startled the people at the table, but she would not give in. "Excuse me, please," she added as an afterthought.

Bjorn paused before following her. "You know she won't sleep until she is sure. I will make sure she doesn't sleep in her cabin. At least not alone." Bjorn hurried to catch up with Tyra.

"They think I'm crazy, but those ships are the only thing protecting us right now," Tyra fretted. "If aught is wrong with them, it won't matter if Grímr attacks. We'll be stranded here until they're repaired. Whether we sail home or sail to Wales, we need them. We won't ride all the way to Wales."

Tyra's long legs carried her swiftly across the bailey to the postern gate. She raised an eyebrow at the guard who hesitated. He scrambled aside when her hand moved to her knife. It was easy for Bjorn to keep up, but he chose not to talk. He understood Tyra needed to lose herself in her thoughts. He was sure she was doing an inventory in her mind and running through the list of things she would check. It was better not to distract her than end up on the wrong side of her temper. She had not shown it much during this voyage, but it rivaled Freya's. She hurried down the cliffside that led to the sandy beach. There were several small fishing boats moored to the sand, so she untethered one and pushed. Bjorn joined her on the other side, and it was only a matter of a moment before it was bobbing in the water. They waded in and pulled themselves into the boat. Bjorn settled on the bench and took the oars while grinning at Tyra.

"You can row us home when we're both tired." Tyra stuck her tongue out at him before giggling. "I like that sound. I told you, you don't laugh like that enough." Bjorn teased.

"I used to. At your expense. You shall have to try harder to be funny." It was Bjorn's turn to stick his tongue out at her, but his look was far more seductive. "Whose cabin shall we check last?" Tyra purred.

"A bed? That will be a first for us. Even at Allenfearn, we fell asleep on the floor before the fire. I'll row faster."

"Ahoy," Tyra called out as they approached. At least half a dozen people were on guard, but she was still unable to determine on which ships.

A head popped over the rail, and Tyra recognized the woman as Helga. One of Freya's best oarswomen. When Helga recognized Tyra and Bjorn, her whistle echoed as other passed it on to the farthest guard. Helga placed a plank between the smaller boat and the ship after Tyra tossed her a rope to secure it.

"We watched you return. There were many more of you than when you left."

"The MacLeods, Sutherlands, and Mackenzies joined us," Bjorn said. "The Sutherlands returned to their keep to see if Grímr headed there. We continued on and discovered Grímr sailed west, or least we think, and will try to sail into the kyle."

Helga looked at the couple and then at the fleet which filled the natural bay below the castle. "How long do you think we have?"

"The night. They will be here in the morning, assuming the weather held for them," Tyra explained.

"That's not very long. The boats are in good condition. The water was sometimes rough. But we docked them far enough apart that they didn't jostled each other. There was one storm that struck with lightning. It took off the mast of one of Rangvald's ships. The one Fritjof sailed."

Tyra shook her head. "He's dead. Killed during our first skirmish."

Helga shrugged. It was a way of life to accept death; it was inevitable for everyone. Tyra watched Helga for a moment before continuing. "Helga, your cousin is dead, too."

"Gunnhild?" Helga was moved by this. "When?"

"In the woods when we made camp one night. Helga, you should know I did it."

Helga glared at Tyra, unable to do anything because of rank. "You murdered my cousin?" She spoke through her teeth.

"I defended myself. She threatened to kill me, because she refused to accept my claim to Bjorn."

Helga's laugh held no mirth as she looked over Tyra's shoulder at Bjorn. "You murdered my cousin over a man you don't even want. Or were you jealous Gunnhild was still sucking his cock?"

Bjorn took a step forward, but Tyra waved his back.

"Much has changed since we left, and that includes my relationship with Bjorn. Gunnhild knew that, as does everyone else. She spoke ill of me to some of the other women and threatened me before them and Bjorn."

Helga looked to Bjorn, but he did not react except for a tick at the side of his jaw. "If it wasn't murder, why are you telling me? Why not let someone else bring me the news."

"Because I would have you learn the truth from me before you heard tales told by those who weren't there. If you don't believe me, and you think Bjorn would lie for me, then ask Solvi and Gala. They were there. Astrid was there to listen to what Gunnhild said earlier. They've told their side to Freya and Erik, who were satisfied with how I handled things."

"Of course they were. Freya is your best friend, and she leads Erik around by the bollocks now. He doesn't dare disagree with his pretty little wife."

Bjorn failed to contain his laughter at that. "Helga, you and I both know that's not true. They still disagree daily, and often neither of them gives in. Someone else decides. You can accuse Tyra, but be careful what you say and who you say it to. If you're a threat to my wife, then I'll kill you myself."

"Wife?"

"As good as married. She's not my mistress, so don't wonder about it."

Helga looked at the powerful couple and knew they spoke the truth. Duty obligated her to defend her cousin, but it did not surprise her that Gunnhild met her end as she had. Gunnhild's jealousy of Tyra lasted her entire life, and she coveted Bjorn for herself for years. Threatening Tyra had only been a matter of time. Helga nodded before turning to point at the bay's opening.

"If we can stop them before they enter the bay, then we won't lose any of our ships. The best thing would be forcing them into a row so we can sink one ship after another," Helga's practical nature ruled. Her arguments in defense of her cousin spent, she reverted to business.

"We form a flotilla to barricade the entrance, but

I want a way to stop them before they even make it to us." Bjorn looked out to the last of the fleet.

"Do you suppose they have enough iron links to form a long chain?" Tyra looked back at the keep. "Perhaps their blacksmith makes something in time, so we spread it across the water further north. We leave enough space for their fleet to sail in, then trap them between two metal chains, or at least we block them with it. If we can, we should attach large fishing nets to the one closest to us. Then archers on either shore attack before our flotilla sails forward."

"It's worth trying." Tyra's tactic impressed Helga, and she begrudgingly admitted. "That's a good idea."

Tyra gave her a tight smile and nod. "Thank you. We need to inspect the other boats and then go ashore."

"Very well. I'm glad you returned."

"Thank you," Bjorn said as Tyra climbed down to the small boat. Once they released the rope from the larger ship, Tyra rowed them around the fleet, weaving between ships to check hulls and speak to the others on watch. When her inspection satisfied her, Bjorn switched with her and rowed them back to shore.

"So much for a bed," Bjorn grumbled. "We'll be up all night, and not the way I prefer."

Tyra nodded in sympathy. Her mind bemoaned the lost opportunity, too. When they reached the shore, they raced back up the path and headed to the blacksmith's forge. The man was just packing up and grabbed an iron poker when he caught sight of the two blond Norsemen running toward him. Tyra held up both hands as they slowed their approach.

"We don't mean any threat. We have an idea and wondered if it was possible." She pointed toward the water. "We need two metal chains long enough to extend across the water from shore to shore. Is that possible?"

The blacksmith looked at them then out to the kyle. "Only if we used all the chains we can collect from the keep and bailey."

"Is it possible for you to do them by morning?"

At the suggestion that the man must work all night, he balked and shook his head.

"Do you want a fleet of Norsemen to enter the bay and attack?" Bjorn tilted his head and raised an eyebrow. "I imagine not."

"Does the laird ken yer plan?"

"Not yet, but I'm confident he will agree to its merit. We also wonder if your fishermen have a fishing net to attach to it. Maybe even an anchor."

"The net might be a possibility, but there is nay way to make an anchor in time. Ye would have to give up one of yers from yer ships."

Tyra looked at Bjorn. "Take the one from mine." She suggested to Bjorn.

"And mine. If we can anchor it at least at both ends, then we can capture the boats. We might even take them once they no longer have crews."

"Speak to the laird. If he says aye, then I will get started."

"I'm positive he will. You should rouse your helpers and get anyone else you might need."

Tyra and Bjorn explained their idea to the others, who agreed it was the best chance they had to avoid full-scale battle on the water. Alex accompanied Tyra and Bjorn back to the blacksmith, who had already relit his forge and had two large young men stoking the fire. He was issuing orders to three other men when they arrived.

"I figured he'd say aye," the blacksmith spoke before Tyra or Bjorn asked.

The three men appeared from the back of the hut with armfuls of iron links. The blacksmith sent them to find more in the keep and around the bailey. Within the hour, there was a gigantic pile of chain sitting outside the hut. The blacksmith was hard at work heating and pounding the segments together. Alex ordered the fishermen from the surrounding village to bring all their nets to the keep. They examined them, and those deemed strong enough were delivered to the blacksmith for him to tie and solder on.

The next day dawned with a thick cloud cover that matched Tyra and Bjorn's mood. They stayed up throughout the night to oversee the project. They finished only a couple of hours before dawn, so they found a spot in the Great Hall and fell asleep. Now they were awake once more and ordering their warriors to haul enormous chains out to their ships. Once they loaded the massive cables, the crews of the two ships set off to lay the furthest chain, then the second one. There was natural cover on both cliffs that allowed members of both crews to wait out of sight.

The sun was trying to make its way out of the clouds when the first of Alex's scouts returned with news that they spotted the fleet. Bjorn and Tyra were still with the ships as they positioned the boats, then tethered them together to make four large flotillas.

Freya, Erik, Strian, and the others were leaving the keep when Gressa ran up to Strian. He had ordered her to remain in the keep on pain of death if she disobeyed. Strian had unbound her hands in case Grímr breached their defenses or an attack also came from land. He would not leave her unable to protect herself.

"Strian, wait!"

"I don't have time, Gressa."

"You have to let me come."

"Absolutely not."

"I'm better than any of your archers, and you know that. I always have been, and I've spent the last ten years fighting with one."

"No."

"Strian," she pleaded.

"I said no."

"Is it because you don't trust me? You fear I'll sabotage this or run away?"

Strian stood akimbo. "Would you?"

"Not until I'm convinced Grímr is dead." The venom that dripped from her words was enough to make Strain pause.

"You said he never forced you."

"Did he give me much choice? It was that or watch you die."

"How can you be so sure he would honor that?"

"Because I already learned too much."

"He might have killed you."

"And I might die in any battle."

"Don't say that," Strian voice cracked as he pulled her in for a deep kiss that left Gressa clinging to him.

"Strian, let me come. Let me do at least this before you leave."

"Before I leave? You think I'm leaving you here?"

"I had hoped."

Strian straightened to his full height which had him towering over Gressa. "Let me dispel that hope. You are coming with me. My thralls don't decide where they go." Gressa lashed out, but Strian grabbed her wrists. "You want me to trust you and bring you along only to tell me moments later that you plan to stay here. I won't let you go, so you intend to run away."

"I intend to kill Grímr and figure out the rest later."

"It's already figured out, Gressa. I don't trust you to stay here. Fool that I am to have considered it. You come with me, but I'll be damned if I give you a weapon. I don't want to die with an arrow in my back."

Gressa gasped and backed away. "You fear that after what I've done, what I've endured, to keep you alive, I would kill you."

"Much has changed, hasn't it?"

Gressa did not miss that he meant both over the years and since they found one another. "I may wish many things on you, Strian, even your death. But it will never be at my hands. Never."

Strian stared down at her for a long moment before grabbing her wrist. "Let's go."

Strian was not sure what he would do with her, but he was willing to admit to himself she was right about being the best archer. He was not ready to voice aloud his capitulation, but he had already accepted he would give in and give her a bow.

As they passed the armory, Strian informed Freya and Erik that he would be on the cliffs instead of his ship. When he grabbed a longbow they brought back, they understood why. Gressa stumbled, unprepared for Strian to pick up one of the Welsh bows and several quivers of bolts. His broad shoulders carried them with ease as he mounted his waiting horse. He pulled her into the saddle in front of him. The jolt of the horse's movement pushed Gressa into Strian's chest. He wrapped his arm around her, and they rode out in silence.

Erik, Freya, Rangvald, and Lorna hurried to the beach where the rowboats ferried them to their boats. The Mackays, Mackenzies, and MacLeods sent archers along the coast, where other rowboats ferried them to the opposite shore while most of their warriors prepared for an attack by land.

Tormod asserted that the Norse might come by water, but the Munros would come by land. A scout confirmed they saw men leaving the Norse fleet just east of the entrance to the Kyle of Tongue.

Once everyone was aboard their ships, there was little they to do but wait. The minutes ticked away into hours with mutters of doubts growing louder. It was late afternoon when the whistle signal passed from ship to ship. They had spotted the enemy fleet entering the kyle. The warriors awaiting the enemy pulled their shields from the sides of the boats and held their swords at the ready.

Tyra glimpsed the prow of the first ships as she waited at the front of the flotilla. It would be on her call that they lifted the first chain. She waited for the signal to come that the entire fleet was within their trap. As the first ships grew closer to the chain and net, she looked around and strained to catch anything that might sound like the signal, but it was quiet.

No one spoke, only the lapping water made a sound. When it was impossible for her to wait any longer without risk of the plan failing, she lowered her raised arm, and the chain snapped into the air as the teams of warriors heaved on each side. It vibrated as water gushed through the links, but it struck the prow of the boats and stopped them. Tyra listened to the enemy's orders to fall back, but arrows rained down from above and from the flotilla.

Grímr's fleet attempted to retreat, but there was not enough room for all their boats to maneuver. His warriors fell to the decks or into the water one after another. Tyra spotted a man she deduced must be one of Grímr's sons. He looked just like his mother, Inga, and bore an uncanny resemblance to Erik, his cousin. She raised her bow and released the arrow. It found its mark deep within the man's neck. She pulled another arrow and shot the next warrior she caught in her sights. So went the rest of the battle. She launched arrow after arrow until there was enough room for them to drop chain and the flotilla to pursue Grímr's boats.

Strian pushed his doubts aside as he handed the longbow to Gressa. She did not look at him but placed the first quiver between her feet. She stunned Strain with how strong she was to pull back the bowstring on a weapon almost as tall as her. She released one arrow after another, and despite the distance, Strian watched as each one found a home in an enemy neck, chest, or eye. The only times she missed was when someone else's arrow struck her intended victim. She wasted few arrows and killed more men that Strian ever had in a single battle.

Grímr's ships retreated to the headland and out of range of their archers. Strian noticed how far apart the enemy's ships sailed. There had never been a chance to pull the second chain and trap them. When a gap formed between those that never crossed the first chain and those retreating from it, he whistled the signal. The second chain snapped up and trapped some of the ships.

"Damn it to *hel*," Gressa swore, using several words in Welsh that Strian was sure were vulgar.

"To your Christian god's hell?"

Gressa glared at him. "No, to ours. The real one." She forced herself to calm. "I didn't get him. He would have been on one of the last boats, so he could make his getaway just like he always does. Shite."

Gressa blinked several times, refusing to cry in front of Strian. He had humiliated her enough times in the past few days. She had an ounce of pride left, and she would not forfeit it before him. He pulled her into his arms, and she dropped the bow, her arms too tired to continue to hold it. She pushed her hands between them, intending to shove him away, but when she felt the strength of the muscles beneath his shirt, she clung to him.

"You will get him. One way or another, he will die. I reckon you have the most right to revenge. I will make sure he dies at your hands, or at the very least, you can watch his slow and painful death."

Now, Gressa did push him away. "Why? Why would you promise me that? A slave. You think I'll fight again? When we return to Wales, you think I will take up arms against my people. My chance to get him has come and gone. You won't give me a weapon again anyway. It is not my vengeance to have."

She tried to storm off, but Strian caught her around the waist. "You still have a lot of explaining to do, and I intend to get that explanation. For now, you're off the hook. We can't wait here any longer. Thank your god, or whoever you believe in these days. I don't have time for this."

TWENTY

"H e escaped. The bluidy bastard escaped." Lorna railed as she pushed the keep door open. Despite her small size, her fury was enough for the enormous door to bang against the door.

"My scouts will tell us which direction he headed. In the meantime, we'll gather as many provisions as we can offer ye, and ye can set sail at first light." Alex smiled at his cousin.

"I'm sure he's going back home. I believe what Gressa said. We killed three more of his sons today, so he has none left. He will want his revenge on Ivar, which means he knows we will follow." Tyra pushed the hair from her face. She and Bjorn had stayed to help untie the ships. They ran all the way from the beach to the keep, catching up with the others."

"I agree with Tyra. We should prepare to go home." Bjorn looked at each of them but paused when Strian shook his head.

"I'm staying."

"What?" Freya burst in. "No, you're not. I refuse."

"To what, grant me permission? Will you try to stop me? Will you stand by as your husband, or your cousin, fight his friend? Your friend?" He looked over her head, "I'm staying, Freya."

"Why? I demand to know."

"I have my reasons, and they are not any of your business."

"It's because of her," Freya pointed at Gressa, and Strian pushed her behind him.

"Freya," he warned.

"Strian," she mocked.

Erik tried to step between them, but Freya shot him a look that promised retribution. He might be her husband, but she was Ivar's representative. He was not entitled to decide for her.

"I refuse to release you. You've pledged fealty to my father, which means you will obey his orders. He never commanded you to stay, but he did command you to fight for him."

Strian's chest puffed out as his shoulders rolled back. "Freya, you have never done this with any of us. You would start now? Now you're the almighty daughter of a jarl because you're not getting what you want. Do you realize how petulant and spoiled you look, not to mention childish?"

Freya hissed as she grabbed Strian's wrist and held it up. "None of us were children when my father gave us our rings. Our childhood ended when we swore our oath. You don't get to decide when and where you follow that oath. Bring the bitch with you. Let her ruin your life all over again. I don't care. But you are coming with us. Bound if we have to."

Freya spun on her heels and took two steps before turning back around. She walked to Strian but looked at Gressa.

"Hurt him again, and I will kill you. I will never forgive you for what you did to him. Never," she whispered so her voiced only reached Gressa and Strian.

"Freya," Strian started, but Gressa squeezed his arm.

"Don't," she whispered. "Not now and not here."

"Very well, Freya. Have it your way. But if anyone is unwilling to forgive, it is now me." Strian turned and wrapped his arm around Gressa. "We're going to my ship."

Tyra and Bjorn watched the exchange between Freya and Strian, stunned at the course of events. They both knew Freya was right, but they were shocked she would treat Strain as she had. Rangvald and Lorna frowned at Erik, as though it was his fault his wife issued such orders.

"They are her people. You know that. Our marriage doesn't change who she is or her right to lead." Erik looked at his parents. "Besides, there is far more going on than anything the three of us know."

Three heads turned to look at Tyra and Bjorn. In turn, Bjorn and Tyra looked at one another.

"Strian and Gressa have a past, but we don't know all of it." Tyra hedged her bets, and wanted to sigh when Rangvald, Lorna, and Erik nodded and seemed satisfied.

"We will oversee the provisions," Lorna looked to Alex who nodded, glad to escape the scene that played out in his Great Hall. Tormod and Kenneth had backed away and given their irate Norse friends space when the argument began. They were uncertain how much blood might be involved.

"We will inform the others. Right, son?" Rangvald formed it as a question, but there was no doubt it was an order.

Tyra turned to Bjorn. "I will check on Freya."

"I will follow Strain."

They exchanged a brief kiss.

As dusk gave way to night, Bjorn and Tyra laid together in the chamber given to them. Neither had made headway with their friends, and both were heartsore. Freya and Strian would never ask them to take sides, but just as Strian was more like a brother to her, he was the same to Freya. Both Bjorn and Tyra recognized Freya was trying to protect Strian because she loved him, but it had gone terribly wrong.

"Do you think they'll forgive each other?" Tyra asked as she drew circles on Bjorn's chest. The little smattering of hair was still damp from their bath.

"Eventually. Whatever his reasons, we all know it's because of Gressa. Something is going on."

"What do you suppose it is? He was intent on bringing her back with him, but now he wants to remain here. I doubt it's to farm."

Bjorn chuckled. "Hardly. He would go to Wales with her. But for what reason, I can't tell."

"What do you think will happen with them?"

"I hope they can reconcile like we did. There is something far greater than a misunderstanding that stands between them."

Tyra remained quiet as she continued to run her hand over his chest as his arm pulled her closer to his side, his hand cupping her bottom. She slid her hand up his neck until she pressed his face toward hers.

"I love you," she murmured.

Bjorn shifted her so their lips met, languid and slow, neither in a rush. Bjorn kissed a heated trail along her jaw until her got to he ear.

"Not more than I love you," he breathed then licked the whorl of her ear. When she shivered, he nipped as her lobe before drawing it into his mouth. Tyra draped her chest over Bjorn's as he found the spot behind her ear that made her moan.

"Louder, Ty. Let me hear your pleasure."

"The entire keep will hear it if I'm any louder."

"Let them."

Tyra pushed up on her hands until she straddled Bjorn's hips. "No more teasing. I want to make love to you."

Bjorn groaned as she encircled his length and stroked. She raised her hips until he glided along her slick entrance. When she positioned him, Bjorn grabbed her hips, pushing down mercilessly as his hips thrust up. Tyra's head fell back, and she did moan unabashedly. She did not care anymore who heard her.

"Gods, Ty. Nothing should feel as good as this. I would stay buried inside of you for the rest of my life."

"I would keep you there if I could." Tyra rocked her hips as Bjorn pressed her onto his length. When she circled her hips, Bjorn was sure he was floating outside his body. He had never experienced bliss like he did with Tyra. "Roll us over, Bjorn. I want you above me. I want to hold you."

Bjorn did not need another invitation. He changed their position and pressed his length into her over and over until she screamed his name. He did not relent until she climaxed again.

"Don't pull out. I have the pennyroyal. My courses should start within a sennight. I will drink the tea soon."

It was impossible for Bjorn to hold back after hearing Tyra's demand. He thrust harder and faster, worried he might hurt her until she pleaded for more. His release ripped through him as he threw his head back and roared her name. Tyra held Bjorn as his arms shook, and she tried to breathe. Never would she have imagined lovemaking like it was with Bjorn. She had enjoyed the times she and Knud coupled, but she never considered it making love, and now she understood the difference. She wondered if it was the same for Bjorn, but they agreed to put the past behind them.

"Tyra, what are you doing to me? I shall either live forever or die a young man. I'm not sure which, but you are unlike anything I ever imagined."

Tyra's throaty laugh made Bjorn's cock twitch. She must have felt it because she moaned and shifted beneath him.

"I could say the same to you," she tilted her hips, needing more of the friction that had already swept her away more than once. She grasped his backside as she moved again.

"Not done?" Bjorn panted.

"Never."

Bjorn rocked his hips as Tyra flexed the muscles of her core causing Bjorn to harden again. "How do you do that?"

"Do what?" Tyra was not paying attention as her body demanded another release.

"How am I growing hard again so soon? I was sure you drained every drop from me."

"Because I can't get enough of you. My body aches for you. It's a need I can't describe, but I can't get rid of it. My body wants yours within me, on me. Everywhere." Tyra realized she made little sense. Her thoughts blurred as her desire propelled her. "Gods, Bjorn. More."

Bjorn buried his nose in her hair as he flexed his hips back and forth. He braced himself on his hands, and Tyra ran hers up and down the corded muscle before scraping her nails over his chest and down the notches of his belly.

"I have never seen anything as magnificent as your body, Bjorn." The reverence rang in her words.

Bjorn pulled one of her legs over his hip as he drove himself deeper still. Tyra cried out as the new position gave her what her body craved, demanded. She concentrated and drew the muscles of her core around Bjorn's length. He grunted as his hips picked up pace and slammed into her. Gone was the tenderness of just minutes earlier.

"Tyra." Her name savage and primal on his lips.

"More." She gasped as she grasped his buttocks and pressed him into her.

"Ty, you're pushing me too far. I'll lose control."

"Good. I've already lost mine. Harder."

Those were the only words Bjorn needed and the last that she uttered. Their bodies moved in unison, and lust replaced love as they raced toward the finish. Their sounds of ecstasy filled the chamber as their bodies collided over and over, the sound of skin making contact drove them to move harder and faster.

"Look at me."

"I can't. Can't keep my eyes open. Want to. Can't." Tyra tipped her back as she arched off the bed, and Bjorn pounded into her. "Bjorn!" she screamed.

"Tyra!" His voice an echo of hers.

Bjorn rolled them so Tyra was once more on top, unable to support his weight any longer. He would crush her no matter how strong she was. He outweighed her by half, if not all, of her weight.

"Are you all right? Was I too rough?" Tyra forced the words from her burning chest.

Bjorn's chest rumbled as he choked out a laugh. "I was going to ask you that."

"Not too rough. Just right."

They lay in silence as their skin cooled and

breathing slowed. After their hearts ceased racing, Bjorn pressed Tyra up so that they gazed at one another.

"Ty, I want you to understand it's never been like that with anyone else. I've never made love to a woman other than you. And I've never lost control like that either. I feared I'd hurt you, but my body couldn't stop."

"You didn't hurt me, and I wanted it just like that. But what do you mean you've never made love? Bjorn, I know you've been with more women than you could possibly keep track of."

"That's not true. There were not that many. I just made the mistake of going back to the same ones. And I coupled with them. I didn't make love to them. How could I when it was you who consumed every corner of my mind, your name I called out?"

"You never had tender feelings for any of them? You never considered marrying any of them."

"No. I never had what you did with Knud." Bjorn tried to keep the jealousy from his voice, but he suspected he failed.

Tyra pushed herself onto her elbow. "I was fond of Knud, but I liked the escape from my family he offered even more. You found out how things ended, how they were between him and me. I didn't make love to him or anyone else. There was only you, my first time. Then not again until the woods."

"It is amazing how feelings change something that people have done since time began. The actions are the same, but they mean so much more when it's with someone you love and desire above all else."

Tyra pushed the hair from his forehead and neck, the tenderness returning after the animalistic feelings moment ago.

"It is. I don't know if other couples in love experience this as we do. I suspect so from Freya, Lorna, and Lena, but I know it's unlike anything else for me. I wouldn't want it to be like this with anyone else."

"I love you, Tyra. I have since we were children, and I will until we meet again in Valhalla. I won't let you go in this lifetime or the next."

They filled their kiss with the devotion born of a lifetime, of being in love and of gratitude they finally shared. They drifted to sleep entangled in one another's arms and the comfort of a bed.

TWENTY-ONE

Their departure the next morning was tense. It was clear Erik and Freya had argued, but everyone said their thank you's and goodbyes to their Highland partners. As they sailed away with Bjorn and Tyra leading the fleet, it was difficult to watch the scene play out between Strian and Freya. There was open hostility between the two of them. Strian glared at Freya, and she returned his looks with smug ones of her own.

Over the course of their journey back home, the tension eased but never disappeared. Tyra kept a close eye on Strian, and her heart hurt as she watched the distance grow between him and Gressa. She worried at times that she might be the cause, but she found it much easier to blame the woman's unexpected reappearance in their lives. There was not the open hostility between Strian and Gressa like there had been when he first captured her, but there was a distance there that had not been present right before they left Castle Varrich.

They did not face any squalls like they had on the way to Scotland, but the seas were rough and gave them no help. Despite all of Tyra's skills and knowledge, there was no way for them to catch up with Grímr's fleet. They caught glimpses of him, but the waves were against them, as though the gods seemed to laugh and make merry at their expense.

"So much for me being the daughter of the sea. We've barely moved at all today." Tyra's pursed lips showed Bjorn her disgust and frustration.

"There is naught to do but have the oarsmen keep going. The wind will shift at some point, and we know where Grímr is headed."

"But he might get there before us."

"There are still more warriors at home than what he set off with. You witnessed how many of his boats we captured or sank. His fleet is limping along."

"The same as we are."

"We're not limping. We're hobbled by the weather."

"Same difference." Tyra tapped his chest, appreciating his reassurance. She returned to the tiller and took it back from her former first mate.

True to his word, Bjorn started the voyage back on Tyra's ship. But the rough seas required him to return to his own boat. His first mate, who he promoted to captain, was an apt and capable sailor, but he had not been at the helm often enough during storms. He did not possess the skills needed to overcome the weather.

"Stay on your boat!" Tyra called to Bjorn as the water washed over the rails. She looked at the other ships and breathed a sigh of relief that the others were leashed to their rails and masts. She had prayed to the gods repeatedly for days, wishing the weather would change and push them toward home. Now she got her wish, and she prayed once more, this time that no one washed away. The swells and troughs slammed their boats like wooden toys. She listened for cracking wood, the sign that a ship would flounder, but nothing carried on the wind because of the noise from the waves.

"Ty, we have to lower our sails, or we will capsize." Freya screamed against the wind.

Tyra shook her head. She was certain they should keep them up a little longer. They needed the tailwind to push them through the waves, or they really would be at the mercy of the sea gods.

"Not yet! Keep them raised. If your boats pitch too much, lower them halfway, but you need them!" Tyra thought Freya must have heard her because her friend sat by her tiller, and no one moved on her deck.

Strian was too far from her ship for him to possibly catch what she said, but she saw Freya signaling him. No matter their differences, they were family and a team. They put aside their differences long enough to stay alive. Even if it was only to argue later. The waves settled hours later, but they had made headway at last. Tyra watched the waves and listened to the whistles and cheers as others spotted pods of dolphins. She breathed easier.

Bjorn remained on his ship for the rest of the journey, but he often pulled alongside Tyra so they could speak. There was no privacy, so talk of navigation and Loki's games with nature dominated their conversations. The trickster god must have been responsible for their frustration. Without a true storm, there was nothing to justify the stronger-than-usual waves. Crossing the North Sea was never easy, but the swells and troughs were far greater than they should have been. It raised the hairs on the back of their necks, knowing the treachery and capriciousness of the gods. Tyra gave up trying to sleep in her bunk as the rise and fall of the hull rolled her around the bed and rattled her teeth. She preferred to stay above deck, where the other ships were visible, and monitor their course.

They had a calm morning midway through their voyage, and the oarsmen on all the ships made steady progress. Tyra stood at the rail speaking to Freya, who maneuvered her ship alongside Tyra's port side.

"Even with this calm weather, we won't catch up to them. We haven't spotted them in days," Tyra mused.

"The weather hasn't blown us off-course, but I doubt any of his captains are as good as you. Do you think he floated further adrift? Have we passed him and don't know it?"

"That's possible, but I doubt it."

"Do you think any of his boats floundered?"

"That's more likely with the waves. We almost lost several of ours." Tyra looked beyond Freya's shoulder, making her friend look back as well. Tyra dropped her voice. "Rangvald's captains are not very good. It's surprising any of his ships survive the tides. They don't steer their boats into the swells, and that forces them to drop into the troughs. They all seem to be racing each other to nowhere. They know not to pass me, and they are still well behind most of our boats."

Freya looked over her shoulder again, watching her husband speak with her first mate. "I know. I've spoken to Erik about it more than once. He's shocked just like we are. His father lost several of his captains in the battles with Hakin and Grímr. He had to replace them with sailors with less experience.

How they haven't crashed into one another is a matter for the gods. I wondered if it was the storm on the way here, but they're not any better in calmer waters. Erik told me his father has been so livid that he refuses to look for fear he will lose his temper and throw his axe at someone. Lorna took more than one to task before we left Scotland. They don't seem to have learned."

The two women continued talking until Freya's barrel man, Freund, who was only a boy of about eleven, called out from the crow's nest.

"Seagulls! I see seagulls!"

Tyra left Freya at the rail and ran to the bow of her boat. She climbed onto the dragonhead and held on with one arm. She shaded her eyes as the rocky coastline came into view and scanned the area to get her bearings. She recognized many of the scattered rocks that jutted from the sea.

"We are another day's sailing from home," she called out. Her crew raised a cheer as word traveled from ship to ship until the entire fleet was calling out and stomping their feet.

Their final day at sea offered them neither wind nor choppy water. The oarsmen battled the waves, but Ivar's homestead came into view. The alarm for approaching ships rang, but they arrived to a warm welcome. Ivar and Lena waited for them on the docks, and Lena did not wait for Freya to come to her. She dashed down the dock as Ivar laughed, but he was close on her heels. She pulled Freya into a tight embrace as she thanked the gods she had both of her children home again. Leif guided Sigrid through the crowd as she hugged her full and round belly. Tyra greeted them and held out a tentative hand. When Sigrid nodded, Tyra placed it on Sigrid's belly. A kick made her jerk her hand back. At Sigrid's laugh, she tried placing her hand there again. This time she was more prepared for the movement.

Bjorn followed Tyra onto the dock but came to a dead stop as he watched her with Sigrid. The awe was clear on her face, and he recognized envy though others would not notice. He approached his cousin and his wife. Before he said anything, Sigrid looked up.

"About damn time."

"Sigrid, they just arrived. Bjorn came straight over here," Leif chastised.

Sigrid shot him a look like he was simple. "No. They are together."

"What?" Leif looked between his cousin and close friend. "You are?"

"Yes." Bjorn wrapped his arms around Tyra's middle. He placed one hand on her belly but covered it with his other arm. The possessive hold did not go unnoticed by Sigrid, but Leif was too stunned to catch it.

"Then my wife is right. About damn time."

Tyra laughed as she twisted to look back at Bjorn. "I'd say that's fair," she laughed.

"Better late than never," Bjorn responded.

Sigrid clapped. "I wasn't sure how much longer I could wait. I was so frustrated with you both."

"So, you knew," Tyra grinned.

"Of course, I did. I've known since I was five-and-ten. That was the first time I had a vision of you two together."

Tyra blushed to her roots. She and Sigrid were close in same age.

"Just what were you shown?" Tyra was not sure she wanted to find out the answer once the question left her mouth, or at least not in front of anyone else. It was Sigrid's turn to blush. That was enough for both of them. Sigrid changed the subject.

"How was the rest of the voyage? I only had short visions here and there. It was not enough for me to tell if things were in your favor."

"Much happened. It would be easier to explain when we are all together in the longhouse," Bjorn interjected. He looked around for Ivar and Lena. When he caught sight them, he squeezed Tyra's waist and nodded in the older couple's direction. "I would speak to them right now."

Tyra's brilliant smile blinded him. She pulled away, but when she reached back for his hand, she just about pulled it loose from his shoulder. It was his turn to smile, pleased at her impatience.

"Jarl Ivar?" Tyra called out.

Ivar and Lena waved and directed speculative looks at the couple.

"About damn time," Ivar muttered.

"Ivar, leave them alone."

"It's all right, *Frú*. Sigrid said the same thing," Tyra assured them.

"Wise woman my son married," Ivar grinned. "I expect there is something you would like to speak to us about."

"There is, Uncle," Bjorn chimed in. "We'd like to marry before the sunsets tomorrow."

Tyra shook her head, and Bjorn's smile faded. "Today," she replied. "I don't want to wait beyond today."

"That is a surprise, Tyra. We were sure Bjorn might have had to chase you to the altar." Ivar teased.

"No, but I will drag him if he is a minute late," Tyra responded.

Lena stepped forward and pulled Tyra into her embrace. Tyra returned it without hesitation, sinking into the comfort the woman had provided since the day of her parents' funeral. Lena stroked her hair and kissed her forehead, much as a mother would.

"I'm overjoyed to have you in my arms again. I worry about you just as I do Leif and Freya. I prayed every day for your safe return and that you would recognize you and Bjorn belong together. But, love, it'll be dark in a few hours. There is much to do before a wedding."

Tyra tried to shake her head, but Lena shushed her. "Please trust me on this. It would be better if you waited until we can all see and aren't rushed." There was a note to Lena's voice that made Tyra relent.

"Very well, but before midday tomorrow. That is as much as I will concede."

Ivar and Lena chuckled as Bjorn crowed. "Who am I to deny her? She might cut off my cock and hand it to me."

Ivar and Lena looked at him in shock.

"There is a story behind that." Bjorn chuckled.

Lena looked at Tyra, who had the good grace to blush.

"I'm sure there is. I look forward to hearing it," boomed Ivar, who called to the others to join him for a feast.

They spent the remainder of the night telling the tale of their mission. They took turns recounting the events, and Ivar's temper simmered until the end, when they warned Grímr was once more on his way. Ivar's grip on the handle of his mug snapped it from the mug. He looked down at his hand, surprised and unaware of how he had been squeezing.

"The bastard wants revenge for the death of his bastard sons? Let him come. Let him discover how long he lasts when he doesn't have his brother or hired thugs to hide behind."

"Father, he still has the men who sailed back with him. There were at least ten ships that survived our attack and escaped." Freya pointed out. Ivar's stare had Freya retreating into her chair back. She nodded before looking at her plate.

"Ivar," Lena's voice softened Ivar's rigid posture. Ivar rolled his neck, the cracking sound ringing around the table.

"We are ready for him when he comes." Ivar's voice was even and controlled.

The meal continued as Ivar and Lena along with Leif and Sigrid told them what happened while they were away. Their story was much shorter.

Bjorn and Tyra retired to his chamber. As Tyra undressed, she looked around the chamber, realizing for the first time that she was in her new home. Bjorn stepped behind her, placing his hands on her shoulders and pulling her back against his chest.

"What are you thinking about?" Bjorn asked.

"Realizing this is now my home. Relishing the fact that I never have to live with my aunt and uncle again."

"This will be your home for as long as you want. If you want us to have a longhouse of our own, then I will look into to it."

Tyra leaned back and rested her head on his shoulder, her eyes drifting closed. "Maybe when this is over, and we no longer have to worry about Grímr killing us in our sleep." Tyra sighed as Bjorn massaged her shoulders. "By that time, though, we might want that farm. Is there any sense to having a longhouse built if we don't intend to live there that long?"

"Perhaps I should ask Ivar for that land sooner rather than later."

Tyra dropped her head as he continued to rub the knots from her neck. "Are you serious about becoming a farmer? You've never known that life. You've lived here, in the settlement, and as a warrior." Her muffled words floated from her bent head.

"That's not true. My earliest memories are of my parents' farm. I remember the animals and the smell of freshly tilled land. I remember my mother sneaking me pieces of warm baked bread before my father came home. I'd like our children to have those memories." Bjorn's arms once more wrapped around Tyra, but this time, both hands rested on her belly.

"And if it's a few years before we make those memories?"

Bjorn caught the uncertainty in her voice. "By the time we finish this sick game of Grímr's, it will be deep into winter, then it'll be raiding season. It'll be a year before we can consider building a home or starting a farm. We'll discover what the gods have in store for us then." Bjorn turned Tyra to face him. "If we have one child, ten, or none, that will never change how much I love you."

"You have developed a knack for saying the right thing."

Bjorn's grin was lopsided and boyish. "I've always had that. You just didn't accept I was right. Rather, you refused to admit it."

Tyra spanked his backside before dashing to the bed. Bjorn caught her, and they crashed onto the mattress laughing. But the laughter soon faded to moans of pleasure as they passed the time before their wedding.

Tyra lifted the embroidered gown from her trunk. She had planned to visit her aunt and uncle's home for the last time that morning to retrieve her few belongings, including her mother's wedding gown. When she told Bjorn where she intended to go, he swore and forbid her to go. She grew angry at the idea he would not allow her to go where she wanted, but he bellowed at her that he would end up killing the last of her family on their wedding day because he would be damned if he allowed anyone to mistreat her or be unkind.

When Tyra realized it was his clumsy way of protecting her, she relented and agreed to him arranging for someone to move her things to their chamber. Now, she kneeled before the chest and looked at the few items she had tucked away from the time when she lived with her parents. She had not dared keep them out at her aunt and uncle's home for fear of being ridiculed, or worse, having them stolen. She laid the dress out on the bed to let it air and prepared to meet the other women at the bathhouse.

Tyra spent most of the morning soaking and talking to her friends and soon-to-be family. She had been unconscious when Sigrid prepared for her wedding to Leif, and Freya refused to wait for the rituals. Tyra wondered why it was so important to Lena that Tyra and Bjorn obey the customs but allowed her own daughter to forego them.

"Bjorn, come here." Ivar called his nephew over who stood with Leif, Erik, and Strian. They were outside, waiting their turn for the bathhouse. The women had been in there for what seemed like forever. "You need the sword."

Bjorn froze as he looked at Ivar. He shook his head and stepped back. He had forgotten about the tradition, and now he looked around in desperation. The memories of his parents' death flooded him. He had been awaiting a glimpse of his bride, and now he wanted to run into the hills.

"Bjorn. Bjorn, are you listening?" Ivar and Rangvald walked over to him. Ivar studied his face and pulled him in for an embrace that was more like a bear strangling him. "Bjorn, your father knew you would need the sword one day. He planned for it already. It's waiting for you."

Bjorn tried to swallow the lump in his throat as he nodded, trying to understand what Ivar was telling him.

"Bjorn, even if he hadn't had the chance, I would have planned for it when I put Leif's sword in the catacombs. You are as much my son now as Leif. Lena and I considered you ours the moment you came to live with us. I will never replace Jan, but I hope you know I love you as much as I do Leif and Freya."

Bjorn only nodded as he returned Ivar's embrace. He once more tried to swallow the lump in his throat, pushing it down to sit heavily in his chest.

"You have been excellent parents to me. I have benefited from your love and generosity. Sometimes it's hard to remember their faces, but it's yours and Aunt Lena's that fill the void. Thank you, Uncle."

Ivar led Bjorn and the others to the catacombs where they buried their elderly and ill. Bjorn grimaced, imagining having to dig through them to find where his father had buried his sword. He glared at Leif, who was ready to tease him in retribution for Bjorn's comments when it was Leif's turn for the same trial.

"I've just returned from battling a madman. I'd say let's agree I'm not a boy and have been a man in my own right for years?"

"No," Rangvald, Ivar, Leif, and Erik bellowed. Only Strian remained quiet. He shrugged and looked at the other men.

"Get it over with, so we can all bathe and prepare for the wedding. The sooner you're wed, the sooner we can eat." Strian reasoned.

"You've always thought with your stomach."

"Among other things."

Bjorn paused to look at Strian.

"I shall remind you of that soon enough." Bjorn began the climb along the uneven face of the tombs. He called over his shoulder. "Any hints to which one it might be in?"

"I'm not sure I remember," Ivar taunted.

"You'd better hope I'm never left to decide which tomb you get," Bjorn grumbled as he pulled away the first stone. The stench made him wobble. He peered inside and grimaced before reaching his hand in. It snagged on a bone, and he yelped but tried to swallow it as a grunt. He failed, and his friends and relatives chortled down below.

"I'm sure it's not that one," Ivar called up.

"Now you tell me," Bjorn muttered.

Bjorn searched through three more tombs before his hand landed on the hilt of a sword. He pulled it free but was unprepared for the wave of emotion that swept over him as he looked upon his father's sword for the first time in a score of years. He landed heavily on the rock next to him as he sat with the sword across his lap. He used his sleeve to wipe the dust and dirt from it.

The weapon had seemed monstrous to him as a child when he was only strong enough to lift the hilt. Now it was like his own sword that he had wielded for years. He laid his father's sword aside as he drew his own. He placed them both on his lap. When he had his sword forged, he had instructed the black-smith to make it as similar to his father's as they both remembered.

Looking at them side by side, they were mirror images. The only differences were the nicks and scratches on the blades. They told different stories from battles long ago and all too recently. Bjorn ran his hand over his sword a final time and kissed the hilt before he placed his sword in the tomb and re-turned the rock. He slid his father's sword into his sheath and climbed back down.

"Thank you." Bjorn looked at the place where his father had buried the final reminder of his life with his parents.

Tyra was impatient. She was dressed and growing rapidly annoyed as Sigrid and Lena finished her hair. She wanted to be on her way to the altar, but she did not dare be rude to her new family members.

"We had better finish, Sigrid, before she runs away," Lena teased.

"The men should be ready now. They left the longhouse a moment ago," Lorna shared.

"They just left? Weren't they ready for ages? Didn't they go to the bathhouse before us?" Tyra wondered.

"No, they visited the catacombs," Freya supplied.

Tyra spun on the stool upon which she sat.

"What? Why would Ivar do that to him? Why would he make him remember he doesn't have a father here today?" Tyra snapped her mouth shut as she looked up at Lena. "I'm so sorry. That was horribly unkind. You and Jarl Ivar have been wonderful to Bjorn. I shouldn't have said that."

"Tyra, Ivar took Bjorn there for the same reason we have been keeping you here. Bjorn's father had already accepted he was dying when he arrived back at the homestead. He buried his sword for Bjorn before he returned to his longhouse. It's been waiting for Bjorn all this time."

Lena stepped to a side table and picked up a dagger. Tyra gasped and shook her head as Lena walked back to her. Tyra covered her mouth with one hand as she shook her other. She was not prepared for Lena to hand her the dagger her father had always carried. It was the same one her mother had given to her father on their wedding day. She wiped her eyes and reached for the knife. She turned it over and over as she remembered the lessons her father taught her with this knife. She assumed it had gone to Valhalla with him.

"They knew to save it. After your mother died, your father brought this to me for safekeeping in case he did not return." Lena reached into the pouch tied as her waist and pulled out two rings. She blinked away her own tears before smiling at Tyra. "Leif and Sigrid wear Ivar's parents' rings. Erik and Freya received Rangvald's. These were my parents' rings. I would like you and Bjorn to have them."

Lena stunned Tyra. She looked between the rings and the dagger, then back again. The knife had been more than she expected, but the rings were more than she could ever have imagined.

"Do you not want to save them for your grandchildren?"

"Perhaps they will one day go to them. Tyra, you and Bjorn are as much my children as Leif and Freya. I regret not bringing you into our home like we did Bjorn. At the time, it seemed best for you to remain with your blood family. Once Ivar and I realized how wrong we were, you were involved with Knud. When that soured, we wanted to invite you to move in, but you raided so often, it seemed useless after waiting so long. My heart is overflowing now that you'll finally make your home in this longhouse, short as that may be."

Tyra leaped to her feet and looked at Sigrid in fear.

"Nothing is happening to you or Bjorn," Lena assured her. "I suspect you will want a farm one day when you both decide raiding is less important than having a family." Lena pulled Tyra into a tight embrace. "I'd say it's time we get you married."

Tyra joined hands with Bjorn before the priestess and the altar. They exchanged their vows as their entire tribe watched. Many were in disbelief that the couple was marrying at last, while others did not understand why it took so long. Bjorn presented Tyra with his father's sword, which she was charged to protect until their son was ready to carry it. Tyra handed her father's dagger to Bjorn.

"Vigo's," he murmured and looked into Tyra's bright eyes. He forgot the exchange of rings as he swam in the hazel pools he had loved since he was seven. It was not until Tyra held them up that he remembered what came next.

"Jan's," Tyra whispered as she handed the sword to Freya then reached out her hand as Bjorn slid the rings from the dagger's hilt and slid one over each of Tyra's fingers before settling it on her third finger. Tyra repeated the ritual until the ring rested on Bjorn's finger. Neither waited for the final blessing. They pulled one another into an embrace, and their lips melded together.

Tyra was sure her soul left her body and floated above them, watching as she and Bjorn sealed their marriage. She was convinced she only returned when the priestess pressed the bowl of goat's blood into their hands. Neither Bjorn nor Tyra had noticed the goat being sacrificed.

The feasting carried on well into the early morning, but Bjorn was only patient enough to sit through one round of toasts before he ordered a thrall to follow him with a tray of food and several pitchers of mead. He swept Tyra into his arms, and ignoring the hoots and calls, he carried his bride to their chamber. Once the thrall left, Bjorn locked and barred the door. He even carried a table to place in front of it.

"You are mine for at least the next sennight," he pulled her into his arms.

"Do you have somewhere else to be? I had planned for a fortnight."

Bjorn nipped at her neck as his hands gathered the material of her gown. He groaned as he found the satiny skin of her thighs and bottom. He let go, careful with the gown, aware it was Tyra's mothers. He eased the gown from her body and draped it over a chair. He looked at Tyra's naked body and was certain he was the luckiest man alive. His wife was beyond beautiful, but she was also intelligent and brave, loyal to a fault, and the only woman for him.

Tyra was not as careful about undressing Bjorn as he had been with her. She yanked his clothes and strew them across the floor. Bjorn lifted her into his arms and carried her to the bed.

"Wife, I intend to make you weep with pleasure."

"Husband, I shall hold you to that."

"I can think of something I'd like you to hold."

"And I can think of something else that will weep."

"Could you be referring to my cock?"

"I don't plan to make you cry, though the ecstasy I bring you may move you to tears."

"I don't doubt that."

Bjorn followed Tyra onto the bed and sank into her as she dug her fingers into his back. They made love throughout the night, dropping off to sleep as sunlight drifted through their window. They slept late into the morning, then woke to make love and talk throughout the rest of the day. They opened the door once a day to receive a loaded platter of food until a sennight night passed. Neither was ready to leave their love nest, but neither missed the fact no one had alerted them to what was happening with Grímr. They had duties they no longer dared to ignore, so they returned to the land of the living in time to continue preparing for their next round with Grímr.

EPILOGUE

"**B**jorn," Tyra groaned.

"Bjorn!" This time it was a scream. "Bjorn!"

The door crashed open as Bjorn charged into their longhouse. He caught Tyra as she doubled over in pain.

"Where is that woman? She was not to leave you alone," he growled as he eased Tyra into a chair, but she would not let go when Bjorn tried to stand up.

"No! You can't go. I need you."

"I have to fetch the midwife. You weren't supposed to be by yourself," Bjorn repeated.

"Bjorn, stop. She needs the rest as much as I do. Strian practically carried her away. You know she's had a hard time with this one."

"And you're overdue. Someone's supposed to be with you at all times, so I could fetch the midwife without worry." Bjorn pulled away despite Tyra clutching to him. He opened the door to their longhouse and looked to the fields. He spotted the boys who helped him on their farm.

"Sven, Harold! Fetch the midwife!" He watched as the boys dropped their tools and hurtled over the fence, running back to the homestead.

"Bjorn," Tyra moaned. He rushed back to her side. "Hold me. This hurts far worse than that axe wound ever did, and that nearly killed me."

Bjorn's face drained of all color as he looked down at his stalwart wife. "Don't say that. Don't remind me and don't scare me," he choked as he lifted her into his lap.

"It hurts, Bjorn. Far worse than I imagined. I believed Sigrid when she told me since it was her second babe and definitely Freya since it was her first. I was there for them both a fortnight ago, but I know now that I could not understand until experiencing it for myself."

She opened her mouth to say more, but pain ripped through her, and Bjorn felt her belly tighten. He ran his hand over her back and tried to comfort her.

"Should I move you to our bed?"

Tyra nodded and clung to him as he carried her to their chamber. He struggled but managed to pull back the bedcover. He laid Tyra down but once more she reached for him.

"Don't go," she struggled to speak around the pain.

"I'm not. I'm not going anywhere until our babe is resting in your arms."

"You'll stay through it all? You won't let the midwife chase you away?"

"The old bat learned her lesson with Leif and Erik. She'll never try to tell any of the men in this family to leave their wives while they deliver. I was sure Leif scared years off the woman's life, but I heard Erik from down the hall."

Tyra laid back against the pillows, enjoying a brief reprieve.

"And I was so sure you would be the worst of

them all." They both looked over as Lena walked in. She spotted them and came to the chamber.

"Where's the midwife? Why isn't she here? What's taking her so long? If you're here, doesn't she realize my wife is in labor?" Bjorn rattled off question after question as he kept looking around Lena's shoulder.

"You *are* going to be worse," Tyra choked the words out before another spasm contracted her belly. She moaned and squeezed her eyes shut. "Bjorn," she whimpered, her eyes still squeezed shut.

He looked to his aunt, pleading for help. Lena smiled and pointed to his side of the bed. "Ty, let go long enough for me to go to my side of the bed."

His wife shook her head, her grip proving she had lost none of her strength despite being away from the training field for months. Bjorn looked back at Lena again. She raised her eyebrows but came to stand next to him. Bjorn kicked off his boots, then carefully climbed over his wife to his side of the bed.

"Tyra, we need to count how far apart your contractions are," Lena stroked the hair away from Tyra's perspiring brow.

"Too close," Tyra cried as another wave of pain made her curl around her belly.

"Will you let me check?" Lena asked as she continued to stroke Tyra's hair. Bjorn noticed it calmed Tyra more than squeezing his hand in her vice-like grip. She made a sound that seemed like consent. Lena moved to the end of the bed and pushed back Tyra's gown to examine her. When she finished, she walked back to stand beside Tyra's head.

"It won't be long. We need to get you out of that gown. Bjorn, help me." The last was not a request but a softly spoken order. Bjorn helped Tyra sit forward as he and Lena worked the gown over her head, leaving her in just a shift. She had taken to wearing gowns when none of her leather pants would fit. Bjorn teased that he preferred the gowns because they were far more convenient when he came home for the midday meal. Rarely did they have time for him to eat, preferring to find interesting and creative ways to make love throughout their home. As Tyra's time drew closer and she grew more awkward, she grew shy about Bjorn seeing her. He put her fears to when she realized he craved making love to her just as much, if not more, now that she was pregnant.

"Bjorn!" She squeezed her hand as tears began to flow down her cheeks. "I need to push. The midwife isn't here, and I need to push. I'm scared."

Bjorn's heart twisted to witness his wife in pain and confessing to it. She was in agony if she admitted it. She never complained of the pain while she recovered from the axe wound or any of the smaller injuries she had suffered.

"It's all right to push. You're ready. Your pains must have started much earlier today." Lena moved to stand at the foot of the bed.

Bjorn looked at Tyra as Lena's words registered with him. "You were in pain, and you didn't tell me?" It was not an accusation, but a question riddled with guilt.

"What could you have done? You have fields to tend. The boys need you to tell them what to do. You know they're lost without your instructions."

Tyra groaned and bore down as her belly contracted yet again.

"I could've gone for help sooner. I could've made sure you were not alone."

Tyra opened her eyes long enough to glimpse Bjorn's tortured expression. She waved him closer and gave him a gentle kiss. "You're the best husband I could ever hope for. You take better care of me than I deserve most of the time. I was uncomfortable all day, but the pain only started just before I called for you. I was alone for maybe ten minutes."

She kissed him again but drew away when her body demanded she push again. They repeated the pattern of Tyra pushing and then resting against Bjorn, who cradled her against his chest. Tyra's pains seemed to go on forever, but their son was born less than two hours after Tyra began to labor.

"For a first child, that was quick." Lena cleaned their babe before handing him to Tyra.

"Quick? That was a lifetime." Bjorn was incredulous that Lena said such a thing.

"It really wasn't *that* long, Bjorn."

Bjorn looked down at his wife as though she had lost her mind, but he watched as their babe nursed, his tiny fist resting against Tyra's bare breast. He reached out and ran his finger over the hand. It opened, and Bjorn placed his finger within his son's grasp. The fist tightened around it, and Bjorn was mesmerized.

"What shall we name him," his voice hushed so he would not disturb their newborn.

"Jan. Jan Bjornson," Tyra brushed her lips against the downy head of blond curls.

"Are you sure?" Bjorn was in awe of his wife's strength and bravery. Now she wanted to name their child after his father.

"I've been considering it for a while. It's just right, now that the three of us are together."

Bjorn looked up as Lena brought a clean nightgown to Tyra. He had not noticed her moving about, cleaning the bedding, or bathing Tyra. He was in a world comprised only him, his wife, and Jan.

"Thank you." Bjorn kissed Tyra's temple before giving his son his first kiss.

Lena slipped from the longhouse without either

parent noticing. They were too busy cooing over the evidence that the gods and fate had planned for them to be together all along.

———

Discover Strian and Gressa's second chance at love, if a secret doesn't tear them apart first in *Strian*.

THANK YOU FOR READING TYRA & BJORN

Celeste Barclay, a nom de plume, lives near the Southern California coast with her husband and sons. Growing up in the Midwest, Celeste enjoyed spending as much time in and on the water as she could. Now she lives near the beach. She's an avid swimmer, a hopeful future surfer, and a former rower. When she's not writing, she's working or being a mom.

Visit Celeste's website, www.celestebarclay.com, for regular updates on works in progress, new releases, and her blog where she features posts about her experiences as an author and recommendations of her favorite reads.

Are you an author who would like to guest blog or be featured in her recommendations? Visit her website for an opportunity to share your insights and experiences.

Have you read *The Highland Ladies Guide?* Learn all the behind the scenes details from my flagship series! This FREE book is available to all new subscribers to Celeste's monthly newsletter. Subscribe on her website.

<u>Get Celeste's freebie</u>

Join the fun and get exclusive insider giveaways, sneak peeks, and new release announcements in

<u>Celeste Barclay's Facebook Ladies of Yore Group</u>

Leif **BOOK 1 SNEAK PEEK**

Leif looked around his chambers within his father's longhouse and breathed a sigh of relief. He noticed the large fur rugs spread throughout the chamber. His two favorites placed strategically before the fire and the bedside he preferred. He looked at his shield that hung on the wall near the door in a symbolic position but waiting at the ready. The chests that held his clothes and some of his finer acquisitions from voyages near and far sat beside his bed and along the far wall. And in the center was his most favorite possession. His oversized bed was one of the few that could accommodate his long and broad frame. He shook his head at his longing to climb under the pile of furs and on the stuffed mattress that beckoned him. He took in the chair placed before the fire where he longed to sit now with a cup of warm mead. It had been two months since he slept in his own bed, and he looked forward to nothing more than pulling the furs over his head and sleeping until he could no longer ignore his hunger. Alas, he would not be crawling into his bed again for several more hours. A feast awaited him to celebrate his and his crew's return from their latest expedition to explore the isle of Britannia. He bathed and wore fresh clothes, so he had no excuse for lingering other than a bone weariness that set in during the last storm at sea. He was eager to spend time at home no matter how much he loved sailing. Their last expedition had been profitable with several raids of monasteries that yielded jewels and both silver and gold, but he was ready for respite.

Leif left his chambers and knocked on the door next to his. He heard movement on the other side, but it was only moments before his sister, Freya, opened her door. She, too, looked tired but clean. A few pieces of jewelry she confiscated from the holy houses that allegedly swore to a life of poverty and deprivation adorned her trim frame.

"That armband suits you well. It compliments your muscles," Leif smirked and dodged a strike from one of those muscular arms.

Only a year younger than he, his sister was a well-known and feared shield maiden. Her lithe form was strong and agile making her a ferocious and competent opponent to any man. Freya's beauty was stunning, but Leif had taken every opportunity since they were children to tease her about her unusual strength even among the female warriors.

"At least one of us inherited our father's prowess. Such a shame it wasn't you."

Freya

Tyra & Bjorn

Strian

Lena & Ivar

THE HIGHLAND LADIES

A Spinster at the Highland Court

BOOK 1 SNEAK PEEK

Elizabeth Fraser looked around the royal chapel within Stirling Castle. The ornate candlestick holders on the altar glistened and reflected the light from the ones in the wall sconces as the priest intoned the holy prayers of the Advent season. Elizabeth kept her head bowed as though in prayer, but her green eyes swept the congregation. She watched the other ladies-in-waiting, many of whom were doing the same thing. She caught the eye of Allyson Elliott. Elizabeth raised one eyebrow as Allyson's lips twitched. Both women had been there enough times to accept they'd be kneeling for at least the next hour as the Latin service carried on. Elizabeth understood the Mass thanks to her cousin Deirdre Fraser, or rather now Deirdre Sinclair. Elizabeth's mind flashed to the recent struggle her cousin faced as she reunited with her husband Magnus after a seven-year separation. Her aunt and uncle's choice to keep Deirdre hidden from her husband simply because they didn't think the Sinclairs were an advantageous enough match, and the resulting scandal, still humiliated the other Fraser clan members at court. She admired Deirdre's husband Magnus's pledge to remain faithful despite not knowing if he'd ever see Deirdre again.

Elizabeth suddenly snapped her attention; while everyone else intoned the twelfth—or was it thirteenth—amen of the Mass, the hairs on the back of her neck stood up. She had the strongest feeling that someone was watching her. Her eyes scanned to her right, where her parents sat further down the pew. Her mother and father had their heads bowed and eyes closed. While she was convinced her mother was in devout prayer, she wondered if her father had fallen asleep during the Mass. Again. With nothing seeming out of the ordinary and no one visibly paying attention to her, her eyes swung to the left. She took in the king and queen as they kneeled together at their prie-dieu. The queen's lips moved as she recited the liturgy in silence. The king was as still as a statue. Years of leading warriors showed, both in his stature and his ability to control his body into absolute stillness. Elizabeth peered past the royal couple and found herself looking into the astute hazel eyes of Edward Bruce, Lord of Badenoch and Lochaber. His gaze gave her the sense that he peered into her thoughts, as though he were assessing her. She tried to keep her face neutral as heat surged up her neck. She prayed her face didn't redden as much as her neck must have, but at a twenty-one, she still hadn't mastered how to control her blushing. Her nape burned like it was on fire. She canted her head slightly before looking up at the crucifix hanging over the altar. She closed her eyes and tried to invoke the image of the Lord that usually centered her when her mind wandered during Mass.

Elizabeth sensed Edward's gaze remained on her. She didn't understand how she was so sure that he was looking at her. She didn't have any special gifts of perception or sight, but her intuition screamed that he was still looking.

A Spy at the Highland Court

A Wallflower at the Highland Court

A Rogue at the Highland Court

A Rake at the Highland Court

An Enemy at the Highland Court

A Saint at the Highland Court

A Beauty at the Highland Court

THE HIGHLAND LADIES ALWAYS

A Sinner at the Highland Court

BOOK 1 SNEAK PEEK

I hate him. I hate him. I hate him. How can he do this to me? How could he pick her over me? That fat sow. Kieran will regret this till the day he dies. He and she both. This is her fault. All her fault. I hate her too.

Madeline MacLeod felt the four walls of her tiny convent cell closing in upon her. Her brother, Kieran, had dragged her from Robert the Bruce's royal court at Stirling Castle and dumped her at Inchcailleoch Priory earlier that week. She refused to accept that any of her words or actions had caused her fall from grace. She'd only spoken the truth each time she told Maude Sutherland how unconventionally curvaceous she was. Why her brother wanted to marry a woman who looked more like a tavern wench than a lady was beyond Madeline.

He just wants a good rut. He'll realize what a dreadful mistake he's made when he takes her home to Stornoway. He will realize that tupping her won't be worth the humiliation of having such a plain-faced, round as a barrel, heifer for a wife. He could have had Laurel Ross!

As Madeline listened to the bells toll for yet another Mass, she grimaced. All she seemed to do was pray these days, but God certainly wasn't listening because she remained at the priory despite her fervent appeals. She kneeled among the other novices, postulants, and nuns eight times throughout the day and night as they followed the Liturgy of Hours. The bells in the background signaled Prime, so she knew it was still very early. She'd already attended Matins in the middle of the night and Lauds at sunrise.

Madeline glanced out the narrow window set high in the wall, thinking that the masons must have designed it so the women couldn't escape. The sunlight, weak and dismal, matched Madeline's mood. When she lived at court, six o'clock in the morning was an hour she'd never seen. Now that she lived at the convent, she'd already been awake for an hour and a half.

Madeline dragged herself from her cot and her introspection. She could feel her anger simmering below the surface, and if she wanted to avoid another outburst—which would result in two days of wearing a hair shirt for penance — she would do well to calm herself. She splashed freezing water from the washbasin onto her face. It was refreshing, but it only reminded her of the austerity she now faced daily. Already dressed in her postulant's dark gray gown, she'd tucked her roughly shorn hair beneath her wimple, and a large wooden cross hung around her neck. The undyed wool of the dress made her skin itch, and it chafed the open cuts upon her back. But it was far better than the hair shirt they forced her to wear the third day she arrived. She'd lashed out at another postulant who bumped into her as they entered their pew. The postulant was formerly a lesser noble, and Madeline reminded her that she, Madeline, was the sister of a laird and a former lady-in-waiting to Queen Elizabeth de Burgh. Madeline's voice carried, but the other woman was more discreet in her own set-down, as she pointed out that Madeline's brother was the one to banish her from court.

A Hellion at the Highland Court

An Angel at the Highland Court

A Harlot at the Highland Court

A Friend at the Highland Court

An Outsider at the Highland Court

A Devil at the Highland Court

His Highland Lass **BOOK 1 SNEAK PEEK**

She entered the great hall like a strong spring storm in the northern most Highlands. Tristan Mackay felt like he had been blown hither and yon. As the storm settled, she left him with the sweet scents of heather and lavender wafting towards him as she approached. She was not a classic beauty, tall and willowy like the women at court. Her face and form were not what legends were made of. But she held a unique appeal unlike any he had seen before. He could not take his eyes off of her long chestnut hair that had strands of fire and burnt copper running through them. Unlike the waves or curls he was used to, her hair was unusually straight and fine. It looked like a waterfall cascading down her back. While she was not tall, neither was she short. She had a figure that was meant for a man to grasp and hold onto, whether from the front or from behind. She had an aura of confidence and charm, but not arrogance or conceit like many good looking women he had met. She did not seem to know her own appeal. He could tell that she was many things, but one thing she was not was his.

His Bonnie Highland Temptation

His Highland Prize

His Highland Pledge

His Highland Surprise

Their Highland Beginning

THE CLAN SINCLAIR LEGACY

Highland Lion **BOOK 1 SNEAK PEEK**

Liam Mackay gazed at the bustling Orcadian village of Skaill, on the isle of Rousay. He thought of how it reminded him of his clan's village, outside the walls of Castle Varrich in the Scottish Highlands. As he crossed the dock, he noticed the massive longboats that Norse traders sailed to conduct trade on the island. With his father's jet-black hair and emerald eyes, few would believe Liam had Nordic heritage, but it had connected his family to Orkney for ten generations. He swept his eyes over the crofts nearest the marina of sorts. He watched as a tall blonde woman stormed out of a house and slammed the door shut. The fury on the woman's face made him think of his mother when she was angry with Liam and his younger brothers and sister. But the woman before him, statuesque and voluptuous, couldn't resemble his petite brunette mother any less. Her tall stature belied her curves until she leaned forward to fill a bucket at the well.

"Elene, come back here. We are not through speaking," an older woman called from the doorway to the croft Elene Isbister left. The younger woman continued to fill the bucket as though no one spoke to her, but Liam watched her face grow red, and it wasn't from exertion. His path carried him toward the well, but he could have continued past to reach his destination. Instead, intrigued by the stunning blonde and the scene playing out before him, he stopped at the well as the woman finished raising the bucket. She poured the contents in her own pail before letting it drop back into the cavernous pit. Unaware of Liam, she jumped when he stepped forward and grasped the crank.

Liam's emerald eyes met deep sapphire, the shade of the Highland sky in autumn. Liam observed the surprise, then wariness, in her gaze as she stepped away. He drew the full bucket to the ledge and dipped the community ladle into the cool water. As he sipped, Elene took two steps back before turning away, disconcerted by the handsome stranger. However, her feet grew roots as the older woman stormed toward her. Liam kept his head down as he lowered the bucket, chiding himself for his nosiness but unwilling to move away. The older woman glanced at him dismissively before settling her attention on Elene.

In Norn, the language of Orkney, the woman continued her chastisement. "I didn't tell you that you could leave. We were in the middle of talking."

"No, Mother. You were in the middle of talking, and I was in the middle of not wanting to hear any more. I cannot believe you're considering marrying him."

"Not considering. I've already decided. When Gunter returns in a sennight, we will wed. Then we will all move home with him."

"Home?" Elene scoffed. "Norway hasn't been our people's home in ten generations. And you are a fool if you believe he will allow me to remain."

"You're old enough to marry."

"Getting married is a far sight different from being sold!" Elene made to step around her mother, but the older woman was just as quick.

"You exaggerate."

"And you believe a slave trader over your own daughter."

"Gunter is not a slave trader. You would smear his name because you aren't getting what you want, you selfish child."

Clearly not a child, Elene stood to her full height as she gazed at her mother, who was at least two inches shorter than her daughter. "Selfish," she repeated her mother. "I hadn't realized Katryne and Johan raised themselves."

"I am their mother."

"But I raised my brother and sister. I lost my chance to marry while you lost yourself in barrels of mead." Elene swung her glare at Liam, who'd remained near the arguing women while he spoke to his two ship captains. Despite speaking Gaelic, Liam sensed Elene knew he understood her conversation with her mother. It explained her accusatory glare.

"That was my grief."

Elene released a dismissive puff of air. "That was your habit. You haven't missed Father in years. You welcomed Petyre into our home almost every night, and Father hadn't been dead two moons."

"We need a man to provide for us," the older woman sniffed defensively.

Elene gawked at her mother before she laughed. "We do not need a man to provide for us. You might need one because you can't stand to be alone for more than a day. But I work our fields and hunt out supper. Petyre, and now Gunter, come into our home and eat the food I provide. I should have accepted Duncan's offer before he grew fed up with waiting."

"You didn't love him."

"You mean like you love Gunter?"

"I do love him," Elene's mother insisted.

"More fool are you," Elene muttered.

"Come inside. You're causing a scene."

"I'm not the one yelling. And I can't. I must bring Bess this water, feed the chickens, muck out the stalls, then milk Bess. I haven't time to argue when I know you refuse to believe me."

"He is not going to sell you!"

"He will. Or he'll force me to bed him. He will not feed and clothe another adult without getting something in return. He told me."

Highland Bear

Highland Jewel

Highland Rose
Highland Strength

The Blond Devil of the Sea **BOOK 1 SNEAK PEEK**

Caragh lifted her torch into the air as she made her way down the precarious Cornish cliffside. She made out the hulking shape of a ship, but the dead of night made it impossible to see who was there. She and the fishermen of Bedruthan Steps weren't expecting any shipments that night. But her younger brother Eddie, who stood watch at the entrance to their hiding place, had spotted the ship and signaled up to the village watchman, who alerted Caragh.

As her boot slid along the dirt and sand, she cursed having to carry the torch and wished she could have sunlight to guide her. She knew these cliffs well, and it was for that reason it was better that she moved slowly than stop moving once and for all. Caragh feared the light from her torch would carry out to the boat. Despite her efforts to keep the flame small, the solitary light would be a beacon.

When Caragh came to the final twist in the path before the sand, she snuffed out her torch and started to run to the cave where the main source of the village's income lay in hiding. She heard movement along the trail above her head and knew the local fishermen would soon join her on the beach. These men, both young and old, were strong from days spent pulling in the full trawling nets and hoisting the larger catches onto their boats. However, these men weren't well-trained swordsmen, and the fear of pirate raids was ever-present. Caragh feared that was who the villagers would face that night.

The Dark Heart of the Sea

The Red Drifter of the Sea

The Scarlet Blade of the Sea